# Defiance

## A Significance Novel
Book Three

SHELLY CRANE

Copyright 2011 © Shelly Crane
This publication is protected under the US Copyright Act of 1976 and all other applicable international, federal, state and local laws, and all rights are reserved, including resale rights: you are not allowed to give or sell this book to anyone else.
Any trademarks, service marks, product names or named features are assumed to be the property of their respective owners, and are used only for reference. There is no implied endorsement if we use one of these terms.
The names and events in this novel are fictional and not based on anything else, fictional or non-fictional.

Editing services provided by Jennifer Nunez.

Printed in paperback 2012 and available in Kindle and E-book format 2012 through Amazon, Create Space and Barnes and Noble.

Printed in the United States

10 9 8 7 6 5 4 3 2 1

**More information can be found at the author's website**
**http://shellycrane.blogspot.com/**

**ISBN- 13: 978-1475009866**
**ISBN-10: 1475009860**

**This book is dedicated to my three best gals:**

Mandy A, Gloria G and especially, especially, Jennifer N.
This book has been the most stressful book for me to write because I had so many personal things going on and injuries and setbacks. You girls were always my online feel-good and pick me up crew!
And Jennifer, I know for a fact that this book, nor the last two, would be available to my readers without you. I know when I give you my book it's in good hands and I know when I have a crisis, personal or professional, you're always there to walk me back to sanityville. I'm so happy that we crossed virtual paths and that I can call you my friend!
I HEART you guys insane amounts!

Laney, Christmas 2013

I love that you love this series. It is without a doubt my favorite. There's a possibility it will be made into a movie. Yay! Hope your Christmas is wonderful - just like you. We love you so much & miss seeing your beautiful face. Can't wait to see you next year!!

Love
Nanny & Poppa

**To my husband, Axel:**

I can't even begin to process or say how much I love you. This past year has been a crazy ride and I'm just so thankful and grateful that you still want to ride with me. It's been almost eleven awesome years of being married to you and I'm looking forward to at least fifty more.

~Infinity~

*One thing was certain in my mind; change was necessary and the truth was always the best option, but that didn't mean that it was going to be a painless journey...*

*- Maggie*

# One

"It's so nice to finally meet you!" she was saying. "Rachel has gone on and on about you for weeks now over the phone," she said, her accent endearing and sweet. But even with that, I could barely concentrate on what the woman, from the Martineze clan of Prague, was saying.

I stared Marla down in absolute confusion and disgust as she chatted with someone. Had she said what I thought she said before? It couldn't be. We'd only been at the 'palace' for less than twenty minutes and I already had a new enemy. Though I guess Marla wasn't new, she'd been working behind the scenes, playing tricks and toying with our minds.

Caleb's hand shaking in mine brought me back to my reality as the woman waved and said her goodbyes to me. I looked over to calm him, but had to stop my breath from catching out loud. He wasn't shaking with fright or confusion, he was shaking with fury. I followed his gaze to Marcus, who was standing and smirking behind Marla. Caleb's mind ran through the multiple times that Marcus had injured or hurt me. The latest being, cutting my hair when I'd fallen asleep at the beach house. His fingers squeezed mine a little too tightly and I flexed them to get his attention. He jerked his gaze over to me and rubbed my fingers gently in apology before turning back to the raven-haired traitor and her family.

Marla laughed as Caleb pulled me behind him as she made her way to us once more.

But she was headed to someone behind us. "Donald!" she sang and lifted her hand in greeting. "You're looking very fit."

"Oh?" an older man said in surprise and smiled, showing a mouth full of perfectly straight, white teeth. "Why, thank you, Marla dear. It's been too long since you've graced us."

"It really has," she answered. "I'm here to remedy that."

"Well, good. And your Champion?"

Marla turned and hid her frown in her hands. She shook her head and lifted her face to him. Her tears might have looked real to him, but we knew otherwise.

"He passed on. A terrible accident just yesterday."

"Oh, my…that is terrible. Poor Sikes. Could we have been notified, we would have held a memorial for him. But as you know there are no phones here."

"Yes, well, his wife wouldn't have wanted the attention anyway. She's quiet and though she did come with us, she's grieving in her own way."

The councilman nodded as if he knew exactly what she meant. Then he said, "I see. It's hard, I know."

"As a matter of fact, I'd better go check on her now," Marla spouted and waved to him as her entourage followed her quickly out some double doors that led into a large hallway. "It was so good to see you," she called over her shoulder.

"You, too, dear." Then he turned to us and he saw me for the first time. Correction - he saw the Visionary. He gasped and fell to one knee in front of me. He took my hand, kissing the backs of my fingers and pressing them to his head before looking back up to me. His eyes took a long time before they left the mark on my neck. I tried to be still and portray the object on display that he apparently thought I was.

Finally he spoke.

"Oh…Visionary. We are so glad you've come. We've waited… long and hard years for your return."

I swallowed my sarcastic response. Waited? Long and hard years? For my return? None of that seemed right. For one, they didn't seem to be waiting. And for two, they sure weren't in hard times. I looked him over. He was wearing what had to be an expensive suit. His shoes were shinier than the marble floor we were standing on, and his eyebrows were perfectly aligned and trimmed. He looked severely pampered. And as for the third thing, the thing about my return? What did that mean? Did he think I was reincarnated or something?

"It's nice to meet you," I said lamely.

"Donald, this is Maggie Masters, soon to be Maggie Jacobson," Caleb explained. He looked over at me and smiled. "My significant."

I had my mind closed off like Caleb had told me to. He had said with all the worshipping going on that my mind would overload for sure in this place. I tried to open up a little to hear the councilman's thoughts. All I heard and felt was disgust. It wafted over me…almost like when Marcus' mind was open to me. Like slime.

I figured I must not be focusing on the councilman right so I backed away from his mind and settled back on Caleb.

"Maggie," Donald tested my name on his tongue. He didn't sound as though he was impressed. "Is that short for something? Margaret, maybe?"

I almost sighed. Almost. "No, sir. Just Maggie."

"Hmm. And Peter," he said clearly, but with a little inflection. He peered around Caleb, and I did, too. Peter was standing there with a smile pasted on his handsome face, a big, fake smile with tight, crinkled eyes. The councilman and Peter stared at each other.

"Donald," Peter said. He folded his arms over his chest, the material bunching and twisting with the tightness, his head turning ever so slightly to the right. "How…nice to see you, as always."

"I'm sure," Donald rebutted with equal amounts of sarcasm. I felt seriously uncomfortable and fidgeted with Caleb's sleeve. "Why don't we get started on the introductions? The Visionary needs to get to know her people."

My heart jumped in my throat. "What?" I squeaked and Caleb eased his arm around my waist.

"It's ok," he whispered. "He just means that he'll announce you to everyone."

"Yes, dear. Unless you'd like to say a few words?" Donald hedged.

"No. No, that won't be necessary," I answered quickly and tried not to gulp.

"As for the rest of you," Donald addressed the rest of our family who stood behind us. "It's so good to see you all again. Please, come in." He lifted an eyebrow and pursed his lips in disapproval. "You don't have to just stand in the doorway like that."

"Donald," Gran drawled and came around Caleb and I. "Don't throw out your condescension on us, now. We're all standing in the doorway because you're blocking our way, you old star-struck fool."

"Oh," Donald said abruptly and looked around. "Quite right. Forgive me, Visionary. You must think me terribly improper."

"No. Um…no," I mumbled.

He waved his arm for us to enter the grand room. I felt someone at my back and turned to find Kyle. His hand was on my shoulder and a sympathetic look on his face. Beside him was Lynne with a tight grip on his hand as she looked around at the golden room. "Time to face the music," Kyle whispered and then patted Caleb on the back.

"You both act like we're going to war or something," Lynne muttered.

Caleb laughed. "No. We just know that Maggie is absolutely going to hate this."

"Hate what?" I asked.

"This," he said and pointed. I looked up to see a room full of people who were just a few seconds ago bustling and talking. Now in the eerie quiet of the room, I could see them all falling to one knee and bowing their heads to me. It was a struggle to keep the disgusted grimace from my face. Everyone just waited. It dawned that they were waiting for me. Crap.

"Thank you. You can…stand," I said.

A few of them came forward to me and each in turn did their little reverence bow; kissing fingers, bowing head and touching it to my hand. When they finally rose I smiled and tried not to cringe into Caleb's side. Everyone else stood and watched.

A few well dressed individuals made their way to a platform that had a long table, covered in white linen. The seven of them sat and then looked our way. At first, I thought they were looking at me. But Gran squeezed my shoulder as she went by. She made her way and stood at the end of the table. They all sat down together, making a total of eight apparently important people.

I was confused. Caleb leaned in and spoke low. "The council. Or the assembly as they like to call themselves. There's a member from each family. Gran represents us."

"Why not your dad? He's the Champion."

"It can't be the Champion. The Champion must always be free for our family and not tied down to any other position. Technically Gran, since she is an assembly member, should live here at the palace with the rest of them. But she refuses."

"Did they pick her?" I asked, thinking the assembly probably wouldn't want such a vocal and, uh…speak-her-mind type on the council.

"Nope. Each family chooses their own representative." He grinned. "Who else would we vote in but Gran?"

I giggled, causing a few people to turn and stare. Caleb just ignored them and put an arm around my shoulder, but I couldn't help but wonder what the strange look on their faces was for. I opened my mind, focusing on one guy in particular who looked pretty upset. His gaze latched onto mine and I immediately felt his jealousy. He wasn't angry, he just wanted. He wanted what he'd been told his whole life was his only way to have a family and to love someone. His mind swamped mine with thoughts of imprints coming back, the possibility of his soul mate being in this very room. That I was the catalyst, the thing that would bring it all back to them. I smiled at him and he seemed shocked by the gesture. He smiled back and bowed his head.

"That's Paul, of the Petrona clan," Caleb said quietly. "And beside him is Philippe. Do you remember me telling you about him?"

"Yes, the other human besides Gran and me." Philippe looked over and saw us looking. He waved to Caleb and bowed his head to me. He started to come our way, but a child grabbed his pant leg and made him stop. He laughed and picked the girl up.

Everyone stared at Kyle and Lynne as well, the looks on their faces with just as much longing. Kyle was oblivious, but Lynne knew what was at stake. She cringed into Kyle's side in an uncharacteristic move from the spunky girl I knew.

Jen was pulled by Maria to stand next to us. Maria took Caleb's and my arm and yawned as she leaned her head against him. He chuckled at her. I looked around the room then, as Donald started addressing everyone loudly. But I tuned him out.

Everyone's mind was the same and they all seemed as taken with me as Donald had been. They wanted what they thought I had to offer; their lives back. Little did they know that I had no idea what the heck I was doing. I really hoped that I could help them because desperation seemed to be the mood of the day.

"Maggie?" I heard and looked back up to see Donald watching me curiously.

"Yes?"

"I wondered if you'd like to say a few words? To your people?"

I looked at him and realized that though he asked me earlier if I wanted to speak, and I told him that I did not, that he wasn't really giving me the option, he was just being polite.

Caleb sighed beside me and I glanced at him to see that he understood all too well that the assembly had no intentions of letting me sit quietly. I steeled myself. I had Caleb's hand in mine, his blood and love running through my veins, and his heart in my chest. I could do this.

*You bet your pretty tush you can.*

I tried not to giggle at his words in my head. I squeezed his hand and turned to face the whole room, a bouquet of different people and colors.

I didn't wait. I just went for it. "I just wanted to say that it's really good to meet you all. I hope we can get to know each other well this week." And since I was in a position for everyone to hear me at once…. "And please, you don't have to bow to me. I'm just like you. I know that you are anxious about my being here, and what that could mean, but we'll figure it all out together. I realize the importance of this and I promise you that I am taking this seriously, but my name is Maggie, please call me that." Then I smiled.

I looked around the room. Some were smiling back, some were just watching, and some were in absolute shock, but they weren't looking at me. I followed their glances over my shoulder to find a red-faced Donald.

"Visionary," he said clearly and I got his meaning by it. No one was to call me Maggie. "I know that you are young, but you have an obligation to our people, being what you are. You can't allow them to treat you as some commoner, because you are not. And you are not some measly human anymore either," he sneered loud and clear.

"I understand," I told him. "I'm not shirking my duties, but I am the Visionary and I don't feel the necessity to treat me as something else other than just…one of you. I plan to try to figure out what it is I'm supposed to do while I'm here."

"Forgive me, Visionary, but we know exactly what you are supposed to do." He came around the table and stood in front of us all. "Welcome home!" he boomed, the echo eerie in the big room. "You are to come here, for good. Rule our people and live with the council as has been planned for centuries."

"I…" What was I supposed to say to that? Peter touched my arm. He gave me a look. I focused on him, assuming he had something to say.

*I assumed they were going to try to do this, Maggie. As much as I love my people, they can be adamant and downright obsessive about tradition and formality. Just…don't get worked up. We'll figure all this out together. I won't let them bully you, I promise.*

I nodded as Peter turned to Donald and smiled that same smile as before. The one that said '*You are seriously full of crap.*' "Donald, Maggie is only seventeen years old and was a human. She has human ties; a father and brother, friends. You cannot expect her to uproot herself completely and come to live here. Not to mention Caleb-"

"What about Caleb?" Donald said smugly. "I extended no such invitation to Caleb to live with us."

"He is her significant," Peter replied tightly.

"And if she chooses to keep him here, he may stay. But that is to the Visionary's discretion how she handles that…situation." My brows bunched in confusion, but he went on. "I understand that she needs his touch to survive, but the Visionary is too important and refined to be consumed with petty, puppy love and insignificant use of her time." Caleb rumbled beside me and I gripped his arm out of instinct. What was the council trying to pull? "Therefore, if the Visionary so wishes it, she may keep Caleb here in the common quarters, as it wouldn't be proper for him to stay with her in her portion of the palace."

"Like hell," Caleb growled.

# Two

"Donald," Peter roared. "I beg your pardon, but are you suggesting that Maggie keep my son here as some sort of...of..."

"Consort?" I finished for him. Just the thought of them suggesting that I use Caleb for such a thing was enough to make my blood boil. And boil it did. The lights began to flicker a little above us.

Everyone looked around in confusion, but I never removed my eyes from the individuals at the table. I looked at them each in turn and told them with my gaze that this was idiocy. They all looked away as if scared of me, or ashamed for sitting by quietly while Donald lorded over everyone. So, if they were scared of me, then why were they pulling this crap? Except Gran, of course. She just smiled and watched.

Donald bristled at my tone and cleared his throat as he took a slight step back. Then he swatted at an energy ribbon as it floated in the air near his head. His eyes bulged when it went straight through his skin. I looked behind me to see that there were lots of energy ribbons in the air. I took a deep breath, understanding the blue menace was coming directly from me. Caleb tried to touch my skin; his hands running up my arms to my face, but in honestly, he was so upset himself that he wasn't calming me much.

"What's going on here?" another assembly member shouted. "Who's doing this?"

"I am," I answered in a hushed voice and everyone stopped. Caleb slid his hands from my face slowly and turned to glare at the assembly once more.

"It's not her fault. Maggie does this when she's upset. So stop it," he ground out.

"It was not our intention to upset you, my dear Visionary," Donald said and made his way back to the table to his chair. I was glad I wasn't close enough to get a good look at the condescension on his face that I could hear in his voice. "What part was it that..." he stopped. I followed his gaze to my wrist. Crap. He turned a couple more shades of red. He glared at Peter, then Caleb.

I watched as his brow shot up in accusation. Or maybe it was curiosity.

"So, you've mutualized with our Visionary?" he asked, causing Caleb's grip to tighten on me. "You...tainted our Visionary before you were married?"

"Now, hold on a second," Peter interrupted. "There's no law-"

"It's a matter of propriety!" he bellowed and stood, banging a wrinkled fist on the table. Jen pulled Maria back to her and looked like she wanted to cover her poor daughter's ears. "Something you should have taught her as the Champion of your clan!"

"Well he's been a little busy saving our lives," I muttered from behind Caleb.

"What was that, Visionary?"

I straightened my back and stood closer to Caleb. I grabbed his hand, letting our wrist tattoos show off our love for each other, but also the fact that we mutualized. It was not something dirty and the fact that he was trying to take my perfect, happy, delicious memory of that night away from me wasn't going to fly. Caleb grinned as he heard my inner rant and chuckled as I turned to the table before me. I spoke clear and loud.

"I said, we've been a little busy trying to stay alive. The fact that I did or didn't mutualize with *my* significant shouldn't matter to you. The fact that we were almost killed by members of the Virtuoso who are in this very room and you're doing nothing about it is what we should discuss. And it's Maggie, not Visionary...sir."

"What is this trickery?" another assemblyman asked. "Are you saying that someone is this room tried to kill you? How? When?"

"Not just me, but yes. On more than one occasion."

"Who?" he repeated louder.

"Maggie's pregnant!" Marla blurted out. I gasped and started to yell back, but everyone in the room, especially the council members, stopped and stared at me. Or wait...no, they were glaring at Caleb. Crap. Things were about to get ugly.

"That is not true," Caleb shouted. "Marla is trying to deflect. The Watsons kidnapped Maggie and kept her for away from me for days. Then, just a couple of days ago, they sent someone to my house and they tried to kill us there, too."

"Now, how can we believe you?" Donald chimed. "The proof that you mutualized with her before you were married is right there for all to see. If you would mutualize with her before marriage, then why not do more than that, hmm?"

"You can believe me because I'm telling you we've done nothing more than mutualize."

"And I say so, too," I butted in to defend Caleb. "I'm not pregnant and haven't done anything to make it so that I was."

"Trust has to be earned," Donald said. "And I'm sorry to say it, but we don't know you well enough yet to trust you like that. Marla has been one of us since birth."

A big, burly older man stood up from the council table and said in a flabbergasted voice, "But she's the Visionary!"

"Assembly, I'm sorry to be the stickler here," Marla continued in a voice that strained with its fake sincerity. "But it would be so easy for them to say that she's not pregnant without any proof. She doesn't want Caleb to be punished."

"Punished?" I yelled and looked at Caleb. "What is she talking about?" I hissed.

He leaned close. "I told you that our kind waits until we're married."

"But you didn't say you'd be punished otherwise."

"Is that a problem, Visionary? I thought you said there was no indiscretion performed?" Donald piped in.

Indiscretion? This whole day was going so far from the way that I imagined it. Before I could speak again, Peter was.

"I informed the council of the Watson's ploys and plans to hurt my family before we arrived. Are you saying that you have no knowledge of it?"

"We received your message, but this is a classic case of he said\she said."

"You wouldn't be bending rules to cover for your family now would you, Donald?"

"How dare you accuse me of such a thing!" Donald roared. "I am counselor and mentor to all, not just my family, as are we all on the council."

"Then, if you investigate the preposterous idea that Maggie could be pregnant, after only being my son's significant for a couple of weeks, then you'll investigate the Watsons and what they did to my family," Peter demanded in a gravelly voice.

"I think you best watch-" Donald started, but Gran cut him off.

"Of course we'll investigate the Watsons, Donald. If such a claim was made against the Jacobsons, we'd investigate that as well. Which is precisely why we have to have a hearing…for Maggie and Caleb." Everyone gasped, including me. What was Gran doing? "When a life is taken, there must be a hearing to determine if punishment is required. Two Watsons were killed at the home of Peter by Maggie and Caleb, and another was killed at the home of Max by another member of the Watson clan."

"You know the rules, Winifred," another member said. "The murder of a member of the same clan is dealt with within the clan. That has nothing to do with us."

"So, let's get on with the dealing for Maggie and Caleb," she said and looked at us. "Who in the family will account for them?"

"I will," Peter said and began to recount everything that happened to us at his house and at Kyle's. While he was doing that, I turned to Caleb and spoke low with Kyle and Lynne huddled in as well.

"What is Gran doing?" I asked. "Why would she want them to-"

"She's not," Caleb assured. He touched my cheek and gave me a sympathetic look. His hand coasted down to wrap around my wrist, his thumb rubbing my tattoo in possession. I shivered even in the tense circumstances. The side of Caleb's mouth tipped up at my reaction, but Kyle smacked his arm. "What?"

"Dude," Kyle complained and rolled his eyes. He looked back at me. "Gran's diffusing. If she brings it up first instead of letting the Watsons tell their side, it'll look better for us. Make us look innocent."

"We are innocent," I insisted in a hiss. "They tried to-"

"I know," he said quickly, "but they don't know that."

"Ok, ok." I nodded to make myself believe everything was going to be alright. This was so not how Caleb described the reunification to me. Caleb and Kyle both made it seem like a big party. Like it was going to be fun, hanging out, dancing and talking. This was just…not.

*I'm sorry. If we had just imprinted and you'd just been you, it wouldn't have been this way. But because you're the Visionary...I kind of expected some of this. Usually the council just sits up there the whole week and we barely see them. But because of what you are, they feel like they've got to make a scene or something.*

*Why do I feel like I should apologize?*

He smiled and pulled me to him, tucking my face into his neck. "Ah, baby," he whispered. "You didn't mess anything up. They're just all a bunch of coots, is all."

"I like that," I told him quietly. "Coots." Then we were jolted as a loud bang was issued. Donald was banging his fist on the clothed table again, face to face with Peter as he leaned toward him.

"I've accounted for the details of what happened. My kids were just protecting themselves, and you can find no fault in that."

"Don't judge and jury me, Peter. This is not some human courtroom where you can play lawyer and weasel your way out of the rules and traditions that were set forth for us centuries ago!"

"That's not what we're trying to do. The Visionary and my son were not only justified in their actions, but would be dead, and many of us dead as well, if they hadn't done what they did."

"Irrelevant and you know it."

"Enough!" Gran yelled and swiped at her hair that had fallen from her bun. "Good grief. You know the rules yourself, Donald Watson." Watson! Ah, it all made sense now…

Gran continued. "A hearing will be set as is customary and we'll vote, nothing else to do about it. Now both of you stop causing a scene and let everyone meet their Visionary."

"Quite right," Donald agreed. "And a pregnancy test will be issued to Maggie to determine that she is not with child."

"Pardon, Donald," Marla called, "but she wouldn't be far enough along to be detected on a home pregnancy test. She'll need a blood test."

As soon as the words left her mouth, I knew exactly what she was planning, though her thoughts were not open to me. Next, she would suggest that her aunt take my blood.

"It just so happens that my Aunt Ruth, Sikes' widow, has the ability to perform the blood draw without any pain or discomfort to the Visionary."

Peter interjected, "This is ridiculous and disrespectful to perform a test solely with the purpose of trying to catch the Visionary in a lie!"

"If she's not lying, there should be no reason she would refuse the test." I knew then that there was nothing I could say. He had us and he knew it, and so did Marla. "It's settled then," Donald chimed, sounding all too thrilled with the idea. When he set his hands on the table, I caught a glimpse of his wrist tattoo, but couldn't make out the design.

I looked to Peter and Caleb, to see if they understood what I had concluded. Marla knew I wasn't pregnant, she was after more of my blood. And there was no way to refuse the test without looking like I *was* pregnant and Marla knew I wouldn't risk Caleb being 'punished', whatever that meant.

Caleb was reading me the whole time and nodded his knowing. He gritted his teeth, but tried to keep me calm. He smiled and rubbed my arm.

*We'll figure this out. I'll go with you. I won't let her keep your blood.*

I nodded back. Peter crossed his arms, his eyes blazing a line of disgust at Donald, but he said nothing. I didn't want to open my mind up to the room, honestly, I didn't want to know what everyone was thinking right then, but I assumed that Peter had come to the same conclusion we had. Rachel came and put her arms around him. I almost smiled as he instantly calmed and looked at her, a grateful look upon his face.

We spent the next hour schmoozing, as Gran put it. I shook hundreds of hands, was bowed to more times than I could count, though I'd asked them not to, and was told multiple names that I would never remember. I also endured the looks from girls who were not happy that I was the one to snag Caleb. I tried not to take their looks of death and then quick smiles - to keep the Visionary from turning them to dust - personally.

Then music started to play. I looked over to see a small stage with instruments…but no one was playing them. The instruments were playing themselves. Rather good too, I might add.

"They're charmed," Caleb explained into my ear. "One of the Gemino clan members can charm objects to do their normal function."

"So he can't make a guitar do the dishes or anything like that?" Lynne asked.

"Nope, just play music."

"Lame," she complained in jest, and we laughed. She was nervous still. People couldn't take their eyes off of us four, all for different reasons, but one common fact. We had imprinted. Lynne hated the attention, but Kyle was eating it up. He loved the fact that he had what everyone else envied.

"How about a dance, pretty lady?" I heard behind me and turned to find Rodney; the one who found me and saved me in the woods that day at the Watson compound. I silently gasped and, without thinking, jumped to grab him around his neck. He held me to him and I felt him chuckle. I peeked over at Caleb, expecting to see a scowl of jealousy, but found only affection. He was still really grateful to Rodney as well. He saved my life, after all.

"I guess that means that you remember who I am," Rodney joked as he put my feet back to the floor.

"Of course I do," I replied. I saw his eyes catch the mark on my neck and the look of affection changed to one of rapture. He smiled and did his bow-kiss-hand thing.

"Visionary," he whispered and smiled wider. "It makes me all the more proud to call you family."

"Please, just Maggie," I insisted, and though he nodded, I knew it would take some persuasion. Then he turned to Caleb.

"Caleb."

"Rodney, man, it's good to see you." They hugged, bumping their fists and pounding backs.

"You, too. And Kyle, I see you've got an addition as well."

"Yes. This is Lynne," Kyle explained proudly. "Lynne, this is our cousin, Rodney."

"Nice to meet you," Lynne said and bumped fists with him. "Are you from Tennessee, too? You've got the whole…" she waved her hand in front of him, "cowboy look going on."

And he did. He was meaty, dark, tanned with jeans and a plaid shirt. All that was needed to top off the picture was a cowboy hat.

"I am from Tennessee, yes, ma'am," he said in an exaggerated southern drawl. "In fact, I live on a farm with fifty horses."

"Nuhuh," Lynne said and leaned closer in interest. "Really?"

"Cross my heart."

"I *love* horses!" she said and giggled in joy. Kyle grabbed her arm and started to drag her away, laughing.

"I better get you away from Mister wild horses over here."

"Aw, don't worry. You can just buy me a horse and then we'll be good."

"Done," Kyle said and though he was laughing, I could tell he was absolutely going to buy her a horse. He nuzzled her neck and they laughed.

I glanced over to see Caleb watching me. "What?" I asked.

"Just wondering what you're thinking, since you've got your brain turned off."

"I'm just thinking that I'm glad Kyle has Lynne," I said without hesitation. "I'm glad he's happy."

"Me, too." He wrapped his arms around me from behind. "And not just because he was annoying the hell out of me over you. I'm just glad that we can be friends again."

"Me, too."

"Me, three," Rodney said and laughed as he clapped Caleb on the shoulder. "I've missed you guys out at the ranch. Mom has, too. She hasn't had anyone to bake sugar cookies for."

"Yeah," Caleb said thoughtfully, "we haven't been out there in months."

"You'll have to come soon. Mom's got a new Clydesdale. It's the biggest horse you've ever seen."

"We'll do that. We've just got to get a few things out of the way first," Caleb said and smiled against the back of my neck.

# Three

The night wore on. I wasn't really enjoying myself. I felt too much on display so I wasn't in a dancing mood. Or an eating mood, as there was a huge spread of fruit. Everyone was whispering and sneaking peeks at us. When I caught one of them they smiled and quickly looked away. I didn't know what to do about it.

Soon, all my thoughts of self-pity flew away when the Watson who had been my poltergeist since I met Caleb decided that the evening needed a little more excitement.

"Hello, little human," Marcus said from behind us. We turned and I held Caleb's arm tight to keep him from charging him. "Nice haircut. Is it new?" he prodded with sarcasm.

Then, there was nothing I could do. Caleb launched himself at Marcus, pinning him to the wall behind him. Caleb's hands gripped his throat and he growled in his face, oblivious of the astonished crowd that watched from across the room. "Don't you speak to her, ever."

"Ah, the Jacobson prince," Marcus replied loudly and laughed. "How lucky for Maggie that she had such a big, strong boy to keep her safe from my insults."

"I said to shut up. We are stuck here with you this week, but that doesn't mean that you can torture Maggie the whole time. She is your Visionary and you will show some respect for that, if nothing else."

"What's going on here?" Donald yelled from behind us. I felt arms around me from behind and turned to find Rachel hugging me, with Peter flanking her. Donald came forward and stood next to Caleb, who still hadn't released Marcus. "I said, what's going on? Answer me!"

"Caleb is jealous of anyone who shows any affection to our Visionary, Uncle," Marcus sneered.

"Marcus, I will-" Caleb started, but Donald cut him off.

"Now, Caleb, I know how you must be feeling." Donald clapped him on the back as if in sympathy. "But you can't be stingy with our Visionary."

"I'm not and have no plans to be. Marcus has tortured Maggie for weeks in echoes and kidnappings and a lot more. I won't let him do that to her this week."

"Neither will I," Donald said sternly. "Of course, anything that happened before was petty and uncalled for, but is over with I'm sure. Considering she *is* the Visionary." It sounded like a warning to Marcus, but Marcus just laughed and tipped his head.

I almost opened my mind to him, but was scared to. I was afraid of what everyone was thinking and was afraid to overload and appear weak in front of all these people who expected so much from me.

"There, you see? Caleb, let him go, son."

Caleb held for a few seconds longer, in obvious protest and his own warning to Marcus, and then came back to take my hand.

"I think I'll take Maggie to her room now," Caleb said. "It's been a long day."

"Of course," Donald conceded and smiled. "Your quarters, Caleb, are on the second floor. Maggie will remain here on the first floor with the rest of the assembly members. This year we've changed a few things around. I'm sure you can understand why."

"No, sir," Caleb replied and laughed a humorless laugh, "I don't think I do understand, but I'm sure there's an implication in there somewhere."

"Caleb," Peter said quietly and came to stand next to us. "Donald, please just tell us what it is that you want us to know. We've all had a long day and would like to retire."

"I'm sure with all the new raging significant hormones that you can see why we'd have to separate the newly imprinted couples. In fact, even Lynne, who isn't a member of the council, will stay in the room next to Maggie's."

"Whoa, whoa, wait a minute," Caleb said, his voice going low and dangerous. "Are you saying that you're separating us for the night?"

"Yes. And not just tonight, but every night. It isn't proper for-"

"Donald," Peter said incredulously. He turned to the rest of the council, who was littered among the nosy onlookers. "You know they will go into withdrawal during the night. Is that what you want? For your Visionary?"

"We've never let unmarried individuals sleep with each other before. Why would we start now?" another assemblyman answered.

"We've never had these circumstances before either," Peter rebutted. "Usually the *individuals,* as you call them, are married within a couple of weeks and it's never an issue."

"Exactly," Donald said and scoffed. "Honestly, Peter, for you to suggest that they sleep together before marriage is just-"

"I'm not suggesting they do anything but sleep, Donald," Peter replied dryly.

"Still. Our ways are best and with good reason. Morals are the highest obligation and responsibility to our people. There are plans for them to marry, yes?"

"Of course."

"Then…" Donald grinned and looked Caleb and me over. "Why not right now? Solve all the problems and be done with it. That would be like five birds with one stone." He laughed at his own joke.

"What?" Caleb said.

"We're all here," Donald explained cheerfully. "You can perform the ceremony, Peter. I'm sure the participants are more than…willing," he said and smiled at me.

"You want us to get married? Like right now?" I blurted out and even I heard the disgust in my voice. From the shocked looks on the others' faces, they clearly misunderstood my disgust. It wasn't that I didn't want to get married to Caleb, but Dad and Bish weren't here. It was unthinkable.

"Are you opposed to marrying Caleb?" someone asked from behind me. "Hasn't he asked you yet?"

"No, he's asked me, I just-"

I was cut off by many replies, from all around me. I cringed into Rachel's chest and gripped Caleb's hand tighter.

"Having a wedding at the palace? That's never happened before."

"Why wouldn't she want to marry him?"

"Humans," a woman scoffed. "They never could cut ties."

"Shh! She's the Visionary, she'll hear you!"

"Alright, listen!" Peter yelled to stop them all. "This isn't right and you know it, Donald. You have spouted nothing but talk about tradition and rules put in place for us by our ancestors since the minute we walked through that door. We've never had a wedding here because it's a sacred thing that is done at the Champion's home and only the families involved are included. How dare you offer to marry them here so callously in disrespect of the traditions for it?"

"I'm just trying to solve the problem that you're so upset about. If they got married, then we would have no qualms about them staying in the same room."

"Marriage isn't just about some ceremony or a piece of paper. It's about family and making a forever commitment to each other in front of the ones you love. For you to try to turn it into something so simple and trivial is ridiculous."

"It's practical."

"You're such a hypocrite!"

I had no idea what to say. I looked at Caleb and realized I still had my mind turned off. Caleb had been awfully quiet throughout the whole thing and now I knew why. He thought I was upset because I didn't want to marry him right now, that maybe after seeing his people that I wanted no part in it.

I pulled from his mother and went the small distance to him. He accepted me into his arms easily and even tried to smile.

"You're such an idiot," I whispered and smiled up at him. How could he honestly believe that I wouldn't want him?

"What?" he said confused, but sucked in a quick breath when I touched his head to mine, opened my mind up, and let him in. I let him feel everything I'd felt since we'd gotten there. I was scared, confused, worried, restless, and had no idea what I was supposed to do for those people. But one thing was for sure. I wanted to marry Caleb…just not because some old guy told me I had to. I wanted exactly what Peter had described. The whole experience, and the sentiment and beautifulness of it.

So I showed Caleb the vision he showed me of that day of me in my red dress, to remind him that this wasn't our destiny. The vision showed exactly what was coming for us: him and me, Lynne and Kyle, my bare feet on green, lush grass, and so many smiling faces.

The council knew that we were going to be married one day and the fact that they didn't trust us to do what our bodies needed during sleep, to keep us from pain, was pretty much a slap in the face.

Caleb lifted his head, a little sheepishly, and looked at me. I bit my lip and smiled, but that quickly slid away as I realized we were surrounded by energy ribbons. I looked up and saw the picture of us twirling in our wedding attire in the air above us. Crap.

I hadn't meant to, but I'd just shown the whole room the very private vision of us at our wedding.

I looked over to see Donald watching. He looked at me differently, I could see that. He was just now realizing that he no idea the things that I could do.

I smiled at him as I spoke to hopefully soften the blow of my words. "I plan to marry him. In fact, it's more than a plan. I will marry him, but as you saw, it'll be on our time. My father isn't here or my brother, and I know that it's tradition for the human to leave her world behind when she joins you, but I didn't have that much to begin with. Bish and my dad are all that I have, and they…" I wondered if I should tell them about the fact that they both knew about us all. I decided against it. "…are really important to me. It's not really an option that they be present at the wedding or not. I want them there and I want to do it at Peter's house. This isn't because I don't want to get married, I just don't want to be told that I have to. I'm sorry if you think I'm being disrespectful-"

"No, no, of course not," Donald said quickly and shortly. Then he gulped as if he recognized that he had made a mistake. He smiled a crap-eating smile. "I understand, and forgive me for suggesting that you do something you weren't ready for."

I opened my mouth to protest, but Caleb grabbed my arm. He shook his head at me in an exasperated way that said not to put in the effort.

"Enough," Caleb said and gripped my hand. "I'm taking Maggie to her room."

"And you'll be dropping her off and then heading upstairs to your own room, right?"

"Of course, assemblyman," Caleb said dryly and turned to his family. "Night."

"Night, you two," Rachel said and hugged us both at the same time. She whispered to us. "Please don't provoke them. We'll get through this." She leaned back. "Caleb, just…hold hands on the way to get as much touch as possible before you leave." She grimaced. "I'm so sorry, Maggie. It's not…usually this way."

"So I've been told," I said with a smile. It wasn't Rachel's fault that this was happening. "Don't worry about us. We'll be alright."

"Alright, everyone," another assemblyman called loudly. "Lights out is in fifteen minutes. Everyone make your way to your rooms, please."

"Come on," Caleb said to me and didn't wait for anyone or anything else as he towed me behind him. I waved at Peter, Jen and our family, who all stood off to the side looking very unhappy. Everyone else bowed slightly as I made my way out of the room.

As we made our way to my bedroom, wherever that was, I couldn't help but ask my burning questions. "Why did Gran stay so quiet? She's always so vocal about everything."

"It's tricky. She can't be biased. She has to seem like she's not just making decisions for our family, but for everyone. If they think she's being unfair, they'll vote her out and the Jacobsons won't have a say on the council anymore. But they can't touch her unless she gives them a reason."

Our shoulders brushed as we walked and it sent shivers through me. One, because he was Caleb and his touch did powerful things to me. And two, I knew I'd be without that touch all night and I didn't even want to think about it.

"I'm sorry. Like I said, it's usually not like-"

"This," I finished for him. "I know. It's ok."

"The council is just scared of you," he said and sighed, sucking his lip in and out, frowning.

"They're just scared of your family," I corrected him. "There is some major hostility there."

"Well, even though Donald is a Watson, and the self-proclaimed leader of the council, we've never had any problems with him before. He's been silent enemies with my dad for as long as I can remember, but I've never heard Donald talk so much in all my life."

"So they really aren't going to punish the Watsons?"

"The law says there can be no murder of another clan member for any reason. It doesn't state anything about attempted murder or kidnapping. The Virtuoso are very strict in their rules, but when there is no specific ruling against something, they won't interfere at all."

"That's crap."

He laughed and pulled me to a stop. "Yeah," he agreed.

"And Marla has my blood….in her," I said and gulped down my disgust and discomfort about that. He nodded and twisted his lips. "And the Watsons are going to be here the whole time." He nodded again. "And Gran is on the council, who wants to keep us apart or force up to marry, and I have to shut myself off every time I go into that room so I won't overload and all those people want me to fix all of their problems," I huffed a breath and kept going to get it all out, "and everyone keeps bowing and freaking out even though I've asked them not to."

"Babe, all that is true, yes, but you've got to get used to it," he said softly. "The only way you can stop them from acting like a bunch of idiots is exactly like you showed me." He looked at me pointedly. "Show them. Teach them. Be the strong, beautiful, amazing girl that I know you are and eventually they'll come around. They won't have a choice but to."

I sighed and nodded. "Ok. I'll try."

He smiled and touched my cheek. "Good. Now, here we are. Your suite, my queen," he said playfully and bowed as he opened the heavy door.

"Don't you start or I'll…oh, my…"

I was flabbergasted. This couldn't be my room. Caleb must have made a mistake. It was huge. It was what I would imagine would be at the penthouse at the Waldorf. Not that I'd ever seen it or ever would. The walls were high and the molding was intricate. The wallpaper was thick lines of white and green and the carpet was seriously plush and thick. There was a huge mahogany poster bed in the middle of the room with white pillows and a white comforter that was as thick and big as a cloud. And the walls were lined with mahogany dressing tables and floor length mirrors, but there were no windows. There wasn't much on the walls, but there was one painting of a city from the hillside.

I think I stood staring, a little intimated, too long, because Caleb finally came up behind me, chuckling as he pulled me against him. He whispered in the skin of my neck, "Pretty nice digs, huh?"

"Are all the rooms like this?"

"Nope. The rooms on the second floor are nice, don't get me wrong, but they aren't like this." He looked around. "I've never even been down here before." He looked back at me. "Off limits."

"And it's still off limits," I said sadly.

"Yeah," he sighed, "and I better get going. If they find me in here, it won't be good."

"Yeah," I replied lamely. I turned in his arms and wasted no time. I pulled him down at the same time that I went onto my tiptoes. His lips really didn't comfort me. I figured that I was just too worked up, too upset, but I kissed the heck out of him anyway.

And boy, did he kiss me back.

# Four

My veins screamed inside of me. Something didn't feel quite right, but my body was so happy that Caleb was here that I didn't dwell on it.

I felt more than heard his growl against my mouth. Gosh, I loved it when he did that. Like he was some animal and he was claiming me, letting everyone else know I was his. I lifted myself even more to be close to him, and just as his hand was sliding dangerously down my back, we heard someone make an annoyed sound to get our attention.

We turned to see a man there. I had no idea who he was, but Caleb apparently did. "Custodian Michaels," Caleb said and huffed. "Perfect timing."

"Caleb," the man chastised, but stood in the doorway and didn't come any closer. "You know the rules. Come on, don't make me be the bad guy."

"I know the rules," Caleb repeated sarcastically. He turned and kissed me once more on the side of my neck and smiled at me. "Goodnight, babe." Then he went to the door. I was a little confused at how easily Caleb had just given in and left like that.

"Bye," I whispered, but they were both already gone. I closed my door and turned to lean against it. No matter how beautiful the room was, it wasn't me. I didn't want to stay here. If felt more like a pretty prison than a vacation. But what could I do now?

I looked around and saw my luggage on the settee at the foot of my bed. I hoped there was a bathroom in my room because I desperately wanted a shower. After exploring a few doors, and finding not only a huge walk-in closet that would put Queen Elizabeth to shame, along with a snack bar, I finally found the bathroom.

I was kind of surprised at how simple it was compared to the rest of the bedroom. It had a white, claw-foot tub on one side and a stand-up stall shower on the other. I decided to shower tonight, but at least once before I left, I'd try out that beautiful cast iron tub. There were even a few scrubs and salts off to the side, making it appear very much like a hotel. The few towels that were there were folded into little designs. Even the toilet paper was shaped into a point, all nice and petite. Who did all this? Were all the rooms this way?

I decided I didn't care and took off my dress. I stepped into the shower and hurried through a hot one. It had been forever since I'd slept by myself. I stood over my open luggage and stared down the dresses I'd brought. Tomorrow I'd have to get all dressed up and pretend to be their leader…

Wait… It hit me like the ceiling had collapsed on me. I was such an idiot! No wonder everyone treated me so strangely and no wonder Donald was such a jackass.

I had acted like a scared little rabbit out there. I shut my mind off so I had no idea what was going on and what everyone was thinking, and I was blindsided because of it. They wanted to use me as a pawn, as an object of worth, and not a person…and I had let them. Oh, how could I be so stupid!

No. More.

Tomorrow, I would keep my mind open at all times. I would not cower behind Caleb's family and I wouldn't let Donald think I was here simply for him to display his traditional side. And Marla and Marcus? I wouldn't let them humiliate me and turn everyone against me before I even got to know anyone.

I was the Visionary for a reason. I was Caleb's significant for a reason. I was brought into this point of my life for a reason. I was me…for a reason. No one was going to take the reins of my own life but me. Tomorrow was a new day and I was going to make it my own.

I pulled on a yellow, polka dot camisole and a pair of white boy-short underwear and climbed into bed. My hair was still wet, and I hated to go to bed with wet hair, but I was in no mood to stand around in that bathroom and see if the wall plugs were compatible in London or not. I wanted to just think.

I lay there, looking at that gorgeous, molded white ceiling. I grabbed my cell off the top of my purse, but there was no signal. I wanted to call Dad, but I guess that would have to wait. I was sure he was worried sick. I'd put him through a lot lately, and Bish, too. Ugh…I rolled over to press my face into the pillow. It smelled like lemons.

It was almost comical how hard it was to fall asleep now. I felt uncomfortable. I rubbed my feet together, but that didn't help. I rolled to my side. I even pulled a pillow down to lay beside me as if it were Caleb, but still no help. I eventually rolled onto my back, slipped the lamp switch, and just decided to strategize about the next day.

I would walk with my head high. I would show them that both of my tattoos, the Visionary one and the mutualizing one, were worn with pride and affection. I would show them that Caleb wasn't some stupid kid who couldn't take care of

things. He was my guy, he was my protector, he was my everything.
And…what…the…

There was a foot hanging from my ceiling– no, through my ceiling. I sat up and blinked a few times to see if I was really awake or had fallen asleep somehow. The foot jerked and moved. I heard muffled curses and then there was a whole blue-jeaned leg…and then two. Then someone fell through the ceiling toward my bed. I somehow muzzled my scream and scooted over just as he fell onto the other side of my large bed with a bounce. Caleb glared at the ceiling.

"You suck at that, just so you know, Uncle Kev."

I looked up to see a man's head sticking out of the ceiling. "Sorry. You're not as little as you used to be, you know," the man grumbled and then changed his gaze to me. He smiled and winked. "You're welcome." A pair of shoes fell through the ceiling as well, landing on Caleb's stomach, and then he was gone.

"Caleb," I breathed as I sat up further. "What are you doing here?"

He grinned and I noticed he was barefoot with his jeans and a white undershirt on. He slid closer on his knees and pulled me to him. "There was no way I was letting you out of my sight tonight."

I giggled silently and hugged him, my spirits lifted. He was the balm to my ache still, and always would be.

His hands drifted up my legs...and didn't stop. I realized he was going to stop at the hem of my shorts, but I wasn't wearing any so he had no stopping point. When he realized the same thing, his hands gripped me, he stopped breathing and his heart beat fast against my chest.

He finally let his breath out slowly as I stayed perfectly still. His hands moved a little to confirm what he already knew I was wearing, and I fought not to shiver. He leaned back and looked at my face closely. "What the hell are these, Maggie?"

"They're b-boy shorts," I stuttered.

"These are not shorts," he rumbled.

"I didn't think I'd see you tonight," I defended in a whisper.

He bit his lip and cocked an eyebrow as he looked me over. "You wore these because you *didn't* think you'd see me?" He chuckled at my confused expression. "I'm just…joking, baby." He sighed a long, meaningful sigh. "I think you better put something on though, before I stop being so in control."

"Yeah," I agreed, but I couldn't help myself. Did he know how incredibly hot he was in his bare feet and white t-shirt? Did he even realize that his hands were still sitting right under my butt on my legs? Did he know how grateful I was to him for somehow finding a way to come to me even when he'd been forbidden not to?

I kissed him with every intention of mutualizing with him. Call me brazen, call me testing his control, call me anything you want, but I couldn't have waited another second. My body – my imprint – demanded for him.

He pushed me back easily to the bed and took my arms to press them over my head. I whispered to him, "Why do you always do that? Hold my arms down?"

"Because if you touched me right now…" He shook his head like he couldn't even think, and started kissing me again.

I opened my mind and waited for the tingle, the spark, the cooling of my blood, but it never came. I was warm. In fact, I was on fire, but that was hormones not mutualizing.

He pulled back and looked confused, too. Then his look morphed to one of anger. He sat back on his heels and laughed humorlessly. "Those bastards," he growled.

"What?" I sat up. "What did they do?"

"They charmed the room," he explained. He ran his hands through his hair. "I thought it was strange before that I didn't feel anything when you touched me, when I was in here earlier. But I just assumed we were both too worked up, too upset, and that was why."

"You mean," I worked it out in my mind, "they got someone to use their ability to make it so that there are no abilities is this room?" He nodded. I hadn't heard any of his thoughts and he was right, I had felt something strange when he'd kissed me before when he said goodbye. It felt weird because it was just us and no imprint. "No healing touch, no reading minds, no…mutualizing?"

"Nope."

I sighed in exasperation. They were testing the limits of *my* control. "And your uncle? The one who shot you through the ceiling?"

"Uncle Kev," he explained.

"Yeah. His ability is to…what? Because if he was the one who did this, I'll…go break all of his light bulbs."

He chuckled silently. "His ability is to do basically what he did. He can put objects, or people, through walls, doors, and apparently, the ceiling." He smiled. "Were you surprised?"

"Uh, yeah." I bit my lip in thought. "So even if you sleep in here with me, we'll still be in withdrawal by morning, won't we?"

"Yeah." His smile turned into a frown. "They had to have done this before we came. They knew we were going to fight them on it. They wanted to cover all of their bases."

"Why is our sex life so interesting to them?" I blurted. He gave me a look that could have melted bones. "I meant, our…mutualizing life…you know what? Whatever, you know what I mean."

He laughed. "You are so cute all flustered."

"Not flustered," I argued.

"Not?" he challenged and leaned closer. I gulped and he laughed again. "Get dressed, gorgeous. I'm taking you out of here."

"Where?"

"Get. Dressed." He grinned as he leaned back on the bed, putting his arms behind his head on the pillows. "Go ahead," he ordered. "Get some clothes on."

I realized he was going to see me strutting around in my boy shorts while I found some clothes. Fine. If he wanted to see, and he apparently did, he could look all he wanted to. I had found my second wind, my reasoning, my gumption and I wasn't going to be silly, little, scared Maggie anymore.

I smiled as I stood up and waltzed over to the suitcase. I pulled out a pair of jeans, my only pair of jeans that I had brought, and started to slip them on. I felt him at my back. Even though I couldn't read his mind right then, somehow I just knew that he wasn't going to be able to just sit there and watch.

It was very empowering.

"Mean," he taunted and kissed the back of my neck.

"I was just doing what you told me to."

"Touché." He kissed my neck once more and looked around the room. "You'll need a sweater or something."

"I have a cargo jacket in that bag," I said and pointed as I buttoned my jeans. I slipped on my blue Converses just as he brought my jacket. He helped me put it on and then put his shoes on quickly. "What about you?"

"I'll be fine. Come on."

"Are you going to tell me where we're going?" I asked as he dragged me to the door.

"Nope." He opened the door and peeked out. He gave me one last look. "Be very quiet. Church mouse quiet."

"Got it," I whispered.

He took my hand and we both stopped for a second as our touch hit us. I could feel him again just by stepping into the hall. I sighed and soaked him up. It was true then, no question, they had charmed my room.

*Yeah, let's not start that again or I'll do something I'll regret.*

We crept down the hall to the next room down. He scratched on the door with his fingernail and Lynne immediately opened the door, wearing a little pink hoodie. She opened her mouth as if to scream while she smiled, but it was silent. She bounced on her toes as she came out of the room and gripped me in a tight hug.

Caleb closed her door quietly and grabbed her hand, too, shushing her as he dragged us down the hall. He took us through some heavy double doors at the other end of the hall. It was all dark, lit only by little gas sconces on the wall. I could hear them hissing as we passed.

Once we were through the doors, he opened the door to some stairs. It was cold and drafty, but he urged us forward. Lynne went first and she was back to her old self; smiley, chipper, bouncy, almost annoying in her giddiness. I understood what she was going through. The assembly and all those people staring at us before had been very intimidating and now she felt free to be herself again.

When we finally reached the top of the stairs, I learned why she was so giddy. She squealed as we hit the cold air of the outside and ran to Kyle, who was waiting there for us. She jumped up into his arms and wrapped her arms and legs around him.

I laughed as I turned to Caleb. "You planned this. All of this."

"Yeah."

"How?"

"I have my ways," he said playfully.

Lynne pulled away from Kyle long enough to laugh and say, "Yeah, your Uncle Kevin scared the crap out of me when he stuck his head through my door to tell me."

We laughed and Caleb took my hand once more. I sighed as I got a heavy dose of his tingly, healing touch.

"Come on, gorgeous," he whispered. "This isn't the surprise. We're just getting started."

# Five

We were on some sort of balcony. The rooftops were surrounding us, connected and strange, like hilltops. Kyle pulled Lynne behind him to follow him.

"We're going on the roof?" I asked.

"Yep," Caleb answered, "and while we're on the roof, with great cell service-"

"The only cell service!" Kyle yelled.

"-I thought you might want to call your dad. I'm sure he's worried. It's daytime there already."

I smiled. "Yes, I do. Thank you." He handed me his cell and I dialed the number as he helped me over the small ridges of the roof. It only rang a couple of times before Dad picked up.

"Hello? Maggie?" he said without waiting for an answer.

"Dad."

"Oh, thank you, God. I've been so worried."

"I know. There isn't any cell service here in the pala…uh, in the house." I cleared my throat and tried to sound happy and at ease so he wouldn't worry more. "But we're having fun. It's a huge, beautiful place."

"Has Caleb taken you to London yet to see the city? It's pretty remarkable from what I've heard."

"Not yet, but…" I had to catch my breath when Caleb pulled me to the top of the last ridge and stood behind me. We were overlooking the city right then, and it was breathtaking. All the lights, the buildings, the people…

"If Jim had only waited another minute to ask you that question," Caleb joked into my ear.

"Maggie? Hello?" Dad said loudly.

"Oh, sorry. Still here."

"What's going on?"

"Nothing. Just…looking at the city now. I wish you were here, Dad," I said and I meant it. "I wish you could see this."

"Me, too, kiddo." He sighed long.

"How's Bish?"

"He had an interview today. Don't know how it went yet, but I've got my fingers crossed for him."

"Me, too. I hope it works out."

"Hey, did Caleb's sister go with you?"

"Um…yeah," I answered carefully, not liking where the conversation was going.

"Just wondering. Bish is doing an awful lot of moping. I thought maybe they could have lunch or something. He needs to get out."

I sighed. Caleb put his forehead against my shoulder and groaned. Even in London, we couldn't get away from the Bish\Jen drama.

"All of Caleb's family came with us, Dad, except Kyle's parents. They are leaving tomorrow…or today I guess it is. They had a couple of things to do first."

"Ok. Well, you've got a package here."

"From who?"

I heard him shaking it and crinkling paper. "It's marked Florida, but there's no return address."

"Oh." I looked at Caleb over my shoulder, who had already heard the conclusion in my mind. "It's probably from Chad, then." Caleb grimaced and crossed his arms over my chest tighter. "Just open it, Dad. It's probably just a sweatshirt from his school or something."

"I'll open it later. I'd love to talk all day, kiddo, but I've got to get to work. I miss ya."

"I know. Me, too. I promise to call when I can."

"Ok. Love you, baby girl."

"Love ya, Dad."

The click told me he was gone and I turned in Caleb's arms. "Thank you for letting me call him. Very thoughtful of you."

"I try." He turned me back to face the city. "If it were daytime, this would look exactly like the painting in your room. This is where it was painted."

"How do you know that?"

"Because Gran painted it," he whispered.

"Gran paints?"

"Mmhmm." He nuzzled my neck. "You like it?"

"It's more beautiful than it should be allowed to be," I said truthfully.

"Good answer." Kyle and Lynne started heading to the other side. Caleb nodded his head for us to go, too. "I know that today sucked," he started. "I have no idea what's going to happen. So, I wanted you to see a little bit of the palace – my favorite parts – before they start all their proper Visionary stuff tomorrow."

"Your favorite part is the roof?"

"No, but this is," he answered and genuinely smiled. I looked ahead to see a huge greenhouse. Lynne and Kyle were already going inside.

We made our way slowly, languidly. I just wanted to enjoy Caleb for as long as possible. I had a feeling that this night was going to fly by.

When we entered the walkway for the greenhouse, I looked around at what Caleb had deemed as his favorite spot. And I immediately knew why. There were roses everywhere. Everywhere! The pathway was lit with little solar lights and littered with stones of every color and shape, pounded into the ground for a smooth walk. The roses were planted, potted, hung and sprouting everywhere. It was gorgeous.

We made our way into the doors and I covered my mouth to stifle some girly squeal that would have escaped. The whole west wall was covered in yellow roses, floor to ceiling, of all size and type.

*It's like it was made for you, huh?*

I nodded without turning to him. "It's beautiful. It's…I've never seen so many in my life."

"I thought of this place, when I saw in your mind that yellow roses were your favorite. I couldn't wait to bring you here." He plucked a small one from the bush and turned me to him. He put it to my nose and I smelled and exhaled. I smiled as he put it behind my ear.

He nodded his head for me to follow him, even though he took my hand and demanded that I come.

Lynne and Kyle were laughing and throwing limestone pebbles at each other. Kyle came and put his arm around my shoulder. "How you holding up, Mags?"

"I'm fine."

"Such a liar," he joked. "It'll get better. It has to, right?"

"Not necessarily. That saying doesn't really hold much water with me anymore."

"Yeah," he agreed in a groan. "I guess not."

"How are you doing, Lynne?" I asked as we all sat down in a grassy area in the middle. Kyle went to the wall and pulled a cord, and kept pulling until the skylight opened up. Without the city lights skewing the view, the sky was pitch black, speckled with stars. I heard Lynne's gasp and knew she forgot all about answering me.

I felt Caleb pull me back to lie against him, my head against his chest. Kyle came over and we all just lay there together and looked up at the sky. It looked the same as it did from my house, or the lake Caleb took me to, or the beach. Same sky, but it may as well have been a different world.

"We used to sneak up here all the time when the ball gowns and fake champagne got to be too much for us," Kyle explained and laughed. I looked over to see him stroking his fingers down Lynne's arm. "We'd lie and say we had to go to the bathroom. We'd be gone for hours and no one even cared or noticed."

"Yeah, you weren't so cute back then. No one noticed you were gone," Caleb goaded.

"Shut up. I was plenty cute. I had just as many girls following me around as you did."

"Hardly," Caleb scoffed.

"Eew," I butted in. "I don't think I need to hear this."

"I second that," Lynne agreed. "I saw them all scoping you out while we were down there. It's bad enough to have to watch it, I don't want to hear it, too."

"Ok," Kyle said to her quickly. "Done. Zipped." He made a zipper of his lips and grinned at her.

"So what's going to happen tomorrow?" I asked. "Is it going to be on repeat all week? Just fighting and standing around?"

"No," Kyle answered. "They always have different events planned for every day. Things will be a little different, because you're here, but I'm sure they have plenty planned to keep us busy."

"Is your room charmed, too?" Caleb asked him.

"Charmed?" Kyle said confused. "What do you…oh, seriously? Wow, cheap shot."

"Yeah."

"I don't know if mine is. And we don't know if Lynne's is…yet," he joked and winked at Caleb. Then he coughed and laughed as Lynne elbowed him in the ribs. "Lynne!" he complained through his chuckle.

"Don't insinuate things," she said in a high voice.

"I would never," he said and smiled. She just melted, and I could see why. Kyle had a new light to him, something I'd never seen on him before. He was so stubborn. He could have been saved a lot of heartache if he'd just waited for her. He thought he was in love with me, but he wasn't. He was in love with the idea of being in love; of imprinting, of starting a new life and being the man of it. I really was happy for him now, and he never looked at me the way he was looking at her.

Caleb rubbed my arm and silently agreed with me.

"And just what is going on out here?" a man's voice said.

"Busted," Kyle said and we all sat up to face our discoverer.

# Six

"Rodney!" Caleb laughed and bumped fists from where we were sitting. "You found us."

"It wasn't very hard, man. We always ran up here to get away from the girls. But this time, you brought them with you." He smiled at me. "Hi, Maggie, long time no see. And Lynne, you're still here? Kyle hasn't driven you away with his not-so-clever wit and lack of charm yet?"

"Shut up, man," Kyle said and pushed his leg as he sat down with us.

"So, you used to come up here, too, and escape all the girl drama?" I said and chuckled when his cheeks turned a little red.

"Nah," he refuted. "It was always these two the girls wanted. The Jacobsons are hot commodities around here."

"Bull crap! You had them eating up those stupid *'I'm a cowboy'* stories and you know it," Kyle yelled. "The one about you saving your sister from the bull was classic. Classic!"

"Eat me," Rodney said, embarrassed.

It was pretty funny how they all kind of talked the same and said the same things. You could tell they'd grown up together.

"So," Rodney said, clearly looking for a subject change. "I guess I'm gonna be your escort for the rest of the week."

"Mine?" I said in surprise. "What for?"

"Well, the assembly doesn't want you to be alone if you're outside of your room. So anywhere you go, I'll be with you."

"Why can't Caleb be with me?" I asked, and quickly turned to Caleb to read his mind, but he had me blocked off.

"You haven't told her yet?" Rodney asked. "Sorry, I just thought you would have."

"Told me what?" Caleb sighed and sat up when I did. "Told me what, Caleb?"

"I asked Rodney to volunteer to be your escort because I knew you'd need one. Because…when we have our trial tomorrow, they aren't going to let me get off."

"What? I…" What was he saying? "Why are you closed off?"

"I want to explain it to you," he said gently and cupped my face, "not have you read it out of my mind and blow up the greenhouse because you're pissed."

I looked up and saw that the glass was rattling in the door next to us. I took a deep breath and gave him a face to tell him to go on.

"You're the Visionary, they won't- no, they can't, by law, punish you. Just like the assembly members can't be punished unless it's something that was done in front of another assembly member." He sighed, his breath warming my face. "But me? They are going to put me in a cell tomorrow."

"How do you know that?" I said, my blood warming in anger.

"Because I know the laws. No one can murder another clan member, for any reason, not even self-defense."

"But it wasn't self-defense," I croaked and cleared my throat, hoping I wouldn't cry. "You killed him to save me."

"I just don't think it'll matter to them. And I wanted someone with you, someone that I trust, so you wouldn't be alone and… scared."

"For how long?"

"When they find someone guilty of something, we have a hearing and then we're put in the cells so that we can't enjoy the week with everyone else. Before I leave, they'll have another hearing to see if I'm banned forever."

"So, if you kill a guy, they put you in a cell and don't let you party? Really? That's the punishment?"

"It's not the only punishment," Rodney chimed in. He gave me a sympathetic look. "He's not allowed any visitors, at all, for any reason."

His meaning smacked into me.

"I won't be able to see him. He won't be able to see me. He'll be in withdrawal the whole week."

"So will you," Caleb growled. "I'm going to try to work out some kind of deal with them. I doubt they'll tell the Visionary to just go and be in pain. They'll probably let me see you for a few minutes a day, just for that."

"This is ridiculous."

"But it's coming, and I wanted to make sure you were taken care of."

"But what about you?" I whispered. He tipped my chin back up when I tried to duck my head.

"I'll be fine. I knew what I was getting into coming here."

"I'll fight them on this," I told him and squared my shoulders. "I'll do something, I'll-"

"Don't, baby. Just…do what they say. Rodney will be with you every day and Dad won't let them do anything crazy."

"Neither will I," Kyle spouted.

I didn't know what to say. I didn't know what to do.

"I'm so mad at you for pretending that everything was ok." I sniffed. "That's why you made such a big deal about coming to me tonight. I wondered why you'd risk it."

"I would have risked it regardless of what happens tomorrow," he said roughly. "I didn't know your room was charmed. I didn't want you to be in withdrawal in the morning, but I guess that was in vain anyway."

I peeked to see the others trying not to look at us, so I spoke in his mind instead. *We're a team, you said so yourself. So why are you still keeping things from me?*

*I didn't want you to spend the whole night upset.*

*But this isn't something stupid and trivial, Caleb. Didn't you think it might be worse for me to not know and then have them throw this on me tomorrow? I'd have busted all the windows in the place. If you warn me, I'll handle myself better. I don't like losing control-*

*I know, I know.* He pulled me to sit in his lap and I didn't protest, though he thought I might. *It physically hurts me to make you unhappy. I wanted to spare you even a minute's worth of hurt. I'm sorry if you don't like it, but I will always protect you, even if you get mad about it. I picked the lesser of two evils.*

*So, what now?*

He chewed on his lip. *I don't know, Maggie.*

*Don't say my name like you're disappointed in me.*

*I'm not.* He looked at me closely. "I could never be disappointed in you. You didn't even do anything wrong."

"But I did, didn't I? If I hadn't freaked when we got here and been so weak and…scared, you wouldn't have felt the need to hide it from me and protect me."

"That is not why I did it. And I don't think you're weak." I looked away because looking into his blue eyes when he was so sincere, so intense, made me want to burst into tears. But he wasn't letting me have it. He pulled my face back up. "Look at me. You are the strongest person I know. What's inside of me, my imprint, my need to protect you, has absolutely nothing to do with what happened today. I think you handled everything great, considering that we were totally blindsided and betrayed."

"But I *am* scared," I whispered.

"That doesn't make you weak." I just stared at him and fought my emotions. He caved, folding like a deck of cards. He pulled my face to his, a constant that I have learned to appreciate so much. "Baby, I'm sorry. I know that you hate to lose control. I was being selfish. I just didn't want you to worry about me all night."

"I understand," I said, and I did. "And I don't want you to worry about me so much."

"Unavoidable and unthinkable." The corner of his lip lifted, his dimple winking at me like it always did. "You don't really want me to be one of those lame boyfriends, do you? Forgetting birthdays? Letting your calls go to voicemail? Being late to pick you up for the movies?"

I laughed and shook my head. "No, I don't want that."

"Then you've got to take it the way it is. I'm the tyrant. That's not going to change, baby."

"I know," I sighed. "And I don't want you to change. I'm sorry. I love the tyrant, mostly."

He chuckled and shook his head. "No, you don't."

"Maybe not," I agreed and smiled, "but I don't want you to change."

"You still mad at me?" he said and cocked his head to the side. His hands slid up and down my back in a soothing motion.

"No. And you're not going to be mad at me tomorrow when I let the council know that this is idiotic and I try to stop them, right?"

"Try away."

"Good," I replied and leaned against him, pressing my face into his neck. "Ok, everyone. The awkward moment has passed. You can all talk now."

"Thank God!" Kyle yelled. "I was about to seriously pretend to be asleep over here."

"Ditto, dude," Rodney laughed. "Even though, technically, it was my fault."

Caleb kicked him with his foot. "Yeah, it kinda was."

We all laughed and settled back into a companionable silence as we lay back in the grass again. Then Lynne broke the silence. "So, does anyone know what we're doing tomorrow?"

"Well," Rodney started and rubbed his short, brown hair, "from what I was told, the hearing is definitely one thing."

"Great," everyone groaned at the same time. We couldn't help the ridiculousness of the moment. We all laughed.

# Seven

I was peaceful, I was calm and warm, and my body hummed with happiness. Like it always did when I woke up with Caleb. Woke up with Caleb…

Crap!

I jerked upright and saw it for myself. We'd all fallen asleep outside and it was morning. Caleb was automatically up with me, feeling my spike of horror. Yes, horror.

Caleb cursed in his mind as he helped me stand quickly and kicked at Kyle and Rodney's legs. "Get up. Get up!"

Kyle immediately realized the same thing, soon followed by Rodney. Kyle jerked the rope to close the skylight and we ran over the hills and ridges of the roof back to the terrace. Kyle jerked on the knob, but it was locked.

"Oh, man. Ah, man! We're dead!" he yelled.

"Move, Kyle," I said and pushed him out of the way gently. I took a slow, long breath and tried the lock. I remembered that it only worked when I got mad so I thought of Donald. It only took a second, and the lock and the door were banging against the wall. The lock flew across the terrace and went over the edge. I cringed. "Sorry."

"No time for sorrys," Caleb said. "Let's go."

"Ah!" I gasped as I finally caught the scene of the city in daylight. "Look at that!"

"Babe," Caleb groaned. "I'll take you to the city one day, or anywhere you want to go, but not today. Today we have to get you back to your room before they come to wake you. If you aren't there, it'll be more than a cell for me."

That got me moving.

We all raced down the countless flights of stairs. It hadn't been weird yesterday when we made it to the top and none of us were winded. I hadn't thought about it, but now, it seemed strange. Hmm. Well, I was winded now and even felt like I should take a breath, but didn't dare. Rodney stopped at the end of the stairway and held a hand up to us.

"Let me go. I'll signal if it's all clear."

"But won't you get in trouble for being out?" I whispered.

"Nah. I'll just tell them I'm coming to see you." He winked at me and bumped Caleb's fist. "Later, Visionary."

I was too worried to rebut. I just waited. He walked into the hall and swaggered his way down it. He was a serious cowboy. I almost laughed. When he got near our room, he flicked his fingers toward us. I took Lynne's hand and started to go, but Caleb moved, too. I stopped. "You're not coming. You still have to make it to your room without being caught."

"I am taking you to your room," he said stubbornly.

"But Rodney is right there," I told him. "You said you trusted him, so trust him. If won't be good for you, especially with what's happening today, to be caught breaking rules. Please." He scowled. "Baby," I added and he sagged against the door.

"Go, gorgeous, before I change my mind," he said, his dimple causing me difficulty.

I pulled his collar so he'd meet my lips. I realized this might be our last kiss before they put him in 'jail', so I put everything into it. The noise he made drove my pulse into overdrive. Kyle bumped us with his hand to get our attention. I sighed and leaned back unwillingly.

Caleb's hair was a cute mess of spikes and ridges. I ran my hand through it and giggled as he closed his eyes, like it was the best thing he'd ever felt. Once again, I felt this awe-inspiring empowerment come over me. I kissed his lips once more and took Lynne with me into the hall. Rodney opened her door first, and she quickly went in and made a silly face at me as she closed her door.

Then he opened mine. "I'll see you in about thirty minutes. We're meeting in the ballroom for instructions on what we're going to do today."

"Ok," I answered. "Hey, why would we have gotten into so much trouble if they caught us out of our rooms?"

"They're really strict about lights out and no one is allowed out of their room before eight o'clock in the morning. It's to keep us from starting up romances with someone who isn't our significant. They started it when they realized the imprints had stopped and people started to marry anyway."

"Oh." Well, I really couldn't blame them too much for that, I guess. "Alright. I'm going to take a shower. I'll be ready when you get back."

"Wear something nice." He wrinkled his nose. "I have a feeling your day of being the Visionary is just getting started."

"'So no fun for me? That's what you're saying?" I joked.

"Sure you'll have fun. You'll be with me," he replied and winked again. "Bye, Visionary."

"Maggie," I corrected. "Please, it's hard enough without you, too. I need someone here to treat me normally. I'm still the same girl you rescued in the woods."

"Ok," he conceded after a pause. "And although you are not the same girl I rescued in the woods, not by a long shot, I'll try."

"Good enough. See you in a bit."

"Yep," he agreed, and waved as his cowboy grin flashed and I shut the door.

"What have I gotten myself into?" I muttered before going to take another hot shower and then to figure out what to wear to my first official day as leader of the Virtuoso.

It wasn't long after I hopped out of my shower that I had a knock on my door. I looked at the wire clock on my wall and knew it couldn't be Rodney. He was way too early and I would be late if I had to entertain visitors instead of getting ready.

I peeked through the crack and smiled as I opened the door wide to let Gran, Maria, Jen and Rachel in. I heard Gran's thoughts first.

*She looks....rested.*

Rachel pulled me into a long hug. I sank into it. She was the closest thing I had to a mother now and she was so good at it. She leaned back a little and smiled sadly, like she could have heard my thoughts. "How are you holding up?"

"I'm ok," I answered and swiped at my wet hair. "But I do have to get ready."

"That's what we're here for," Jen said and picked my hand up to look at my nails. "Do you have some clear polish?"

"What? What are you-"

"We're your ladies-in-waiting," Maria chimed. "Isn't that what they're called, Gran?"

"Something like that, Miss *I Read Too Many Novels,"* she answered and hugged me to her. "Pretty girl, the council wants you to be prepped and pampered in good hands this morning…since you're certainly in withdrawal from Caleb…from being away from him all night," she said wryly and quirked a brow at me.

"Oh, yeah." I cleared my throat and turned away from Jen and Rachel's smirks. "I do feel just terrible," I said flatly, with a double dose of sarcasm. They all laughed and Rachel shook her head.

"I knew he wouldn't stay away." She smiled in pride. "That's my boy."

"So they sent you here to dress me?" I asked.

"Yep," Gran continued and went to my suitcase. "Put this on." She handed me a dress. A knee-length blue sundress. "Can you imagine!" she gasped and put a hand over her heart. "The Visionary dressing herself!"

"You don't have to do this," I told her.

"Oh, shush. I want to. I just don't like *them* telling me that I *have* to because they think the label Visionary also means incompetent. You should be truly insulted, child. Even the Queen puts her own clothes on."

I laughed. "I'll try not to be insulted. I'm glad you guys are here." I caught the croak in my throat and swallowed it down.

"Whatever happens today, Maggie," Rachel started and I saw her tearing up. I had to look away. "We're here. You will always be our family."

"Even if we have to kidnap you and be a rogue clan," Gran muttered under her breath.

"Gran!" Jen chastised in a whisper. "They'll kick you off of the council for saying stuff like that."

"Let 'em!" she huffed. "I've about had it with those old coots anyway. They lay one more ounce of insult or hurt on my girl," she rubbed my hair, "and I'll hog tie 'em all and we'll road trip it on out of here."

I giggled against my tightly closed lips. Then Rachel giggled. Then we all laughed.

"What's *'hog tie them'* mean?" Maria asked. "Are you saying they're pigs?"

"In the truest sense of the word!" Gran cackled and went back to picking out some earrings for me. "Coots and pigs, the lot of them!"

"Well, I just don't understand what the fuss is about," I said. "I know I'm your…I mean I'm a…"

"Our leader?" Gran supplied and grinned at my discomfort.

"Yes, that. But, even leaders put their pants on one leg at a time like everybody else. I promise that I will try with everything in me to be what I'm supposed to be and figure out what I need to do, but I think the biggest reason that they were being punished by God, or whatever it is that controls your power, is because of this kind of stuff. I shouldn't be put on a pedestal just because of a mark on my neck. I should be put to work. Working on figuring out why the Visionary is here and what needs to be done now."

"Spoken like a true leader. Do you really have to still question why you're the Visionary?" Gran said knowingly and plopped some silver teardrop earrings into my hand.

"I hope I don't let you down," I mumbled

"Not possible," Rachel said as she brushed my short hair. "We love you, Maggie. And we believe in you."

"I love you, too," I said truthfully.

It was the first time that I saw Gran stunned. She stared at me and then broke out in the biggest smile. "Child, you are a gift from God. I don't doubt you for one minute."

Then Jen broke out the flat iron and blow dryer while Maria started painting a thin veil of clear finish on my nails. I gave up. I laid the dress across my lap and sat on the bench at the vanity. I closed my eyes and let them make me beautiful.

~ ~ ~

Maria held my hand as we walked the long corridor. Rodney was on my other side. He was surprised when he knocked on my door to find a cackling bunch of women, instead of just one. We all walked together and my stomach growled at the spread that I saw when we reached the ballroom door. I waited and didn't go in yet. Who cooked all of this?

"Do they hire someone – humans I mean – to come here and cook and things like that?"

"Nope," Rodney answered and tipped his head to indicate a group of people off to the side. "We take turns serving. Everybody has a job at least one day for the week that we're here."

"Soon it will be the Jacobson's kitchen day," Rachel said. "My favorite day of the reunification, if you ask me." I laughed and she kissed my cheek. "Be strong today, honey. Everything is for a reason." I nodded.

Jen gave me a sympathetic look. "I wouldn’t want to be in your shoes, that's for sure." I nodded again as she hugged me.

I whispered, "I talked to my dad last night." She stiffened. "Bish is doing some job interviews in Tennessee."

"He deserves something good. I hope it…works out for him."

I leaned back to see her face. She looked on the verge of hysteria. I realized what I'd done. I noticed it before. Even though they hadn't imprinted yet, their bodies knew it was inevitable. Their imprints were reaching for each other. She was in withdrawal and she didn't even know it. As much as she wanted to just pretend that she wasn't in love with my brother and could be normal, I knew that wasn't true. This thing would drive them both mad at some point. I had to find a way to stop the vision. Had to.

She seemed to understand some of my revelation because she pulled away and licked her lips nervously. She took Maria's hand and turned back to me. "Be careful today. Donald is very…cunning, like the rest of his family."

"Thanks."

"Wait here for Caleb," Rachel said before turning to go. "You're supposed to be in withdrawal, remember?"

I nodded and clung to the wall with my back. Rodney stayed, as I figured he would. I tried to imagine what my day was going to be like. I had promised myself not to be a rabbit, but a sheep. I could be meek and soft, but butt heads if I needed to. The first thing I did was open up my mind. No more cowering in the corners of my own thoughts.

I needed to know what my enemies had up their sleeves, and I needed to know what my allies thought about it all. As soon as the door of my mind swung open, Rodney's thought hit me.

*Whew. You can do this. She needs you. Caleb is going to a cell today, no doubt about that, and they'll drag it out and make it painful because they're a bunch of sadistic jerks. But you have to keep her calm, keep her from blowing the place up. Caleb said she was powerful. She might hurt herself without meaning to. She might bring the mountain down on us...*

"Rodney," I said softly.

"Yeah?"

"Please stop." I looked at him closely, but with a smile. The last thing I needed right now was my guard to be scared of me. "I won't bring the mountain down."

His jaw dropped, but then he looked sheepish. "Crap, I forgot about that."

"Sorry, I wasn't trying to eavesdrop. I just…I kept myself closed off yesterday and I regret it now. I have to keep my mind open, so I know what's going on. So I know what certain people have planned."

"Sorry. I wasn't trying to say you were out of control or something."

"No, it's ok. I do get out of control easily, and usually Caleb's touch is the only thing to bring me back down." I smiled. "So this should be fun, huh?"

He smiled, but stopped. "I just want you to understand something. They will play their games, and they'll eat and drink and act like everything is fine. Then they'll spring it on you. Caleb will go to a cell today," he said with surety. "They obey the law to the T, and even if they seem like they've forgotten it, they haven't."

"I'm prepared now. I've thought long and hard about it. I have a plan."

"Really? Does it include busting council heads? Because I could get in on that action," he grinned.

I chewed my lip. "Well, my plan is to go with my gut. I guess it's not really a plan at all, but I've got to start being this Visionary and I think a good first action would be to spring my husband from jail." I shrugged.

"Husband," he said softly and chuckled under his breath. I hadn't even realized I'd used that word. I smiled. "I'm really happy for Caleb. He deserved to imprint."

"So do you," I said. He shrugged, non-committal. I peeked around the doorframe to look into the room and he stopped me with an arm. His skin hit mine, and I had the first vision I'd had since we got there.

# Eight

I gasped, as it always took my breath away, and held onto him so we wouldn't fall over. All we saw were feet; bare feet. They were swaying, dancing. Several sets. I looked puzzled at it. Usually the visions were pretty clear as to what was going on, but this one was strange.

Just as I came out of the vision, I felt Caleb at my back. He sighed into the back of my neck and said, "It's a wedding." He 'borrowed' my ability and had seen everything we'd seen.

"What?" Rodney wheezed. "What was that? A wedding…"

"Your wedding," Caleb clarified and wrapped his arms around me. "The vision she had was *with* you, which meant it was about you. That was your wedding, man."

Rodney's face took on an enraptured look. His mouth opened and closed several times before he finally said something. "My wedding."

I nodded. He gulped. He looked at me and spoke desperately. "Tell me it's real. The visions you have, they come true, right?"

"They have so far, unless I stop them."

"So you're saying that I'm going to imprint? Because I'd never get married without being imprinted," he said hurriedly.

"Then I'd say, I guess you're going to imprint." He jerked me from Caleb into a hug and I 'oomphed' against his chest.

"Dude," Caleb complained, but laughed. "Easy with the cargo."

"Oh," Rodney said and released me gently. "I'm sorry, please forgive me. I just-"

"I get it," I said and laughed. "It's fine."

"Really?" Rodney said once more. "Like, really? I'm going to find her?"

"Really."

"Maggie, I can't tell you what I…" he tried, but had to stop. I kissed his cheek and felt a slight burn and tingle when I did. My imprint scolding me for being so brazen. "Thank you. When I find her, I'll never be able to thank you enough."

"No thanks needed. You'll be helping me plenty today anyway, I'm sure," I said, suddenly remembering the gloom of the day.

"I'll let you two have a minute," Rodney said, still dazed as he walked into the room.

Caleb turned me to him, took my face gently, and kissed me. It was just a kiss. It wasn't a goodbye. I understood that. He leaned back and smiled. "Mom and Gran did good."

"You knew they were coming to primp me?"

"Dad told me." He nodded his head behind him. Peter was there and had been there the whole time, through the vision and all, because he had a similar enraptured look on his face.

He came forward and kissed the top of my head. "My son is always right. You are amazing."

I blushed and pushed my hair behind my ear. "It's the Visionary, not me."

"It's you, not the Visionary," he corrected. "The Visionary isn't some alive reincarnated being as the council likes to think." He held his chin between his thumb and fingers and thought, looking off into nothing. "I've always known it would be someone incredible, if it ever happened. I had always been on the fence about whether it was a fairytale or not myself. But you're real, you're humble, you're in control. The Visionary is just an add-on to you, Maggie. No matter how out of control you feel sometimes, you are in complete control. It's your decisions that will define my people from now, and the Visionary part of you is just a tool to do that."

I nodded and straightened. "I'm done being scared of this thing. I won't disappoint you."

"Not in a million years," he said and clapped Caleb's shoulder before waving his arm to the door. "Shall we?"

"Yes, but first," I turned to Caleb, "don't be mad at me later. I know what they are going to do, but I know what I have to do, too. And I'm not going down without a fight."

He smiled a devilishly, sexy smirk. "This ought to be good."

"Let's hope I don't explode Donald's head," I mumbled as we made our way.

"Oh, I don't know," Peter mused. "That sounds pretty entertaining."

Caleb and I laughed as he took me to the buffet and I almost lost my step. A spread as long as my hallway at home…and it was half filled with honey buns.

"Who told them?"

"Oh, I'm sure they have their ways," he said and chuckled as he loaded up his plate. I took a deep breath and tried to be normal, not focused on anything in particular, but not shut off to anything either.

*Ah! She's eating the honey buns! Yay! I hope she likes them!*

*What is she wearing? She's a walking fashion ad from last season!*

I turned at that and quirked my eyebrow. The two women who had been watching me both turned quickly.

"You're wide open," Caleb mused. "Is that a good idea?"

"I think so," I replied and smelled the coffee from the cup in my hands. I made a noise of delight at the heavenly aroma, causing Caleb to laugh and lead us to one of the tables in the middle. "I decided yesterday that I would have known all Donald's thoughts, his tricks and all the councils' plans for me, if I'd just opened up. I can't be closed off. I need to know what's going on. I'll just try to keep a hold on it."

"I agree. I just want you to be safe."

"I'm safe. I'm ok."

He nodded and rubbed my leg under the table as he watched me devour my honey bun with a dimpled smile. We were soon joined by Lynne and Kyle.

"These are nowhere near as good as Rachel's, ok?" Lynne spouted, even as she scarfed half of hers in one bite. "Just let it be known."

I smiled. "So does anyone know what they have planned for today?"

"Usually, the first full day here, we race," Kyle said matter-of-factly.

"Race?" I asked.

"Yeah," he said through a mouthful. "They have all these races we do, games and stuff. The three-legged dog, the cherry picker, the rat race."

"My love," Lynne said sarcastically, "will you please explain all that and don't make us beg you."

"But I like it when you beg," he said low and chuckling.

Caleb came to the rescue. "Did anyone ever tell you that you're completely inappropriate?"

"They have. And you know, I had a little talk with myself about it. It turns out I'm cool with it."

We rolled our eyes while Lynne acted like that was the most comedic line ever delivered. Then Kyle explained.

"Ok, uh…the three-legged dog is where two people tie one of their legs together and then run. The cherry picker is where they fill a tub full of cool whip and toss a whole bunch of stemmed cherries in there. You have to pick them out with your teeth and not get any cream on you. And the rat race is the most fun." He grinned.

"You've never played," Caleb told him. "You have no idea if it's fun or not."

Kyle continued on as if he hadn't been interrupted. "It's where they blindfold the men, the imprinted men, and we have to try to find our significant mixed in with everyone else. But the kicker is that they get Barcelona over there," he pointed to a tall, thin man all by himself in the corner, "to charm us so that we can't sense each other until the game is over. And…we can only touch each other's hands."

"That doesn't sound so hard," I said, thinking that I knew exactly what Caleb's hands felt like.

"You'd think that, but it's harder than it seems. And whoever the guy picks has to be his date for dinner that night, even if it's not his significant."

I grimaced. "That doesn't sound good at all."

"It's a camaraderie exercise, to get us to all keep in touch with each other and not form cliques or stay within our family the whole time. It's supposed to make us mingle. Usually they do silly dances that night, like the Waltz and the Shuffle, so it's fun and not weird, you know?"

"Hmm. I get it."

"But I doubt they'll let their precious Visionary play our games," Kyle sneered.

"On the contrary," Donald said from behind us. We all turned to see him standing there, a pretty blonde on his arm. "The council could devise its own version of the rat race just for Maggie." He looked at me and smiled. I tried to read him, and once again I got nothing. No thoughts, no memories, nothing…but malice. I felt it all over him. He hated me. And for some reason I couldn't read his thoughts, but the rest was loud and clear. He hated my guts. And not just mine, he hated the Jacobsons as a whole.

"Come on, dear," the blonde said. "I'm hungry."

"Very well, Priscilla. Maggie, I hope you enjoy this exercise and take it to heart," he said with a hard voice.

I smiled a genuine smile. "I plan to. Thank you."

He bristled at my kindness and walked over to the coffee bar.

"Kill 'em with kindness, sister!" Lynne said triumphantly. She reminded me so much of Beck. I missed her. I nodded to her and then looked to my left as we were joined by another couple.

"Philippe, right?" I asked. He and his wife both looked surprised.

"Yes. And this is my lovely wife, Marcella," he said, his accent was thick and gravelly as raw sugar. I smiled wider when she waved and went right back to her breakfast. When he turned to his wife and said something in French, they both bowed their heads to me and I was grateful that they at least listened yesterday and hadn't done a full on show.

I bowed mine in return and saw the spark in Philippe's eyes, but he quickly recovered.

*She's so humble...she's so human...*

I pressed my lips together.

"Are you reading my thoughts, Visionary?" he asked, the corner of his mouth rising. "It's all right. I wasn't trying to embarrass you. Anyone who has nothing to hide shouldn't mind if the leader, the one who's here to help us all, can read their thoughts or not, right?"

"Hmm," I mumbled. "I doubt that most of the people in this room would agree. I'm not trying to read your thoughts," I told him. "It kind of…chooses who it wants to read or not when I'm wide open this way."

"I understand. Don't worry, you have an ally in me," he whispered conspiratorially and then leaned forward. "Caleb! How are you?"

"Doing pretty good, Frenchy," Caleb goaded and put an arm around my shoulder. "Doing pretty good."

"Ah, you Americans." Philippe shook his head. "So chipper and happy." Caleb laughed and they bumped fists. Does everyone do that around here? "Marcella doesn't speak much English, but she said she'd love to have tea later."

"Um…sure," I replied. "That sounds good."

"Everyone, please, your attention!"

We turned to see the big, burly council guy again. His gray hair was coiled into a perfect sweep and his eyes were just as gray. His eyes swept over everyone and stumbled over me before moving away quickly and going to something on the back wall as he gulped.

*Oh…Is she reading my mind right now? Is she going to get a vision for me? What if she finds out about that time I gambled away a whole paycheck in New Zealand, and lied to my family and said I was mugged. Oh, crap! I just told her! She can read my thoughts! Visionary, please forgive me. Don't condemn to a life of solitude for my sins.*

He was begging me, speaking directly to me, knowing I could hear him, and everyone else was just staring at him, waiting for him to finish his announcement. I gripped Caleb's hand for a second and then stood. The man's eyes bugged as I made my way to him.

"What's your name?" I asked softly once I reached him.

"Paulo," he answered in a low voice. "Paulo, my Visionary."

"Well, Paulo, I'm Maggie." I held my hand out to him. He took it, but didn't move. I had to do the shaking. "I know that I'm the Visionary, but I'm not here to judge you. I'm here to change the way we do things from now on," I said where only he could hear me. "I had a vision of your people…"

Then I realized that everyone needed to see, not just Paulo. I turned to the room and started to say something, but the look on Marla's face stopped me. She had something up her sleeve given by her gleeful smirk. I had to be smart about this. I focused on the room.

The first thing I felt was Caleb's anger. He was reading everything through me, and could see the look on Marla's face as plainly as I could. I swept over the faces with my gaze. Every time I found a malicious looking person, someone who wasn't wondering what I might say, but looking on with an anticipation that made me shiver with anxiety, I focused on them extra hard…

And got nothing.

I got random thoughts from others in the room, but it was as if every Watson member of the family was blocked to me and I wasn't able to tap into their thoughts…like Marla.

Holy wow, I was such an idiot! Of course Marla would give each member of her family my blood. She already tested her theory at the club alley that night in the limo. She knew that her thoughts were safe with my blood in her veins, and she had something planned for this week, that I was certain.

She gave all the Watsons my blood so all of their thoughts would be out of my grasp. So I'd have no idea what they were going to do. Dang! Blindsided again.

I kept my head. I smiled and turned back to Paulo. "Go ahead and make your announcement."

"All right," he said shakily and cleared his throat uncomfortably. "Everyone, sorry for the delay. Uh…I just wanted to start the games for today."

*Don't give up so easily, Maggie.*

I cringed and took a step back when I heard the voice in my head. I looked around, but couldn't figure out who it was coming from.

*Things aren't always as they seem. Pay attention. You're smart enough to figure this out, to stop this from happening.*

*What? I'm not giving up.* I thought back, though I was sure he couldn't hear me.

"Maggie?" Jen asked and took my arm. "What's the matter? You look spooked."

"I don't know. I heard something…uh, someone." I raked my fingers through my hair, still feeling the weirdness from it being so short. "I can't figure out who it is and they're being very cryptic. I think Marla's playing tricks."

"Don't let her get to you. It feeds her ego."

"I'm not trying to." Caleb joined us and he didn't look any happier than before. "You heard?"

"Yeah," he said gruffly. "No idea what it means, but he better stay out of your head."

*How's your father?*

I looked around again in exasperation as the voice made another appearance. What did he mean, how's my father?

*Shut up. Don't talk about my father.*

"Come everyone!" Donald was saying. I put everything aside and put what I assumed was a pretty smile on my face. I needed to look in control and without fear.

Caleb took my hand and whispered, "I think you're right about your blood. It's the only thing that makes sense as to why you can't hear them, and only them. Don't go anywhere without me or Rodney, ok?"

I nodded.

"Friends!" Donald chimed and raised his hands in show. "Let's get started with today's activities! Would everyone please pick your partner while today's staff gets everything cleaned up?"

I made my way with Caleb, as he was explaining the game. No abilities could be used and we had to walk in zigzags instead of a straight line. Someone drew the outline for our paths on the floor with their ability and I saw that this would be challenging for sure. The paths weaved together and we had to outmaneuver our opponents.

As Caleb started to tie our legs together, with gold rope, what else, I was tapped on the shoulder by someone I couldn't read. Donald. Another revelation hit me then. He had my blood as well, which meant that he knew about everything Marla was up to.

I smiled at him. "Yes, Donald?"

"It's not fitting for someone of your stature to play these games, Visionary. We have selected a fitting game for you another day. For now, come sit at the assembly table with us."

"What better way to get to know the people I'm supposed to be ruling than to do what they do?" He bristled, but I kept right on smiling. "Maybe the council should play as well?" I suggested and heard his disgusted grunt. "In fact," I spoke louder, "assembly members, why don't you join us?"

"Visionary," one of them muttered. The big, burly one. "We know you are young-"

"Young is in the heart, not the body," Gran interrupted as she practically sprang from her council chair. "Or has your heart grown old and wrinkled, Lucius?"

He scoffed and went back to sipping his tea from his fine china. A couple of the council members made their way down, albeit after much internal deliberation, but most stayed put, looking every bit the pompous coots they had been labeled as.

Gran touched my cheek. "You're doing pretty dang good for your first day, pretty girl."

"Yeah, well, it's just getting started," I said and blew a much needed breath.

"That it is," she said and kissed Caleb's cheek. She went to grab Maria to be her partner. I saw Jen's leg being tied by someone, a guy I'd never seen before. He was nice looking, and his thoughts were innocent and clean. He was freaking out because he had no idea that Jen would have said yes when he asked and now, he was afraid the crush he'd had on her since forever would come shining through like a stain on a white collar shirt.

"Maggie," Caleb said to get my attention, clearly not interested in looking through his sister's non-existent love life. "Are you any good at this?"

"That sounds like a challenge," I countered and laughed as we almost fell over. Caleb's strong arms could hold us together pretty good though. "I'm good enough, I guess, though I haven't played this game since Kindergarten."

"And you sucked back then, if you want to know the truth," Kyle said from our side. "Just FYI."

"Oh, bite me," I laughed out.

"Mmm," Caleb grumbled low and wrapped his arms around me in a prison of arms. "That sounds like a challenge," he repeated to me.

I bit my lip and then grinned before kissing his dimple.

"Ready?" he asked. "I'm not in a losing mood, so let's teach them how the Visionary kicks it."

"Ready."

# Nine

We won eight out of ten rounds.

Caleb was ecstatic. All that was missing was the puffed up chest. It was pretty adorable. At the beginning, I was thinking it was pretty silly. I mean, I was pressed against Caleb so it's not like I was really complaining, but it just seemed childish, I guess, to play these games. But I quickly learned how much fun it was, and how much it brought everyone together.

The cherry picker was the worst. It sounded easy, but it wasn't at all. Kyle won and gloated endlessly about it. I kept getting cream on my nose right before I could maneuver the stem into my mouth. Kyle said it was because I was 'nosy'.

I tried not to laugh, but he was the old Kyle. The Kyle I used to hang out with and goof off. The class clown.

Even the council members who decided to join us seemed to be enjoying themselves. I think Peter and Rachel were probably the cutest. They were all proper and at attention, but as soon as the whistle rang – the whistle that blew all by itself because it too had been charmed – they took off, all business. Rachel even squealed when they won, but soon composed herself. Then just as Rodney had said, Donald sprang the trial news on us out of nowhere.

"Friends," he clapped his hands together, his scarf getting caught in his hands, "it's so good to see everyone having such a good time. Sadly, there is still business to attend and the assembly needs to convene to discuss the matter. So, if the council members will come forth, and we'll meet in the green room when we're finished."

"The green room?" I asked Caleb.

"They color code the rooms," he answered as he watched them head to the council table. "They don't want to seem biased so if they call the room a color, instead of a function, then it seems more appealing and less threatening." I gave him a questioning look. "What would the green room be called? The sentencing room?"

"Oh," I replied and swallowed. "I get it. So this is the gold room?"

"Yep."

I nodded and licked my lips that had suddenly gone dry. "They are deciding our fate in that room, and we don't even get to see it?"

"No one is allowed to make decisions on matters of discipline but council members."

"So this is a monarchy?" I snorted with annoyance.

"Pretty much," he said softly. "It'll be all right."

"Now," Donald started and I wondered if anyone else on the council ever got a say, "we have had an accounting of the events that took place the day that two from the Watson clan were murdered."

"Killed," Peter corrected. "In self-defense."

"Apples and oranges, right?" Donald taunted and continued. "Now, I have no doubt that Caleb thought he was doing the right thing by protecting his significant, the Visionary no less, but that doesn't mean that it's acceptable to take a life."

"Not even when they tried to kill you first?" Kyle yelled.

"Not even then," Donald ground out. "I know this seems harsh, but laws are laws and we must be in accordance with them. Now, we haven't convened yet, but I'm sure you all know that the Visionary will be granted clemency for her actions regarding this matter, as she must have seen the need to do so-"

"You can't just let me off and then hang Caleb out to dry!" I yelled. Everyone looked, but I kept my eyes on the table of people trying to take the love of my life away. "If I had a good reason, then what's to say that Caleb didn't as well?"

"I say!" Donald yelled so forcefully, I leaned back a little involuntarily. "The laws are laws, missy, and if you think that just because you have that tattoo on your neck that you can come in here and change the way we've always done things so they can fit neatly into your human little box, then you are going to be sorely disappointed…Visionary."

"Donald!" Peter roared.

"Don't you ever," Caleb yelled in a growl, "talk to her that way again."

"Laws are laws, " Donald repeated even as Lucius tried to pull his sleeve and make him sit down. "It can't be denied that she was chosen, she has the mark, but that doesn't mean that she's capable of-"

"I suggest you sit before you piss off your Visionary and she does something that she might need to be granted clemency for," Caleb continued and pulled me closer to him. Then he pulled me behind him completely when Donald stood.

He gasped. "Don't you dare act as though I'd hurt her! I'm merely acting as a voice for our people!"

"A voice?" Peter asked. "It seems that you're the only voice anyone can hear. There are quite a few members beside you who have the same amount of authority as you and you have yet to let them speak."

Donald looked down the table both ways, as he was sat in the center. "Well? Someone else have anything to say?"

Lucius went to speak, but Donald cut him off without even looking. "See! They don't need to speak when it's clear that I'm being diplomatic and just. Laws are laws. And you know the one thing more important than laws? It's keeping and enforcing those laws. We can't be lackluster mentors and keepers of the way."

"That's a real pretty speech," I heard myself say, my eyes focusing on his face. I didn't want to miss a thing. "But I was sent here – the Visionary was sent here – to change things. I had a vision specifically about this– Wait, isn't there some record of the last Visionary?"

"Of course there is," Donald spouted and smoothed his shirt front. "But the records are sealed. Only someone who–"

"Are you saying the Visionary can't read the records on…the Visionary?" Caleb said and sighed in annoyance. "Come on, that's not even a good argument."

"I don't know where all this hostility has come from, Mr. Jacobson," Donald said snidely, "but I don't appreciate it and I don't think anyone else here does either."

"It's coming from you trying to underhand my girl, who also happens to be your leader. I can't see where you have the authority to tell her what she can and can't do. You have to let her do what she was sent here for."

"Donald, enough," Peter said, the Champion in his voice clear. "Caleb is right and I'm not just saying that because he happens to be my son. We were all as star-struck by Maggie as you all were when we found out about who she was. She doesn't only deserve your respect, but your allegiance. Not to Maggie, but what she stands for. You can no longer pretend to still be the link that holds us all together, Donald. Give her the records."

"Yes, Donald," Lucius said harshly, "and shame on you for speaking to the Visionary in such as way."

Donald looked around and saw that the tables had turned. I could see it in his face. He thought his long years of 'service' would win him the vote over anything we said, but insulting the Visionary was apparently going too far. I tried not to take it personally that they were all worried about the Visionary and not me.

"Clearly, there has been a misunderstanding." He steepled his hands in front of him against his chest. "I am merely trying to wake the Visionary up!" He laughed. "She's been a meek, silent watcher since she arrived. I wanted to stir up something to bring out her fierceness," he growled and shook a fist as he grinned as if in triumphant. "And it worked! Look at her!" He smiled affectionately at me. "We've waited many years to see that spark. Thank you, Visionary, for coming back and taking your rightful place among our people."

Then worst thing that I could have imagined took place. Everyone stood up, clapped and bowed to me. I smiled and bowed in return, but I knew then that this was now a game. And I needed to understand all the rules before I could play.

Donald was using me for something, and I needed to figure out for what, first thing. But for now, I played my part; the sweet, but spunky, Visionary.

~~~

They eventually settled down and wanted to start their last traditional game before lunch. The game was the Rat Race and I was prepared to be touched by every man in the room who was in search of his significant.

All the men who'd imprinted were corralled into the middle of the room and the ladies stood on the outside. I still thought this was silly. I mean, guys had to know what their wife smelled like and what her hands felt like, right?

But I was wrong.

Once they were charmed and all their senses were stripped, they were like blind mice looking for a hole in the wall. I watched as several of them tried to decide which set of hands was their wife's. There were only two people who weren't married. Caleb and Kyle.

A couple got them right, most got them wrong, but no one came down my way as of yet. When it was an older guy's turn, he seemed to walk right to me. He turned his arm as if beckoning me instead of trying to find me. His family crest was half of a black raindrop, or blood drop. The Watsons. When our skin touched, I had a vision and felt stupid for not knowing that every guy who touched me would have a vision.

His vision was hazy. It fought me and I actually had to focus to see what it was. But I felt an urgency – a need – to see this vision. So I grabbed onto his hand and held on. He tried to pull away, which made me want to see it more. What was he hiding?

I heard my name being called, and then gasps and noises of surprise. Then I felt a familiar warm hand on my elbow and knew that Caleb had joined me. His touch seemed to give me the extra oomph I needed and the vision became clearer and in real time.

I saw flowers and a sidewalk. I saw and felt a man's footsteps as he made his way down the path. He waved to a mailman with a flick of his fingers and then
~~~

went around a kid on a bike. He stood in the grass and watched as another man rang a doorbell on a house.

It was a dark-haired man in a black leather jacket with a blue dragon on the back…and he was standing outside of my house.

The vision was torn from me with a roar. I saw the man standing away from me, holding his hand like I'd burned him, which I did, or he burned me rather with an offense mark.

"What were you doing outside of my house?" I asked calmly, though I was anything but calm on the inside. I held my hand to my chest and didn't even think about the offense mark. This guy was at my house!

"I wanted to see where the Visionary lived," he answered slowly and stood taller. Marla came to stand beside him and soothed him with pats on his arm.

"Don't go to my house again," I said. "That's not even my house anymore, and my father has nothing to do with this."

"Understood, Visionary," Marla said dramatically and over-bowed. "He only meant to pay homage, I'm sure."

"Doubtful," Caleb refuted behind me, his hand still wrapped around my wrist. "Stay away from that house, and stay away from Maggie."

"Of course," Marla dragged out sweetly and batted her eyelashes at him. "We're not in the habit of disobeying the ones who rule us." She turned to her minion. "Are we, Gaston?"

"Nope," he replied curtly and glared at me.

"There! All better," Marla soothed and took Gaston's arm. "We'll be on our way."

I watched her leave with a burning coal in my stomach. What was she up to?

Caleb turned me to him and I felt the offense mark sizzle away as he held on to me. I realized no one had seen the mark but Caleb.

Donald must have sensed that this round of the games was over and he called everyone to order. Then he explained how it was time for my pregnancy test, very loudly and unnecessarily.

I wondered if this was a diversion. Were they trying to keep me from barging into Caleb's trial by keeping me preoccupied? Once again, I couldn't say I wasn't going to take the test because that'd make me look guilty.

"Come on," I told Caleb. "They can't have your trial if you're not here, right?" I started to drag him with me, but he stopped me.

"We aren't allowed at our own trials, Maggie. I'm coming with you, but that won't stop them if they're trying to deflect attention from that to you."

"Well…I still want you to come with me."

He scoffed, "Of course I'm coming with you."

I smiled. "Of course. Come on."

He apparently knew where he was going. He took us down several hallways before we came to a plain white door that was marked 'Infirmary'.

He tapped on the door and then it opened to reveal Sikes' wife; the woman who took my blood when they kidnapped me. She didn't look ill, or mentally unstable from grief. In fact, she looked way too happy. I heard her in my mind.

*Thank the good Lord...*

"Maggie," she sighed and seemed to be relieved. "I'm glad you're alright. Come in." But she stopped Caleb. "Not you."

"I'm coming-" he started, but she moved to the side to show that she wasn't alone. There was a man there, not a Watson though. I caught something in his mind about being an unbiased chaperone and figured that Gran had probably insisted someone other than a Watson be present.

"The assembly is very thorough," she said dryly. "I'll be finished in no time."

Caleb ran one hand through his hair angrily and watched me as she closed the door. I sat on the bed, as there was no use in fighting.

She eased onto the bed next to me and reached across to the bedside table. I looked away.

"I remember you hating needles." She smiled as if there was no history between us. "I'll make it as painless as it was last time."

"Yeah," I said sarcastically. "The last time you took my blood and gave it to them."

"Circumstances are the same as they were then. I am a Watson, that can't be changed even if my husband is no longer alive," she said softly and glanced up at my face for a split second.

I thought about what she said. I thought about what she'd done and where she came from. I remembered that she'd said she was human, and her touch wouldn't hurt me like the others who wished me harm. I remembered that Caleb didn't know about her being human…

"How come the other clans don't know that you were a human?"

"Because Sikes didn't want them to know, and Sikes always got his way. Always," she said. I heard the bitterness in her voice.

Her fingers touched me and I jerked from the cold of her skin. She apologized in a whisper as she guided the needle expertly into my skin. She was good at it, and it didn't hurt too badly, but that didn't mean that I didn't feel it this time.

I winced and Caleb stuck his head inside the door. "Everything all right in here?"

"Yes, prince," my guard said sarcastically as he crossed his arms in the corner. "A needle stick isn't supposed to feel like cherries in springtime."

I snorted a laugh. Caleb raised his eyebrow at me with a twist to his lips. "I'm ok, I promise," I told him.

He nodded reluctantly and backed out.

I turned to look at her, but the needle was still pulling my life from me so I swallowed the bile and turned my head again. "You're taking an awful lot," I mused. "Seems strange to take so much for one blood test."

"Honey, you know I'm not doing a pregnancy test."

I jerked my gaze to her, surprised by her candor. "You're not?"

"Marla wants more of your blood, and I am bound to do what she says."

"And why is that?" I asked and looked at the guard who stood silently. He never looked our way, though I knew he could hear us. "Why would you even tell me all of this?"

"Because," she began and stopped her ministrations to look me right in the eye. "I know what it's like to have your life taken from you one day with no rhyme or reason, no cause, and no way back."

"What are you talking about?"

"I didn't imprint with Sikes the…conventional way."

"What?" I said with as much irritation as I could muster at the woman with the needle in my arm.

"I was like you; human, alive, a typical teenager where everything that happens to you is the worst thing ever. Because it is. It is the worst thing ever when you haven't lived yet. Sikes pulled me from the street one day, took me to his compound and performed test on me. Blood test."

She looked at me poignantly and I knew the next words out of her mouth were about to change my world. The Virtuoso world, too.

"He was exactly the same back then as he is now…well," she blanched, "was." She cleared her throat. "He was determined to gain the upper hand over his race. He was determined that the key was in the blood. He kept me for a couple of weeks, and I wasn't his only prisoner. He had several of us down there."

"But," I was baffled, "you helped him kidnap me. You acted like you… loved him."

"Oh, honey, I did love him. And he loved me, after the imprint of course." I just shook my head in confusion so she went on. "You see, he used my blood, and the other's blood, to perform experiments on each other. He was certain that he could force an imprint." She sighed and took a long breath. "And he succeeded."

"What?" I gasped.

"When he was performing his experiments on me, he wound up giving me his blood. Then one day, for no particular reason, he touched my hand to feel my pulse…I felt the imprinting. I saw the visions. I felt his attraction to me. I knew he had some sort of feelings for me…because he never made me scream."

"What do you mean?" I asked, though the ice in my veins as I read the answer out of her head begged me not to ask her.

She took a long breath, one filled with regret, longing, and guilt. "During the experiments, he never made me scream like the others did."

# Ten

The bile was rising just as Caleb burst back into the room. I could barely think, but soon understood that my heart was beating a mile a minute. I pressed my hand against my chest just as Caleb jerked me from the table, putting me behind him and assessing the threat of the room. The older, graying woman and the man who had yet to move a muscle didn't prove to be what was causing me so much terror.

He turned to me, while keeping an eye on the other two. "What's wrong, Maggie?"

I had to ignore him for now. I had to understand what she was saying. I moved around Caleb toward her and he turned me back to face him. I felt his fast heartbeat reach into my chest, and I knew that I needed to calm him first. "I'm fine. It's ok."

"What happened? Did she do something to you?"

"No, just told me something that I didn't like." I nodded toward her. "I have to finish this. I'm ok," I assured him.

"I'm right here," he said as I turned around, "and I'm not going anywhere."

"Uh…what's your name?" I asked her before I went further.

"Ruth," she answered in a whisper.

"Ruth, what did he do to you?" I asked and felt Caleb pulling the answers from my head behind me. He grunted when he found what we were talking about and he gripped my hand like he'd never let go.

"At first he did stupid things. He would try to bully them into a reaction from their body. He tried to scare them into it, like their body would choose that over death or pain. But it doesn't work that way, and when we imprinted, it changed things. He wasn't able to give his blood away anymore."

"Why not?" I asked in enraptured curiosity.

"Because I was jealous," she said and smirked. "More than that, my imprint demanded that he be only mine."

"So you really loved each other?"

"Yes," she answered carefully. "We were bound, we were together, and we belonged to each other. But it wasn't right. It wasn't the same as everyone else."

"Ruth," I said in exasperation, "you're talking in circles and it's making me a little crazy. Will you please not make me pry all the answers out of you?"

She sighed and nodded once. "It's just that I've never told a soul any of this before. I wasn't allowed to when Sikes was alive and now it still feels like betrayal." I started to ask her why, but she held her hand up. "I'm getting to it, Miss Impatient."

I fought not to roll my eyes and gave a motion for her to continue. I sank back into Caleb's chest, feeling the need for his calm and soothing. I had a feeling she was saving the best for last. She continued.

"I wasn't allowed to go against him. I wasn't my own person. I practically belonged to Sikes, and not in the romantic way that you two belong together. He controlled me, whether he wanted to or not. My body submitted to his every subconscious will. His blood in my veins made some sort of connection in me that allowed me to imprint with him, but it wasn't real." She looked at us both and curled her lip a little. "Sikes never looked at me the way that boy looks at you."

"But you said you both loved each other?" I argued.

"And we did, but it was because I had no choice. You know, it's as if you have a family member who had hurt you. You still love them, but you don't like them?" she tried to explain. I nodded. Yes, I knew what that felt like all too well. "From the moment we imprinted, I knew that things were different for us, that we were one of a kind."

"Wait," Caleb said gruffly behind me, his breath breezing over my ear. "The imprints were still working then. Sikes would have imprinted the natural way if he'd just waited. What was he trying to accomplish?"

"The Watsons started losing their imprints long before the rest of the clans," she answered and I felt Caleb jerk. "They just didn't tell anyone. They were ashamed and didn't want to appear even weaker to you. It was only a few at first, and the clan covered it up. They hid those men away and didn't let anyone know. When Sikes reached imprint age and realized he was going to be one of the ones to be stuck away in the compound with the rest, he refused to submit to that. So he began his secret experiments. No one ever went down to the well compound. It was old and wearing down. He knew he wouldn't get caught there, and he didn't."

"This whole time, every time I've seen you, you're saying that your imprint hasn't been real?" Caleb said slowly.

She lifted her wrist. I saw the half-black water drop on her wrist. "This is a tattoo," she revealed and rubbed it with her fingers. "A real tattoo. And it hurt like the dickens."

I gaped at her. "You didn't get your tattoo when you…" I blushed at what I was about to ask her.

"No," she said and gave a sweet little chuckle. "Sikes and I never mutualized. We were unable to. He even had to go and have my name tattooed on his crest. It never appeared and he didn't want anyone to know that it wasn't real. When he revealed me to his family as his significant, they were skeptical. He was a little older than most, but they didn't question it once they saw our tattoos and the way we could read each other's minds."

"Why didn't Sikes tell anyone? He could have imprinted his whole family that way," I said and was truly baffled. If he had the power to do it, it was unbelievable that he had not.

"Because he knew it was wrong." I scoffed and she looked at me sharply. "I'm not trying to justify him. I loved him and hated him. I wanted him and wanted to run away every second of every day. I needed his touch and craved it, but also wanted to vomit every time he touched me. He felt the same. It wasn't right, it wasn't a life. It was a prison, for us both. Yes, we gained abilities, yes, we could communicate with our minds, yes, we healed each other, but the intimate parts, the soul bonding parts of the imprint were missing. For us, it was all chemical. All physics and alchemy, and Sikes always regretted what he did to me."

"Why?" I whispered because I couldn't stop myself.

"Because he loved me. Whether he wanted to or not, he loved me, and it was against his imprinted nature to hurt me."

"Ok," I replied, soaking everything in. "So, if that was the case, then why did he make you help him and why did he kidnap me?"

"Well," she began and I heard her thoughts.

*Oh, boy…this is where it gets hard*

"Just touch me then," I told her. "Let me read it all through you, if you don't mind."

"That would be easier. I have no secrets anymore," she said sadly and gave me her hand. It was the swiftest, most eager vision I'd ever had. I guess because she was offering it instead of me taking it. It jerked my senses alive and I felt her emotions as raw and real as if they were my own.

I saw her with Sikes. They both looked so young as they were new in their relationship. It was awkward for them, even more awkward than it had been for me, but they couldn't deny the need for each other. The attraction was mostly on his side; he'd felt strange about her ever since he'd kidnapped her. He felt something in him that was protective of her. Then after they imprinted, he felt guilty. Ruth was swamped by his guilt of how he'd entrapped her, when in truth, that was what he'd been trying to do. Instead of reveling in his accomplishment, he wallowed in his shame and pain. Over the years, that turned to bitterness.

When Caleb and I imprinted, it was the final straw. He made it his new mission to remake the imprints in his family, regardless of the consequences to the ones involved. He knew their imprints would be broken and faulty, like his was, but it no longer mattered. He was blinded by rage.

Marcus was his first apprentice. He clued him in on everything, about the forced imprint on Ruth, about how he planned to take me and use my blood to set their family free. About how Marcus was going to be the first one to imprint after Sikes figured out how to do it again. He hadn't been a very good scientist.

She laughed, shook her head and spoke out loud. "He was so furious and rage filled when he started it all, he didn't even perform his tests in a constructive way. He had no idea why we imprinted. He long since stopped giving me his blood. The imprint seemed to be a fluke, but we knew better."

"I'm sorry, but you didn't tell me anything so terrible. Why were you so worried about telling me that?"

"The part I was reluctant about, is telling you that Marla gave me her blood. Not just me, but every Watson. Which, in turn means that we all have your blood as well."

"Maggie already figured that out," Caleb dismissed. "There's something else you're not telling us."

"Wait," I said. "If she gave you my blood, I shouldn't be able to read your thoughts."

"I know," she replied. "I'm the only human. I can only guess that is why. But Marla doesn't know that you can. I am, however, bound to her blood as a Watson. Something happened when I imprinted with Sikes that made me under their power. Even though Sikes is no longer here, I have her blood, therefore I have to follow her."

I processed all that with a sigh. Caleb was doing the same behind me, his arms still manacles to keep me from harm. "So what is it that Marla wants?"

"And there's the kicker; I can't tell you."

"Why?"

"Because she forbade me to. She didn't say anything about telling you my past, but she specifically said not to say anything else about what we're doing here."

"Well, at least she's keeping things interesting," Caleb grumbled.

"So, I was right? Everyone who has my blood in them is immune to my ability. But why? That doesn't make any sense to me."

"As I'm sure lots of things don't," she said softly and I remembered the man in the room with us. I glanced at his wrist. His tattoo was a half of a cloud. He wasn't a Watson, for sure. So why was she speaking so freely in front of him?

I turned my gaze to him. He squirmed appropriately and coughed. "I'm Rodrigo, Visionary," he answered my unspoken question and bowed. He looked back up to me and grinned. "Shall I kiss your fingers?"

"Not gonna happen," Caleb said. Whether it was out of jealousy at Rodrigo's blaring thought of how delicate and delicious I looked or because he knew I hated the bowing was unclear. Ok, it was pretty clear. "You can get up now, *Mister* Gonzales. I'm sure Mrs. Gonzales wouldn't appreciate your leering at the Visionary."

"You know him?" I asked Caleb.

"Babe," he said sarcastically. "I know everyone. I was born with these people."

"Oh, yeah, that's right."

Rodrigo smiled. "Yes, Caleb was such a rambunctious child," he explained with a heavy accent. "I see he has grown to be quite a rambunctious young man as well."

"You trust him that much?" I ignored him and asked Ruth. "He's not of your clan."

"But," she started, "he is the one who charmed this room so that no one could hear our conversation in here."

Charmed the room....something was working in my mind. I gasped when I got her meaning.

"You!" I accused him and pointed my finger. "You charmed my bedroom!"

"I knew who did it," Caleb confessed. I turned to him. He placed his hands on the top of my shoulders. "I knew *who* did it, I was just mad that the assembly would *make* him do it."

"Make him..." I pondered. "So he can't say no or they'll think something's up? Is that it?"

"Basically," he answered. "It's not uncommon for them to use our abilities if the situation calls for it."

"Use our abilities," I mused. I turned back to Rodrigo. "Sorry."

"It's all right," Rodrigo interrupted and smiled. "I didn't actually think you'd be happy about it, but I didn't really have much choice. I also thought it would take you a while to realize it...since Caleb was supposed to be in his room last night...and not in yours," he remarked with a quirked brow and a smirk.

I tried not to blush again. "So, you're helping Ruth. Why?"

"Because, like her, I know what it's like to be used for her abilities. And I don't want things to stay the same any more than you do, Visionary." He came to me and knelt on one knee, but I wasn't upset. I could tell this was something more than blind worship. "I am willing to help you in any way that you will allow me, but I have to play my part for the assembly as well. We all do. When I heard that the Visionary was here," he smiled brilliantly, "I knew that change was coming. Me, and my family, are happy to be of service to you."

"I understand and I appreciate that. I have no doubt that we'll need all the people that we can get." I turned to Ruth as Rodrigo stood. "Does this mean you're with us, too?"

"I think you know the answer to that," she answered. And I did. She wanted to help, but couldn't. She was bound to Marla's blood and couldn't do anything to go against that, her body wouldn't let her. But she wished us all the best and would help if she could.

"So not everyone is so blindly devoted to the assembly as I originally thought?" I asked no one.

"No," she answered and squeezed my hand, "but they all have their part to play, too."

"I know the feeling," I whispered.

"But Marla isn't what you think. She's a spoiled, selfish child with an ego the size of Delaware, but she's been trained from birth to think that she's better than everyone else, either because they are human and she's above them, or because they aren't a Watson and therefore aren't as good as she is. Sikes brainwashed her just as he did Marcus. She's smart, she's quick thinking, and she's cunning, but she's cocky. She thinks she can't lose. But she's wrong."

I nodded. I had one more question for her. One I knew that Caleb would blow up about if I was right, so I blocked him, but he immediately caught on to me. "What are you doing, Maggie?" he asked me roughly.

I opened back up, looked at Ruth and steeled myself. "I have another question, and I want you to tell me the truth." I felt Caleb's understanding slam into me. He waited with breath held. "Sikes killed Caleb's grandfather in an echo, didn't he? It wasn't a heart attack."

She stared at us silently for a long time and we had our answer. Caleb sighed roughly and I swiftly turned and hugged him to me.

Why did I do that? Why not just let him believe that his grandfather died of natural causes? Because their family needed to know the truth, that's why. I loved them. I loved Caleb's family. They were sweet, and they were strong and faithful to one another. They were efficient and hard-working, but they weren't upset. They weren't passionate about making change. They couldn't really be on the same page as the Visionary, and truly be on my side, until they got angry. And knowing that their Champion was murdered was enough to do that.

"I'm sorry," I whispered into his neck. "I'm so sorry."

"I always knew," he said, the anguish marking his voice. "I always knew it was something else. Ah, man, Gran…"

I began to regret my thinking process. Maybe it wasn't worth his family's pain to bring them to the surface of the problem.

"No," Caleb refuted me. "No, they need to know. You're right. We may not have been the problem, but sitting by and knowing something was going on and not doing anything to stop it was bad enough." He sighed his frustration across my face. I pressed my palm to his cheek to draw off some of his anguish. "We've got to tell the family."

"Caleb, maybe you should think about it," I started, but he pressed his thumb over my lips.

"No, you're right," he said and kissed the tip of my nose.

"I'm so sorry about him. I wish there was another way, but I bet your grandpa would have done whatever was necessary to bring them around, huh?"

"You are absolutely right, Visionary." He smiled at my frown. "Don't scowl at me," he said playfully and pulled me closer. He pulled me up by my chin to kiss my lips and then spoke against them. "I love you, baby."

"I love you." I started to go back in for more of those kisses when I saw movement out of the corner of my eye. Rodrigo was slipping out the door. "Wait. Thank you."

"Don't thank me, just do what needs to be done and don't let them intimidate you. You have everything you need right there with you and within you," he said ominously.

"Ok," I barely voiced, but he was already gone.

"Let's go," Ruth said and pushed me gently with a hand on my elbow. "I don't want Marla suspicious because we're taking too long." I saw the blood vials wrapped gently in her fingers. She followed my line of sight. "I have to," she said.

"I know." She had to take the blood to Marla. She didn't have a choice. "Don't worry about me, we will figure all of this out." I closed my eyes and tried to focus. "As soon as I figure out where to start."

# Eleven

The walk back to the gold room was quiet. Caleb was thinking about how to go about telling his family. But as soon as we walked into the ballroom, I knew we wouldn't be telling anyone anything right then.

The family was scattered all over the place as they watched Kyle juggling in the center. He was laughing and then he started to dance. He moved his feet and kept the rhythm of the oranges he was juggling. Caleb and I went to stand next to Gran as everyone watched with big smiles on their faces. When he started doing the Moonwalk, I lost my composure.

He was so good at it! Caleb and I laughed uneasily, and Gran slapped her knee in her joy as she chuckled. Lynne was jumping up and down, clapping and laughing as she watched. When he was done, he collected his oranges and bowed. Lynne jumped at him as he made his way to her and he almost fell over as she wrapped her arms around his neck.

As everyone was laughing at the spectacle they were making, Maria made her way to us. She hugged me around my middle and smiled before saying, "Uncle Caleb, will you play for me?"

"Play what, M?" he said and leaned down to hear her over the ruckus.

"The guitar. Mom's going to play piano and I want to sing *Brighter Than The Sun*." Caleb groaned in jest and Maria pressed her palms together in front of her face and pleaded. "Please!"

"Oh, all right," he conceded and turned to me. "I'll be back. A little public humiliation never hurt anyone, right?"

I saw in his mind that he played every single time they came together for the reunification. He was just being modest,

I laughed and accepted his kiss to my cheek. While he was getting started, Gran looped her arm through mine. "Did you get your blood tests done?"

"Yes, ma'am," I answered. "Did y'all convene about Caleb yet?"

"No, ma'am," she said and nudged me to make sure I understood her joke. "I'm sure they'll bring it up sooner than later."

"Do you enjoy being on the council?"

"Not a minute of it," she admitted, "but it was appointed to me and I figured my Raymond would've wanted me to do it."

At the mention of Caleb's grandfather's name, I winced.

"What's wrong?" she asked with concern.

"Nothing, I just…" I stalled. Caleb wanted to tell his family all together about his grandfather. It was such a shock to lose someone. Once you had a significant, you could always be healed, so early death was not common among their race. The fact that it wasn't an accident, and he was murdered so maliciously and deviously just made things even worse. "I'm just trying to…strategize," I told her.

I smiled at Caleb as he strummed along and Maria's sweet, melodious little voice carried across the room to the tune of Colbie Caillat. He winked and I couldn't help but grin at him.

"Well, get to strategizing, girl," she said, "cause here we go."

I started to ask what she meant, but I saw Donald coming across the room with a posse of council members behind him. Maria was just finishing her song and Caleb stood with a grimace before making quick strides to my side. He took my hand and pulled me behind him. I wanted to tell him it wasn't me that was in danger, it was him.

"Come, Winifred," Donald commanded. "We will begin the trial at this time."

Gran went with them silently and they all left without another word.

The rest of the long, waiting day was spent watching everyone who wanted to perform for us. They all had talents, some to do with their abilities. Some were pretty hilarious and some were fantastically masterful.

Caleb wrapped his arms around me from behind. I could feel his chuckles as we watched a guy with blonde hair and a green bowtie do magic tricks. Caleb was trying to put my focus on other things and not what was going on in the room back there. I was grateful to him for it, but I wasn't about to let it go.

"Everything will be all right," he said into the skin under my ear. He kissed the same spot. "I promise."

"You're right, it will." I smiled. "Because I'm going in there."

"Maggie "

I turned to him. "I told you, I wasn't going to sit by and watch."

He lifted his hands as if to say, *whatever, go ahead,* his dimples in full swing.

I kissed him and made my way to the room that the others had gone through. Peter caught up to me.

"I can only guess what you're going to do," he said wryly.

"Caleb wouldn't just sit out there while my trial was going on, would he?" I asked. I saw Peter's face light up. His mind still, even after weeks had passed, couldn't wrap itself around the fact that his son belonged to me, and that I was just as gung-ho about his safety and happiness as he was about mine.

"I know that this won't change anything," he said carefully. "Their decision is set in stone already, but it makes me so proud that you would try."

"I have to," was all I could say. I made my way to the 'sentencing room'. I figured you should just call it what it was.

I stayed in the hall, waiting for the right time to burst through with my proclamation of Caleb's release from responsibility from this. He was saving me, shouldn't that count for something?

I waited….and waited, and waited. They talked about everything but Caleb. I was there for over an hour waiting for them to get to the point. When they started discussing the cracking ceiling in the gold room once more, I slid down the wall to my haunches in aggravation. What on earth was wrong with them? They were talking in circles.

Then I realized the conversation was exactly like before. Word for word. Daggumit!

The room was charmed! Just like when Ruth had Rodrigo charm the infirmary room so no one would hear what we were talking about. I tried to focus on the room, to hear what Gran was saying and what was being said, but I couldn't. Their thoughts were all blocked and I had my definitive answer.

Those jackals!

I dallied no longer and burst through the door of the room. They all looked up surprised as they sat poised behind a rounded table so they could all face each other. They stood and bowed slightly. This room was not lacking in embellishments either, but I turned to the problem at hand. Before I could speak, Donald addressed me in his formal, irritating way.

"Ah, Visionary. We were just discussing your pregnancy results and it turns out that you are not! Isn't that wonderful?" he beamed and waited to see if I reciprocated.

"I already knew that," I replied starkly. "I'm here to ask for clemency for Caleb. I want to explain what happened so that you understand that what he did was absolutely necessary."

"We never doubted that Caleb *thought* he acted accordingly," Paulo said and bowed slightly to me again, as if just now remembering. "Visionary. Our concern is that the law states no matter the terms-"

"I know, I heard this earlier. I'm saying that it wasn't self-defense though. He did what he did to save me. One of the members of the Watson clan was coming after me with a gun."

"A gun!" Donald roared and laughed loudly. "Why on earth would an Ace need a gun?"

"Because they have no abilities," I reminded him, though it made me feel almost sorry for the Watsons to have to resort to that. What else was a villain with no power to do?

"A gun," he mused again and chuckled, annoying the heck out of me. "If you had said a knife maybe, or even a baseball bat, it may have been more credible."

"What are you saying, Donald?" Paulo hissed, his eyes darting furiously in indecision.

"I'm just saying that I think our Visionary is stressed…and maybe a little confused." He stood menacing and tall. "I spoke with Marla on this matter and she informed me of all of your little problems with your new power; breaking glass, light bulbs. We even saw your little display yesterday with the…blue things."

"Energy ribbons," I snapped.

"Yes, those. I don't think there's any shame in admitting that things are getting to be too much for you."

"It's not," I answered, but the glasses on the table started to rattle, sloshing drops of water all over the wooden surface. I took a deep breath, praying Caleb didn't bust in here to see what was the matter. "This is just backlash of what happens when I get upset. Or angry," I said harshly to Donald. "It doesn't mean that I'm not in control and my view of what happened that day isn't confused with helplessness. I remember everything perfectly clear. Caleb was shot in the stomach," I saw Gran flinch, "and I had to save him with my touch. As a matter of fact, I'll show you."

I opened up my mind to do so, but forgot I needed Caleb to do these kinds of things. "Wait just a second. Let me go get Caleb and I'll show you-"

"Caleb cannot be present at his own trial!" Donald refuted earnestly. "Visionary, there are rules!"

"But I'm telling you it wasn't his fault," I argued. I'd never felt so temperamental in all my life. They were bringing out my worst teenage girl attributes and it was pissing me off even more. "I need Caleb to show you what I'm talking about. He's the trigger for my Visionary abilities."

"Preposterous," he said slowly, but his eye lit with something I didn't understand. "There's no way your ability needs someone else to make it work. The Visionary is her own power, her own ability."

"I'm telling you the truth," I bristled. "And I'm getting kind of tired of you calling me a liar."

"Forgive me, that's not what I meant," he replied, but the exasperation in his voice refuted any apology in it. I stared hard at him and squinted, letting him know that I knew his thoughts weren't available to me. "I just mean to say that there are laws and rules that cannot be broken for anyone, no matter the reason. The laws are what we've lived by for centuries, and we can't change that for one boy who broke them in hopes of using his significant as a free pass."

"Caleb didn't ask me to come in here. I came on my own, for my own reasons."

"We will continue the trial," Donald said as if I hadn't spoke, "and get everything settled. Visionary, please wait outside while we deliberate. It wouldn't be proper for you to be present during sentencing because you're so emotionally involved, otherwise you would be more than welcome."

"Isn't the verdict already in?" I said sarcastically and looked to Gran. She stood stoic and still. "Hasn't Caleb's fate already been decided?"

"Pretty girl, some things can't be changed by will alone," she said ominously. I squinted at her. "Some things just are," she said pointedly.

*Unless you change them. You have to play by their rules until you're in a position to do something different.*

I sighed and tried to play off like Gran wasn't speaking privately to me. "Fine," I ground out and looked at Donald and only Donald. "This isn't over, for me or the Visionary."

He gulped angrily, but nodded once in concession. I stomped out of the room and made my way back to the gold room. I was fuming, but also trying to process what had happened. Gran was clearly trying to send me a message that I needed to take the reins, but I didn't know how or where to start.

I was worried about Caleb. I was worried about how I was supposed to teach or lead these people. I was just worried. When the gas sconces started to shake from my worry, I was done.

I put my forehead against the cool wall and begged. I begged whoever or whatever it was that was in control of all of this to give me a little sign, a little hand out, a little clue, something. I was lost. I was floating in a sea of self-doubt and uncertainty. I had the desire to do what was needed, but didn't feel like I had the tools. That was when I felt it.

The feeling of cold water rushed over me, touching all of my senses, inside and out. I shivered in the realization that this was the answer to my prayer. I got a feeling like I'd felt the day I found out I was the Visionary. A knowing calm, but an intense wave of emotion came over me. I knew what I was here to do now.

The council had to hit the dusty trail. That was number one.

Number two, was that I had to stop the Watsons. Too many years, they played with the loopholes in the Virtuoso laws so that they could practically do anything they wanted, because human laws were of no consequence to them. They had hurt humans for years, and although it seemed that a lot of people knew something strange was going on, nobody was jumping up and down to do much about it.

And that had to change.

A soon as I recognized the task and let it grab hold of me, I felt myself start to warm back up. My mind cleared, so thin and light, and everything just seemed more open to me. I could hear everyone, almost at once, as they laughed and joked over their supper. I could decipher and know who was who and what was what. It was very different from the way it was before, where I had to strain so much and focus to catch glimpses. This…

It was like a new world had opened up to me.

Was this what had been wrong with me all along? I had fought the Visionary and not embraced it. I whined and complained when I should have understood the magnitude of such a gift. I could see things. I could see the future! I had been fully content to squander that to go back to being a normal teenager. But no, I couldn't. And you know what? I didn't want to. Not anymore. I had a hunger now after seeing Caleb's kind; the good, happy people who just wanted peace and imprints so they could have their lives back and a future to look forward to.

Before, did I even fully understand that this generation would have been their last if the imprints didn't come back? I assumed they were, deep down I assumed, or hoped. And, as much as I was angry with the Watsons, they were desperate just like everyone else and instead of sitting by, they were trying to be proactive. Yes, they were cruel and sadistic, but at least they were doing. And the rest of the Aces better get to *doing* too so we could catch up. We needed to counteract the Watsons, learn from their cleverness, and expel their hate and bitterness from the people as a whole.

We didn't need some convoluted system with a bunch of people who didn't have our best interests at heart to rule us. I didn't want to rule us either. Our people were strong and able to carry themselves. It wasn't that hard.

Why couldn't everyone just follow the Golden Rule? Why couldn't everyone just live their own lives and then meet back up once a year for a reunion? Was it so hard? It may be naïve thinking, but for now, I was going to focus on just that. Getting these people to realize that they had power and, though they may have forgotten it because the imprints seemed to leave them helpless, they were far from it.

So I watched them. I stood in the doorway of the grand gold room and watched them all without any rose-colored glasses on, without any blinders, without any notions. I just watched, and smiled. They really were a good people. They just let things get out of hand. I laughed into my fist as Maria threw a grape into the air and caught it in her mouth. Jen was opened mouth in awe about it and laughed as she demanded her to do it again.

Peter and Rachel were the same as always, a picture perfect example of poise and worry. They were discussing in their minds to one another about tonight when they take Caleb. About how I'll react, and how in the morning I'll be in withdrawal. Caleb and I both will be.

They were just as worried about me as they were about Caleb. I was upset about it. And Rodney, sitting with Caleb, Kyle and Lynne, was dreaming out the vision I'd had of his wedding. My eyes slid passed Caleb, who had been watching me the whole time with his signature smirk, and I tried not to giggle, to Kyle and Lynne. He was rubbing her thigh and Lynne was scolding him for being so brazen, though her giggling probably didn't solidify her argument.

Philippe, his wife and their young daughter were mowing down some chips. The whole place smelled of delicious cod and chips, but I just couldn't make myself eat. I was too wired, too full of anticipation.

Then I took in the rest of the room. Everyone looked so normal and human; an extremely proficient façade. I fought it as long as I could before forcing my eyes to the Watsons. They had quarantined themselves off to the side with purpose and dedication to being the villains and outcasts. I glared at their backs as I crossed my arms and silently told them all they were going down in a fiery crash of justice and humiliation. And I would enjoy it immensely.

"A fiery crash of justice and humiliation?" I heard off to the side and looked over at Caleb. I shrugged and went back to my glaring. "That's a witty revenge."

"I'm in a witty mood," I said dryly. "And I'm not hungry, so no, but thank you," I answered his questions before he asked.

"You need to eat, babe," he ordered softly and sighed. "It's gonna be a long night."

I knew what he was talking about, but still didn't want to eat. "Come with me?" I asked, and held my hand out with a coy smile.

"Avoider," he accused and smiled crookedly as he took my hand. The lights went off and on once to indicate it was almost bedtime. "Whatever. I'd rather take you to your room than watch you eat fish anyway."

I bit my lip at his words and gave him a sideways glance. He chuckled silently and pulled me under his arm as he kissed my temple. We walked silently to my room. The gloom that had plagued me all day settled back in as I realized that our night was almost over, and the outcome of tomorrow was uncertain. I listened to him try to calm me.

*I don't want you to be under some assumption that everything will just work out tonight in our favor. Please don't freak out.*

"How can they do this though, Caleb? I just don't know what it's going to accomplish other than puffing up their chests."

He grunted his annoyance which matched my own.

"I don't know," he said and watched our hands locked together between us. "I don't know what game they're playing."

"The last time we were separated was…" I shuddered thinking of being in the Watson compound. Now I was surrounded by Watsons every time I turned the corner. It just wasn't right. It didn't feel right, and the fact that the assembly was a tit-for-tat ruling machine made me feel even more unease. What a bunch of hypocritical coots.

"Don't think about that," Caleb commanded softly and ran a hand through my hair, scalp to neck. I shivered, but not because I was cold.

Caleb had been very greedy of my touch ever since we got here, as if he knew that the assembly was going to try to pull something like this. He and his father both were magnificent. They defended me, our family, our actions and reasons for killing the Watsons, all of it. But in the end, it didn't matter, and though I'd been granted clemency because I was the precious Visionary, Caleb's fate was up in the air and undecided.

He said he wasn't worried. He told me it would all be alright, and by the end of our night here in London, in this beautiful underground castle that was as sinister as it was pleasing to the eye, I almost believed him. But now, as we stood in the long corridor of rooms that were presented in elegance by 'rank' among the Virtuoso, I looked around me. The place was just dead. If I peeled a scrap of that pretty golden wallpaper off with my fingernail, I wondered what I'd find. Concrete? Prison bars? Or something much more alive and malicious, like a ghostly presence that seemed to blanket everything within view.

The lights flickered in the hall, which was what they told us would indicate 'lights out'. Yep. I was engaged, I was almost eighteen, I was in London with my fiancé's family, I was the Visionary – an esteemed and revered artifact of an ancient race – and I still had a curfew.

And this would be Caleb and my first night here and first real night apart. He breathed deeply, his fingers digging further into my hair, and dragged me against him. The assembly has spoken of propriety, of morals, of rules and regulations, ceremonies and a slew of other things that Caleb and I were supposed to be either doing or already done. When they'd seen our tattoos, marking us as mutualized significants, they had blown an old coot gasket.

So, what was I to do when being placed in a position where I was being controlled and told exactly what I was going to do, with no say in the matter? Naturally, I said, 'Screw you, propriety.'

# Twelve

I turned and pressed Caleb's back into the wall, letting his arms crush me to him. When he murmured against my lips, I pulled back the barest inch to hear him.

"I said, I like you like this. You should be pissed off more often," he said low and chuckling, but he was dead serious, too. I ignored Lynne and Kyle as they made their way swiftly to the room next to mine. He kissed her and she slipped inside. He grinned at us before walking to the staircase on the other end of the hall.

"Will there be lots of interruptions now that it's time for lights out?" I asked breathlessly.

"Nope." He kissed my jaw. "They'll all take the south stairwell. It's closer from the ballroom to the second floor that way."

"So…no more interruptions?" I said slyly.

Caleb pulled my lips back to his, knowing we were already breaking the rules by not being in our separate rooms at almost curfew. His hand splayed at the small of my back, bunching the fabric in his fist, the back of my dress lifting slightly. His other hand worked into my hair, as if he couldn't get me close enough.

As I gripped his neck, I heard the thoughts of others right before we were interrupted. I pulled back, but Caleb pulled me behind his arm, the protectiveness wafting off him. I wondered why, but when I looked back at the others, I saw that they were guards.

Oh, no. The assembly has convened about Caleb already, and it didn't look as if they were extending clemency any further. They were taking him to his cell.

"No," I said involuntarily.

"It's alright," Caleb said and turned to me. "It's ok. I'll figure something out."

"You always say that," I mused and smiled sadly up at him, "but it's not all figured out this time, Caleb." I took a deep breath, gnawing my bottom lip. One of the guys behind us cleared his throat and made a noise that said *'hurry up'*.

I reached up and put my hands on his face, causing him to grunt with the force of my touch. We both soaked it up with ferocity. I dreaded this, but needed to be strong and put together. I needed to show Caleb that I would be ok. If he thought for one second that I was about to breakdown, he'd throw a fit to stay with me. I needed him to be calm, and I needed to slow my heartbeat.

"Let's go, Caleb," one of them barked.

Caleb looked back with a glower. "You can wait a second, Wayne, while I see to my significant. How's Michelle, by the way?"

Wayne flushed and looked away uncomfortably.

"I'm ok," I assured Caleb and pulled him back to look at me. "Just go with them. Don't hurt anybody," I said quickly.

He smirked and laughed silently. "Don't hurt anybody, huh?"

"Yeah." I straightened and smiled bravely, but he saw right through it.

"I don't know how, but I will make this ok," he promised in a hard, compelling voice and looked at me until I nodded. One of the guys tried to grab his arm and Caleb jerked his arm back. "Don't you touch me. I can walk on my own." He looked back to me. "I know right where we're going."

He kissed me sweetly on the lips, lingering and stalling.

*I'll see you soon. Remember, don't leave the room without Rodney.*

I nodded and he went with them down the long hallway. I watched and waited. I didn't really know what I was waiting for. I knew the council wouldn't come to their rooms until later, knowing I'd want an altercation with them now.

I decided I better go into my room and just wait. Wait for what, I didn't know, but standing around the hall and looking on after Caleb was already gone wasn't helping a thing.

The door opened easily, without a creak or sound. I slipped my shoes off by the door and went into the bathroom. The white bathroom was so bright and loud with its simplicity that it almost made me mad. I didn't want to be bright, I wanted a dark room so that I could wallow, but that wasn't what I needed. I needed to be awake and sharp. So I took a hot shower, the steam drifted out into my room from the open bathroom door it was so hot.

I lathered my hair, washed my body, shaved, though it seemed silly now. I brushed my teeth, stark naked and wet. I walked back into my room, still stark naked and dripping onto the fine carpet. It was my small rebellion; the only thing that seemed like it could be in my control tonight. I sat around my room, or paced rather, and thought about the next day. I wondered what was in store; more games, more dancing, more food, more of the same.

I decided I needed to start talking to the others. I needed to introduce myself properly, not only as the Visionary, but as me. They needed to see me as someone who they could talk to and approach if they had a problem. The gloom that had blanketed the palace since we got here wasn't just from our family, it seemed to emanate from everyone. And I needed to figure out why. Not to sound arrogant, but wouldn't they be happy that I was here? The Visionary? Wasn't this what they'd been waiting for?

I decided to rebel further as I put on some sleep pants and a small *Metal Petals* t-shirt that Caleb must've slipped into my bag. I smiled at his gesture, but quickly became stoic once more. I lifted the small keychain that Caleb had given me and rubbed it in between my fingers. Then I picked up my star bracelet and slipped it back onto my wrist, like I did every time I got out of the shower. I found my flip-flops by the door and cracked it open. I had no idea where I was going, but I knew exactly what I was looking for. I just hoped that the Visionary part of me was working full blast tonight.

I opened my senses as I made my way stealthily down the hall. Truly all that was missing was Mission Impossible theme music, but if I was being honest, it was playing in my head anyway. I almost laughed at myself for being silly, but I was a new me. And I had a plan.

I could hear Lynne's thoughts as she picked out her outfit for the next day as I passed her room. She was deciding between a green dress or a pink sweater. She really wanted to wear both, but wanted to be respectable for Kyle's sake. All of the other rooms were empty.

I arrived at the stairs at the exact moment that I heard voices behind me in the hall. They weren't there yet, but would be in seconds. I swung open the heavy door and pressed my hand to the back of it to keep it from slamming. It eased to a close and I peeked down the hall to see the council finally going to their rooms. Apparently, lights out wasn't meant for them.

They were fighting. Though they had lowered their voices, I heard them each in my mind, except for Donald. They were arguing about what to do with me, my withdrawals. Donald was telling them it would be perfectly acceptable for me to visit Caleb in the cell for a few minutes every morning.

It was still so strange to me their way of thinking. Not that I believed Caleb was meant to be in a cell, but the punishment for killing someone was just that? To be put in a cell for a week and then possibly banished? Seemed a little like a grain of rice weighing up against a bag of sugar.

But I saw in their minds that they believed the law was the only way to keep peace, however inconsistent and sometime silly it seemed. They believed you couldn't teach someone not to kill by killing. Ok, it sounded logical when you said it like that, but in reality, that wasn't the way things worked. Everyone needed boundaries, and if you did something wrong, you needed a consequence that was a deterrent to keep you from doing it again.

I realized then how my idea of a Utopian society where everyone just handled their own was an impossibility. I also realized that someone was going to have to rule. Dang it! I almost complained out loud, but kept my composure. They all separated and went to their rooms. I inched up the stairs and looked for my target.

They were so many rooms on the second floor. It was huge! Corridor after corridor, hall after hall of rooms. I heard them all behind their closed, heavy gray doors as they bustled to get ready for bed and took care of their families. I stomped my foot in frustration as I knew it was going to take a miracle to sift through everyone to find him.

Then a miracle happened. From my outburst came a few energy ribbons. They hovered in the air in front of me as if waiting to see that they had my full attention. I stared at them as they huddled into a little ball. There were only about ten of them and they started a slow trail down the hall. They left a little ethereal matter behind them in an eerie blue trail, but I looked up and was being left behind, so I scrambled to catch up.

They took me down several halls to a door. I sighed in relief when I realized that Rodney was behind that door. Then I heard his thoughts…jail break? I busted through his door without knocking and gawked at him. He stared at me with surprise as he held his shirt in the air, half on, half off. He'd been dressing and me – the idiot I was – had barged in. Thank goodness that it was his shirt I'd caught him without and not his pants. I quickly turned.

"Visionary?" he asked, the humor in his voice causing me to blush as I peeked back and saw him slipping the shirt on. He tucked the front into his jeans, letting his belt buckle show. It had the letters JR on it. I wondered what that meant. Jacobson Ranch?

He made a deep noise in his throat to get my attention and I jerked my gaze up to see his amused face. "If you were any other girl, I'd worry that you were flirting with me."

I blushed even more. "I'm sorry. I was just admiring…I mean looking at your belt buckle." Jeez, that was no help. "I'm sorry I barged in, but I needed your help and when I heard your thoughts- Not that I was trying to read your thoughts, I was just trying to find you…by reading your thoughts… This isn't coming out right," I muttered in embarrassment.

He laughed. "It's all right. I was just coming to get you actually."

I looked him over, objectively of course, and saw that he'd been getting dressed in day clothes, not night ones. "Coming to get me?"

"I knew there was no way that you were letting Caleb sit in that cell." He grinned. "I was trying to hurry before you left without me, but I guess I was just too slow."

I smiled and bit my thumbnail as I looked around his room. "Am I that predictable already?" His room was really nice, but not as elaborate and fancy as mine.

"Pretty much," he said. "Let's get going."

"I want to make a pit stop first, at the library or wherever it is that they would keep the Visionary's journals."

He squinted in confusion. "The Visionary's journals? Oh…You're the Visionary, duh. Of course you'd want them. I don't think it's what you think it is though."

"What do you mean?"

"Well," he said carefully, and his mind was blank. Not like he was hiding something, but like he didn't know. "I've never seen them before, but from what I've heard it's not a book." I shook my head to tell him I still didn't get it. "Let's just go and you can see for yourself."

"Ok," I agreed. "Lead the way, cowboy."

"Ha!" he laughed. "Don't listen too much to their stories about me. I'm not as much of a rodeo hero as they make me out to be."

"I'm sure," I joked. We opened his door and he peeked out. He grabbed my arm to guide me out the door instead of talking. I jolted only slightly from the warning my skin gave me. He looked back at his arm and then my face.

"Did I hurt you?" he whispered, horrified at the thought.

"No," I assured him. "It's nothing, I'm fine. Let's go."

We crept out and he shut his door quietly. The hallway was barely lit by the gas sconces, but we could see well enough to creep our way down the hall. Once we reached the end, he looked before taking us down another. I heard a lot of thoughts as we passed, but one in particular seemed to be louder than the rest. A guy was in the halls, a guy who'd been assigned to be on guard tonight.

I pulled Rodney back before he peeked around the hall where the guy was. He bumped his back into the wall and gave me a strange look.

*What the…*

I mouthed to him, 'Someone's there.'

He mouthed back, 'Who?'

I shrugged and looked at him incredulously as I mouthed back to him, 'I don't know these people!'

'Ok, sorry. We can go back this way, but it's longer.'

I shook my head before mouthing, 'I've got it.'

I looked into the man to see what he was thinking. He was picking at something under his nail – gross – and then used that same finger to scratch his nose. He was bored and so not paying attention.

I peeked my head out really quickly and did a count of how many lights lined the hallway. I counted ten before the next hallway turned. It was like a maze there. I wondered if that was where Peter got the idea for his house. I looked back to Rodney and mouthed, 'Follow me.' He nodded.

To get myself mad, I thought about how Marla had snidely and slyly suggested that I was pregnant, and it didn't take long before I had all the lights dimming all the way down until they were dark.

"What the…" the guy said, and I wasted no time.

I grabbed Rodney's hand and we ran down the dark hall, letting the wall guide us so we didn't run into anything or anyone. The guy had been on the opposite side, I hoped that was still true. When I knew we were clear, we picked up speed. As soon as we reached the end, we bolted toward the new hallway and waited, leaning against the wall. No footsteps pounded and the guy said nothing further, except muttering under his breath as he fumbled in the dark toward something he thought would help him.

I turned to Rodney and mouthed, 'Now where?'

'You're a genius!' he mouthed back.

I rolled my eyes and let him help me up from my squat. He led the way. Hallways became stairwells, stairwells became more hallways, and finally, he stopped at the bottom of a set of spiral golden stairs in the middle of a wide room. They were so tall, made of steel and mesh wire, I had to crane my neck to see the top.

"This is it. The library's up there, but like I said, I've never been in there before."

"Why not?"

"Off limits," he said and smiled sadly. "Caleb made the reunification out to be something totally different, didn't he?"

"Why do you say that?"

"Because every time I mention something like rules, you grimace, which leads me to believe that Caleb was so excited about you coming that he may have been blinded to how strict and organized it all is. It is fun, but we always have rules and boundaries out the wahoo."

What was a wahoo?

"Maybe a little," I admitted. "He told me all about this before we found out I was the Visionary, though. He may have explained things differently if he'd known."

He nodded in agreement. "Probably. Ready?"

I took the first step and gripped the handrail tightly. "You realize this is like three stories of steps, right?"

"Four," he corrected and started up the stairs behind me. It wasn't a walk, it was a hike! A ridiculous hike that made me question the sanity of the person who built them, or the palace for that matter.

"Why on earth would they put these stairs here, in the middle of a room like that, and then make them go up four flights?" I shrieked, only a little out of breath, and tried to calm down.

He laughed and said, "Your answer is at the top, milady."

When we reached the top, I got it. They built the library, and I use that term loosely, in the vortex of the building. The room was circular, only about as wide as a normal, middle-class American family's living room, but the ceiling went on and on, all the way up to the top of the roof where a sky light was placed, but wasn't offering much light. Rodney turned on a lighting system of candles. I watched as he lit one candle and that candle tipped to the side to light the next candle, and the next one did the same, and so on and so on, all the way across the circular wall. It was almost magical and romantic.

"I would have to say this is what you're looking for," he interrupted my gawking. I looked over at him and saw him nod his head to the wall. I inched closer to see that there was writing on the wall. Little, beautifully written and carefully spaced words filled the walls in bunches. Each grouping seemed to have a theme and they were old, the penmanship something I'd always longed for, and the calligraphy look of it making me envious.

There was a quill, a long black feather, in a pen well on a little table in the center of the room with a stack of old parchment paper. There was a chair and that was about it. The rest of the walls were filled with shelves, and where there weren't shelves was the writings. I ran my fingers down the shelves to read the book titles. Almost everything was women's literature and poetry. It wasn't a very diverse library if you asked me.

Rodney seemed to be doing the same as me, just looking around at everything. It was extremely dusty, telling me no one else had made that insane journey up the stairs lately. I came to the one wall that had no writings and no shelves. It did have a string pull near the top of the wall, so naturally, I pulled it.

I yelped and leapt back as the wall came crashing down at me. Rodney ran over and put his arm out as if to shield me…from the dusty hideaway bed that I'd just pulled from the wall.

"Sorry," I mumbled just before hearing Caleb in my mind.

*Hey! What's the matter?*

*Nothing. I just got scared...of something. A spider.*

I immediately shut my mind so he wouldn't see our plan. He'd try to talk me out of it.

*Maggie…*

*I love you, Caleb, but not now.*

I kicked him out altogether. I hated to do it, but I needed to get this done so that I could go and save his cute butt. As mad as I knew he was going to be, I needed to do all this. And it had to be now, tonight.

"Why would there be a bed up here like that?" Rodney mused and pushed it back up into the wall. "In the library?"

"Wait…a library full of chick lit, a wall full of Visionary ramblings or whatever they are, and a bed. This is where the Visionary stayed. This was her room."

"But why would she want to stay here all by herself in the middle of the palace like that?"

"No idea," I answered and then ran my hand through my hair. "But I was hoping for a book or something that I could read later. I'll never remember any of this and I wanted to read all of it." I touched the wall, rubbing my thumb over the word *restitution*. "This just isn't going to do me much good. I can't sneak back up here every night to read it."

"You girls and your worry," he scoffed and smirked at me. "Did you really think I came unprepared?"

"What?" I asked as he pulled out his cell phone and started snapping pictures of all the bundles of words. I laughed. "Oh! You're a genius!"

"It must have rubbed off from you," he said in jest and once he got them all done, he turned back to me. "Shall we go rescue the husband now?"

"Please," I said and was already starting to feel the ache in my back from being without him

I went first, but the stairs were a lot easier on the way down. Once we reached the bottom, he led me down another passageway different from the way we came.

"How do you know where everything is in this place?"

"I've been coming here all my life. Me and Caleb and Kyle," he shook his head as his memories ran through in his mind, "we always ran around and tried to find secret passageways and things like that. We played pirates on the roof when we were six, hide and go seek in the halls when we were nine, and ran away from the girls with cootics when we were thirteen." He chuckled to himself. "We spent a lot of time together when we were little. Not so much lately, though." He bumped my shoulder. "I blame you."

I smiled bashfully. "I accept the blame. I've always been a troublemaker."

"Now I don't believe that for one second, missy."

"Oh, you just don't know. Kyle used to get me into all kinds of trouble." I couldn't help but smile as I thought about it. "He always started stuff at school, pranks and stuff, and then would drag us all into it with him. He'd start chants in the middle of the Principal's speeches and we'd help, but in the end, we all got in trouble. We all went down with the ship," I laughed.

"I could see Kyle doing that." He laughed, too. "You know, I know it might be awkward for you, but I remember the first time Kyle told me about you."

"Kyle talked about me to you?" I asked in quite curiosity.

"Yeah," he replied and smiled sadly. He hooked a thumb into his pocket. "He told me there was this girl, and she was human and he was going to have her." He laughed, but shook his head. "I told him he was crazy. That his parents would kill him, that you, the girl, would think he was nuts once you met our family, but he wouldn't listen. He had it all planned out. He was going to ask you out Graduation night, and if you said no, he was going to puppy dog eye you until you caved." My mouth opened in shock, because that was exactly what Kyle had done. He laughed at my expression. "Then he was going to take you out to eat and to a movie, then to the park where he planned to spill his lovesick guts. Tell you that he'd been in love with you forever and he didn't want to be your silly friend anymore."

Wow. It really had just been hours away from bad timing. Caleb had stopped me from that when I saved him. Though Kyle and I went on a date, he left the park and the confession out. I wondered what I would have said to him if he'd laid it all out for me and there was no Caleb involved. My heart ached a little in a pulse at the thought of that.

"Wow," was all I could say.

"Yeah," he said wryly. "So it's kind of strange for me to see him so happy with Lynne when he was so content to be miserable waiting for you." I shot him a look and he held up his hands and laughed. "Just sayin'. But that's how imprints work. The ones who haven't imprinted complain a little that it seems to steal your choices, but it doesn't. Kyle eventually would have given up on you and when they went to the summer house in California, he'd have bumped into Lynne at that club anyway. And they would have started something. It's fate. But fate just gives us a nudge in the right direction on the fast lane. I guarantee she doesn't have her hands in your pockets while she's doing it."

I squinted at him. "Is that cowboy logic?"

"Yes, ma'am, it is," he replied in his best southern drawl and grinned.

# Thirteen

"And here we are," he said and put his finger to his lips and whispered. "They have guards down here with him, no doubt."

"Guards," I scoffed. "You mean someone who got assigned to be a guard for the night and really just wants to go back to their room?"

He moved his head side to side. "Pretty much."

"I'll handle them," I said confidently, but really didn't know what I was going to do. I stood tall and sauntered into the low stone stairwell he'd led us to. I heard him sputtering behind me, trying to stop me, but not wanting to yell. I kept going.

"Hey, who's down here?" I heard someone ask and metal scrape, like a chair moving.

*Maggie, dang it, get your butt out of here!*

*No, Caleb. I'm already here. May as well see the accommodations.*

He sighed raggedly in my mind.

"Hey! I said, who's down here?" the man repeated just as I turned the corner. He blanched and bowed. "Visionary, I'm sorry. I didn't know it was you."

"Does it make a difference now that you know it is me?" I asked sarcastically.

He gave me a sad smile. "I'm sorry. I know this doesn't seem right to you, but our laws and traditions are all that we have."

I was sick of rules and traditions. I dove right into his mind, knowing that now that I'd claimed my destiny and embraced it, I embraced my power as well. His past memories were normal. His family was beautiful, and he was such a good father. He was patient and loving as he showed them the way. He explained why certain things couldn't be done, and the way he did it wasn't "Because I told you to."

His eldest son was almost twenty two now and the man was worried that he wasn't going to imprint like the rest of them, that he'd never have a family of his own, that he'd never know what it was like to be joined with someone; body, heart, soul.

"No," I told him and when I opened my eyes, I knew he'd seen everything I'd seen in his mind. "No, you're wrong. Rules and traditions aren't all you have. Those things in your mind? Those memories? That's what you have. Those are the things everyone here should have if they don't. I'm not trying to come in and take over. I'm trying to give you back the one thing that means everything to everyone; your future. If the imprints don't come back, our kind has no future. This generation will be the last. That can't be what everyone wants."

His eyes watered and he fell to his knees, shaking his head. "No, I don't want that, but we've been told ever since we were born that one way was the only way. We've followed the laws laid down by the first council our whole lives and for you to so openly break them and defy the council is a direct violation of the law. I'm just…I just don't know what to do."

I saw flashes of things in his mind as he rapidly processed everything. Rules for working a job; there were only certain trades you could be in and it had to be one of respect and wealth. Rules for family; no one was allowed to marry/be 'friendly' with a rival clan member where they had ever had any kind of conflict because it could cause a rift in the race. Rules for school: everyone went to college, no matter if you wanted to or not, because college bred people of propriety and society. Rules for council: the assembly rules on every issue, and their word is final and they rule by the Virtuoso law only. Rules for health: parents must watch what their children eat closely, because obesity was not permitted among someone young who'd not imprinted. Granted you'd heal each other once you were imprinted, that wasn't an issue, because you healed each other even from that.

It struck me that Gran was the only one that was on the hefty side of all the people I'd seen.

There were rules for everything in their life. Whoever these people were that wrote all these rules didn't have their kind's best interest at heart. They may have thought they did, that by restricting them so tightly that it would mold and shape them, but the rules only addressed things on the surface. As far as character and morals and….and…happiness! That was not a concern.

"Let me pass. I'm getting my significant out of here and I'm addressing the council tomorrow to let them know that things have to change."

"I…" He shook his head. "I wish I could help."

"You can," I said and smiled. "Don't tell anyone you saw me in my pajamas," I joked and he choked on a surprised laugh.

"You're so different. They always said you'd be this beautiful, regal, magnificent woman. And you are," he said quickly, "we just didn't think you'd be a human, and we definitely didn't think you'd be imprinted. The last Visionary wasn't. She was just one of our kind and the Visionary mark showed up on her one day as she had the gift. We just assumed you'd be the same."

"Sorry to disappoint," I muttered.

"No, no, no, it's not a disappointment at all. It's a miracle. If you're to take the place on the council, then it's better that you are truly one of us, an imprinted significant, to be able to relate to us."

"I agree. And this imprinted significant is already in withdrawal," I groaned and pressed my hand to my stomach. "Please. Let me pass."

"I'll come with you. I think the council figured you might try this." He smiled sheepishly. "They put eight guards down there with him."

"Eight?" I croaked and looked back at Rodney, who looked very much in awe at the moment. "Well, we have no choice. Let's go."

He picked up a camping lantern and took us down the stone stairs. When we reached the bottom, I blew a disgusted breath at the smell. What was down there other than people?

"Who goes there?" a deep voice rumbled and then his eyes went wide. "What are you doing bringing her down here?"

"I came to get Caleb." I looked behind the man to the cells, but he moved to block my view. I glared at him and he stepped back and gulped.

I was confused. They were afraid of me, but they were also just as afraid of the council. I didn't get it. It was like the council and I weren't even on the same side and everyone knew it.

"Let her go," Rodney said in exasperation and came to stand beside me. "Do we really have to go through the whole spiel with each person individually?"

"What spiel?" the man huffed.

Rodney crossed his arms. "The spiel about Maggie being your frigging Visionary and you better show some respect or she'll fry your tail."

"Uh..." The man's eyes darted from Rodney, to the other guy, to me. "Fine." He waved his hand for us to go. "You won't get very far anyway."

I pushed past him and ran my face straight into the chest of a tall man. "Ow," I muttered and looked up before seeing his face. Donald.

"Are you quite finished making a fool of yourself?" he said pompously. "I don't even know you and yet you're so predictable. This is why the Visionary shouldn't be imprinted. You're letting your emotions get the best of you instead of doing what's right."

"And what's right is keeping someone locked up for protecting someone else?" I replied evenly.

He sighed. "Visionary, you are completely unreasonable. Law is not ruled by emotion and passion."

"It should be!" I yelled up at him. "If you're not passionate about it then how can you even say you're invested? All that should matter is what's right and what's good for these people. Caleb being locked away as some silly punishment for defending me isn't right! And you keep saying that I'm the Visionary," the bars next to us started to rattle. He glanced over nervously and then back to me. "And you keep saying that I'm important and I need to lead, so let me. Move out of my way!"

Donald glanced over my shoulder. "Is this your pathetic excuse for backup?"

"No, they're just watching the show. And as mad as I am, there is going to be a huge one if you don't move."

He scoffed. "Are you trying to pull rank on me?"

"I'm trying to pass." He just gawked, so I let my feelings go and when the energy ribbons came, he backed away and inched around me. He hadn't seemed too fond of them the first time he saw them either.

I know it seems like I was just bullying them all into doing what I wanted, but I would explain everything tomorrow when they were all together. I couldn't let Caleb stay stuck down there.

I followed Donald with my eyes and saw him motion to a few others standing off to the side. At first, I thought he was ordering them to attack me, but they followed behind him up the stone steps. Ahh…he was using them as a shield from me.

Coward.

I turned back to the cells. There were four of them and Caleb was in the last one, in complete darkness. My energy ribbons illuminated his arms stuck out the bars as he rested his elbows there. I ran to him like I hadn't seen him in weeks.

He grabbed my face and sighed as we both were released from the coiled aches. I caught all of his emotions at once. He was mad I put myself in 'danger' to come and get him, but he was so happy and proud of me. To watch me stand up to Donald… I thought he'd be angry about it, say I had acted childish for pulling the Visionary card, but instead he was overflowing with pride.

"Open it," he said gruffly.

"Keys?" I called to Rodney and the guard.

"They don't use keys down here, babe," Caleb explained. He motioned to the bars and I noticed there wasn’t a lock. I pulled the door, but it wouldn't move. I looked at him questioningly. "It's charmed."

I huffed, "Is everything charmed in this place?"

"Yes," he answered softly. "It is. Our abilities are what we all have in common when we're here."

"So can't you just borrow their power and get yourself out?"

"The inside of the cell is charmed. They aren't that stupid." He motioned again. "Open it. I'm ready to kiss you like crazy." I almost smiled as I tried to yank it again. He corrected me. "No, babe, magic for magic. Your human strength won't open it, but your ability will."

I understood. I did what I had to do and yanked it open with my mind. It slammed against another cell and I squeaked as I moved out of the way. Caleb stumbled forward and engulfed me in his warm, broad arms. With his lips on my forehead, he spoke against my skin. "Mmm, you're in so much trouble." He looked down at me and grinned. "You refuse to listen, don't you?"

"When it's about you and jail? Yes." I grinned back. "Come on, gorgeous, let's go."

"Hey, that's my line," he laughed and winced as he stepped on something. I looked down and saw that he was barefoot.

"Where's your shoes?"

"They took them. I think it's a humiliation thing." I felt my lips purse in disapproval. I bent down closer and saw that he was stepping on bones. Mouse bones. "Ew!" I squealed and practically dragged him to the stairs. "Gross, disgusting. Real prisoners in real prison are treated better than this!"

Caleb smirked at me in humor and then turned to Rodney. "Dude, I thought you were going to watch her."

"Hey!" I bristled.

"I meant *look after*," Caleb admonished sweetly. I knew he was throwing me a bone, but I fell for it anyway. Especially when he added his arm to my shoulder and kissed my temple.

"This is me looking after her," Rodney said. "If I didn't come, she'd have come by herself."

"And you, Aleza," Caleb said, hard and angry. "What are you doing here?" The man who I'd talked into letting me get to Caleb stood awkwardly and looked down at his shoes. "Aleza, you put me in that cell yourself, so why would you help her get me out?"

"For the same reason I did," Rodney replied. "Your girl here can be pretty persuasive. The fact that she can pretty much do anything she wants, and just hasn't realized it yet, is the scariest part of all."

Aleza looked up. "I did it because she made me see that some things are more important than my loyalty to a blind cause."

"I hope it stays that way," Caleb said begrudgingly and pulled me to walk in front of him on the steps. I could feel the pull and tingle of my touch as I healed Caleb's feet. Aleza parted ways and Rodney walked with us to my door. Or Caleb and my door, I should say, because I wasn't letting him out of my sight tonight. Or any other night for that matter.

"Well, I'll let you two get to bed," Rodney said and went to turn. I grabbed his arm and hugged him around his neck.

"Thank you."

"Thank you," he whispered, "for looking out for my boy."

"I'll always do that."

He leaned back and smiled, winked at Caleb, and then he was gone, stealthily down the hall.

Caleb pulled me into the room without a word and went straight to the shower...leaving the bathroom door wide open. He took his shirt off with one tug from the back over his head and then he unbuttoned his pants, letting them hang loosely on him as he started the water. He turned and watched me as he let them fall to the floor and he was only in his boxer briefs.

Boxer….briefs….

My body was reacting strangely as I leaned against the wall of my room. I gulped, breathing was a thing of the past, and my eyes refused to blink for fear of missing something. He didn't smile, he didn't smirk or wink, he just watched me. He hooked his fingers into the waistband and pulled them down.

And like an idiot, I closed my eyes at the best part.

I laughed at myself, at my utter ridiculousness. He was my fiancé, he had seen me naked already. I wondered what I was scared of, but in truth, I knew. I was scared of starting something that I wasn't ready to finish. When I opened my eyes, he was already in the shower. This charmed room kept his thoughts private, and I was almost glad for that for a split second, that it kept my secret as well.

I walked toward the bathroom door. I could see his silhouette through the frosted glass of the shower stall. Ok, Maggie, you are not a child anymore. You are going to be eighteen in a couple of days, you're about to get married, and you're about to *technically* lead a race of people.

I boldly walked forward to the sink and grabbed my toothbrush. I picked up the toothpaste and spread a fat line that dropped off the end and dripped into the sink. I shook my head at myself and scolded my shaking hands. It was just brushing teeth. This was not intimate.

I turned on the faucet, wet my toothbrush and put it in my mouth. As soon as I started working the bristles around, I straightened and watched Caleb. He was washing his hair and my stomach got a funny knot in it as I watched his arms flex and move. I continued to brush my teeth and looked at the girl in the mirror.

Wow, I really wasn't the same girl anymore. It wasn't just my looks, but my eyes, even I could see the change, the determination in them.

The shower cut off and he pulled the towel from off the top. Then a few seconds later the stall door slid open and he was standing there, the towel low on his hips. He watched me with fascination. I smiled slightly around my toothbrush before spitting, wetting my toothbrush and brushing again. When I straightened back up this time, he was behind me. I watched him in the mirror as I rinsed, then I turned.

He shook his head slowly, his lips parted. Then he moved toward me, reached around me, and opened a drawer beside us. There was a stockpile of bathroom toiletries in there, all laid out neat and straight of course. He pulled a new toothbrush out, opened the wrapper, and went to the side of me to brush.

I stayed right there. I think we both knew this was a new step for us; being normal, being human, doing human things around each other that were considered an intimate, but necessary thing. This was something married people did.

When he finished, he stood and looked at me. I leaned over and kissed his scruffy chin. He smiled as I ran my knuckles over it. He walked over to the shower, got my razor and shaving cream out, and stood in front of the mirror. He wet his face and started to dab the shaving cream on and smooth it. Then he picked up the razor - my razor - and began to shave near his sideburns, then downward towards his chin. I hopped up onto the counter and watched him. Every now and then, he'd glance over my way, looking at the exact spot my eyes were as if he knew every time right where they would be, and he'd hold my gaze for a few seconds before getting back to work.

When he was done, all rinsed and dried, he tilted his chin my way and finally, the smirk was there. He was waiting for me to inspect and give my approval. I pulled him to stand between my knees. He leaned forward a little and put his arms on either side of me as I kissed his chin again. I made an objective face, like I was just an unbiased spectator. Then I ran my knuckles over his jaw and nodded my head. Then I ran my cheek across his, and then his chin and jaw. Finally, I kissed his top lip, just once, and leaned back.

I nodded and he laughed silently. He leaned down then, wrapped his arms around my waist, and pressed his head to my chest. His ear… He was listening to my heartbeat. I felt his breaths against my neck and chest through my t-shirt. I reached up and ran my fingers through his wet hair, loving the little spikes and curls it made.

"The sound of your heartbeat…is my favorite sound in the whole world," he said, his voice gruff and husky. I realized then that not a word had been spoken since we'd come into my room until now. We'd had a hundred conversations with our eyes, with our senses, with our hands and movements, with not a word spoken.

He lifted his head and looked at me before dipping his head and kissing my neck. I sucked in a startled, gaspy breath at the feel of his warm lips. He smiled against my skin. "And that is my second favorite sound."

When he looked at me this time he was still smiling slightly, but it wasn't any of his normal cockiness and playfulness.

"I didn’t say thank you for coming to save me," he said softly.

"I didn't think you would," I answered truthfully.

"I'm not mad," he said even softer, "I just hate that you had to do that. I hate that you're seeing all the bad parts of my people and none of the good."

"I've seen enough to know that they're just scared. They don't know who or what to trust and when you have not only yourself, but a family to keep safe, it's a big responsibility. I'm proud of them at least for taking that responsibility seriously. I just need to show them that I can be trusted, and that I have their best interests in mind."

He smiled at me and even without our abilities, I could see the pride oozing out of him. "And you will." His smile eventually turned into a grin. "Now, unless you want to get another chance for a sneak peek, I suggest you go into the room. Now."

I practically scrambled to get out of there. I heard him laughing, but he didn't shut the door. I went and straightened the bed a little bit. Then I thought I might smell. I had been traipsing through the palace and up spiral stairs and through dungeons. Caleb had just taken a shower, so I might need another one. A quick sniff of my shirt said I was in the clear.

A minute later, he emerged in all of his boxer brief glory. I covered my mouth loosely with my fingers. I watched him as he went over to the light switch and flicked off the lights. I stood in the pitch black of the windowless room and waited. Without a sound, he made his way to me somehow and I didn't jump when I felt his hands on my waist. He edged us toward the bed carefully, but I still tripped over a flip-flop and we laughed as we fell onto the bed's edge.

I wasn't surprised when he pushed me to lie down and leaned in to kiss my laughing mouth either. He was in a strange mood. A mood that was mature and intimate...and seductive. He didn't attack me though, he just kissed me. After a while of some serious kissing and swollen lips, he pulled us up to the pillows and covered us with the duvet. I didn't explain to him that it was purely ornamental and the real blanket was underneath us, I just snuggled against him.

With every breath he took that resounded in my ears, I recognized how quiet it was. I pressed my ear to his chest and just listened to our hearts beating there. I had almost expected not to find my heartbeat there, because of the charm on the room, but I should have known that it would be. I doubted anything on this earth could take my heart from his chest, not hell itself. I imagined Satan trying to bargain for it and Caleb telling him to screw off.

"What's funny?" he asked in the quiet. I must've laughed at my daydream.

"Nothing. Just thinking."

"You know," he shifted, moving his arm out from under me so he could run his fingers through my hair as he spoke, "I know it sucks not being able to read each other's mind. I know in the morning, it'll really suck, but this is almost a gift."

I looked up at him, but couldn't see him in the dark. He explained further. "We would never have known what it was like to just be normal. I've always known how you feel about things, how far I can…push you," he told me, his voice low and husky to tell me what he was referring to. "It's totally different when I have to guess what you're thinking. When I have to decide for myself if what I'm doing is just because I want to do it, or I'd think you'd like it and want me to." I felt his head shake. "We're practically human right now."

I nodded my head. "Yeah. I feel like that, too." I ran my hand over his now smooth cheek. "You're right though. It's kind of nice…to have to guess. It's also nice knowing everything there is to know about you, though."

"Yeah," he replied low, "that is definitely nice."

I switched gears. "Tomorrow, I'm going to have to address everyone." I swallowed, the sound loud and almost embarrassing. "I'm going to have to tell them that the laws are what's keeping us from thriving."

Caleb sighed and I honestly couldn't tell if it was a good sigh or a bad sigh. I waited, tensed, and he seemed to know that I was confused.

"I've heard you say all day…us, our people, our kind." He rolled so that he was over me a little. "It makes me very happy that you no longer have to think about if you're one of us or not."

"I'm one of you," I told him with certainty. "For better or worse."

He kissed me again and then settled me against him protectively, and we slept in the comfort of each other's arm, just out of reach of our healing touch, but for now, this was all I needed.

# Fourteen

I knew it was coming; the pain, the aches, the tightness in my bones and muscles, but waking up to something I hadn't felt since I was kidnapped was a blinding shot of painful reality. I groaned as I pressed my face into Caleb's chest and used his arm as leverage as I pushed myself up. The alarm clock on the dresser said it was seven o'clock, but I could barely see it as my vision bounced, making the red numbers on the face of the clock blurry and streaky.

Caleb stirred under me and groaned, stopping mid-stretch as he felt the aches lance through him, too. "Gaaah…Maggie?"

"I'm awake," I said breathlessly, but my arm wouldn't hold me up anymore and I fell back to his chest lamely.

He rolled me over off of him and my jaw dropped for a split second before he hefted me up into his arms and fumbled his way to the door. He opened it and carried me in the hall. As soon as we passed the threshold into untainted air, the healing touch hit us so hard that we both fell against the wall. Caleb let my feet go to the floor, but held my face in his hands and groaned as we both felt the muscles release, and even our back joints seemed to pop back into place.

I was in his head again. And he was pissed.

I opened my eyes to see why he was so upset and he was watching me with a scowl. "What's the matter?"

He growled his words against my forehead as he leaned there. "How could they do this to you knowing what would happen?"

"They've known you longer and they did it to you," I argued.

He sighed long, which turned into a grunt as he thought that over. "I'm ready for this week to be over. I'm ready to take you home."

I wondered where home was for me. He heard my thought and I felt the slam of his thoughts as he blocked me out. He started to open his mouth to say something, but quickly shut it. "Let's go get dressed."

I looked down at him and saw that he was in his underwear still. I couldn't help but smile, but then we heard a door open. Gran came out of her room, stopping dead in her tracks at seeing her grandson in his skivvies.

I waited for her to blush, or something, anything, but she just stood there. Caleb coughed uncomfortably and pulled me in front of him. It was the first time he'd ever put me in front of him to shield *him*. Usually it was the other way around. Gran's cackle started. She laughed so hard and pointed, even doubling over as she did so.

"Gran, come on," Caleb complained to her and then bent his head to look at me when I started laughing, too.

"I'm sorry," I said, "but it's funny."

"Caleb," Gran laughed and gasped for breath, "just tell me you didn't walk all the way from your cell that way and I'll be fine."

I stopped laughing. "You knew he was in a cell last night…but you don't look surprised to see him here." I heard her thought, she knew that I would go and get him. She hadn't been worried for one second that we'd spend the night apart. I gawked at her as she winked and walked down the hall, still chuckling.

Caleb jerked me into the room and quickly shut the door as he flipped on the lights. "Well, that was just great," he said sarcastically.

"I'm sure she's seen your cute behind before," I told him as I went to my suitcase. "I'm sure she changed plenty of your diapers."

He grimaced. "I don't want to think about it."

I just laughed at him more. He went to the bathroom and put on his clothes. I knew he had to head upstairs to put on some real ones that weren't dirty cell clothes. He came out and stopped in front of me.

"I'm going to have to take another shower." He smelled his shirt and wrinkled his nose. "The cells were pretty disgusting, but I'll be back down as soon as I can. Let Rodney walk you, ok?"

"Yes, tyrant," I said sweetly and kissed his dimple.

"I'll have you know, this is not the tyrant," he replied playfully. "The tyrant would have you getting dressed and then coming with me. I think that I'm doing pretty good, considering."

"Considering what?"

"That my fiancé can kick my tush without moving a muscle. Makes a guy feel a little unneeded."

"Aww, and what a cute tush it is," I goaded and he grinned through a fake scowl. "I need you," I said soberly. "I need you a lot, especially this week. Especially today. Don't ever think I don't need you."

"I know," he said, letting his fingers tangle and jingle my star bracelet.

"Do you?" I asked him sincerely.

"Absolutely," he replied with certainty, his blue eyes locking on mine. "Hey, I'm fine. Why are you all of a sudden so worried about me?"

"I just don't want you to think that because of everything….the Visionary stuff, that I'll become some kind of robot that just handles everything and doesn't-"

"You're such a girl," he interrupted sweetly, putting his head to mine. "I am completely secure. I trust you more than anyone. Don't worry about anything. We aren't going to change, no matter what happens this week." I licked my lips and nodded. He leaned in to kiss me. "I'll see in a few minutes, ok?"

"Ok," I told him and watched him go to the door. "I love you."

He turned as he opened the door. "I love you, babe."

As soon as he was gone, I started getting ready for the day, though entailed details I wasn't privy to. I had no idea what to wear, casual or dressy, and if I was going to bring my A-game today, I needed to be prepared.

The knock on the door drew my attention and I went to it. I peeked out only to find my handmaids once more.

"Ah," I sighed. "Thank you guys so much. I'm freaking out about what to wear."

I let Gran come in first and Rachel was right behind her. Jen walked with her hands on Maria's shoulders before Maria ran and bounded into the air to land in a giggling heap on my bed.

"Hmmm," Rachel said as she eyed me. "Once again, you seem to be well rested and in good spirits, but no Caleb in sight. Hmm."

I looked at Gran, sure she had spilled the beans about Caleb being in his skivvies in the hall. She just winked. Our secret, I got it. I smiled and then sat on the bench at my vanity. I didn't argue or wait. I just closed my eyes and let them work on me. They seemed so excited to do it and I was excited for one less thing to worry about.

When I finally opened my eyes, Jen had just now finished my hair. She'd curled it with a big curler and it hung in fantastic curls that framed my face. The earrings someone had slid into my ears were little silver feathers, and when I looked at the dress Gran had laid on the end of the bed, I bit my lip. How did that old lady have such good taste?

It was a strapless blue, knee-length dress with a silver belt. Maria was holding the silver flats in her hands and looking at the glittery bow on the front with envy. "Why can't shoes like this fit me?"

"One day," her mom promised. "Those are big girl shoes."

I laughed. "They look like comfortable big girl shoes. Thank you for that."

"You're welcome," Rachel said and beamed at me. "I told Caleb to tell you not to bring anything, but he said you'd insist on bringing your own things."

And he was right. Even though technically I hadn't worn anything of mine but pajamas, just having my stuff there and knowing I could wear my own stuff was enough to stroke my need to seem like I was in control.

"Thank you guys," I said and heard the catch in my voice. I cleared my throat. "I know you all had to get ready so much earlier than me and then to come in here and help me…and I know that you do it because it's me and not the Visionary. Thank you."

"Oh, shush, girl, or you're gon' make me cry," Gran said and pulled me from the bench. "Arms up."

"I'm sorry?"

"Arms. Up," she said haughtily. "You ain't got nothing I ain't already seen."

My mouth made the 'oh', but the sound never left my mouth as I obeyed her. She removed my shirt and then my bra. I felt my cheeks heat to furnace levels. Then Rachel helped her put on a beautiful blue strapless lace bra before slipping the dress over my head.

I looked at myself in the mirror as Rachel zipped me up. Man, I loved this dress.

"Your shoes!" Maria said as if I'd forget and leave without them.

"Oh, thank you," I said graciously for her benefit as I slipped them on.

"Today is the dignitary luncheon," Jen explained, "and then tonight is the dance."

"Dance?" I asked, suddenly feeling ill.

"Not like what you're thinking I'm sure. A different family each reunification picks a dance native to their region and teaches it to all of us. One year it was the Waltz, then the Rumba, last year it was the Tango," she laughed. "That was so much fun!"

"But…" I was confused. "I don't understand. Rodney said that they do lights out for the purpose of keeping people apart so as not to build…relationships outside of imprints that won't work out in the end. So why would a dance, especially dances like those, be allowed where people are going to be all over each other?"

"Oh, only imprinted significants can participate, but it's still fun to watch."

"Can't your uncle just teach everyone the dance real fast like?"

"Yes, but then there'd be no fun in watching them all fall and trip trying to get it right," she laughed and pointed at Rachel who rolled her eyes graciously. I assumed there was a story there, but with the charmed room, I had to assume only.

"All right, let's go," Gran said. "I've already peeked in there and the Vanderbilts have cooked up something yummy."

"The Vanderbilts?" I asked.

"Yep. A different family prepares the meal each day."

"Huh," was all I said.

We made our way out to the hall where Rodney was waiting for me. He looked about ready to fall asleep right there in the hall. I didn't understand, but then wrinkled my nose as I remembered that he'd guided me all over the palace last night and didn't have a significant to reenergize him like I did. "Ouch," I sympathized and he jerked at the sound.

"What?" he groaned. "I'm sorry, what?"

"I said ouch. I'm sorry. I didn't think about you being out so late with me."

"Are you kidding?" he replied good-naturedly. He bowed slightly and spoke clearly and with a new fervor. "I am always here to serve you, Visionary."

"And I'm grateful, but please don't bow."

He stayed bowed. "After seeing you in action last night, with my own eyes, seeing the Visionary in her element and with purpose, I can't pretend that you're just some girl anymore. You are the Visionary and it's only proper that I treat you as such."

"Oh, boy," I grumbled.

"What is it?"

"I just thought out of everyone I could count on you to keep a sane head about all of this." I humored him playfully and curtsied to him. "You may rise, my humble guard. There are things we must attend to on this beautiful morn."

"Ha," he said and laughed as I took his offered arm.

"Well, if you want to treat me as some spoiled princess, I'll act like one."

"Ok, point taken." He stopped and looked at me. "But no promises. If you met the President and he tried to bump fists with you, would you, or would you feel awkward because you were being disrespectful?"

"I'd do what he wanted," I countered. "If I'm *so special,"* I said smartly, "shouldn't my wishes count for something?"

"Of course," he conceded. "I apologize."

"I don't want you to be sorry; I want you to be normal."

"I've never been normal," he chuckled. "You're out of luck there."

"I'll take what I can get at this point." I sniffed the aroma that could only be described as divine as we got closer to the room. "What is that?" I asked dreamily.

"Smells like pancakes." His eyes lit up. "Oh, it's the Vanderbilts! They make these pumpkin and banana pancakes that are so good, they will make you want to slap your momma."

"I already want to," I muttered under my breath.

"What's that?"

"Nothing. Let's go. Caleb will be down soon."

"Awww," we heard behind us and turned to find Marcus. "Is our little Visionary imprinting her way down the Jacobson line?"

"I suggest you walk on, Marcus," Rodney said in a voice I'd not heard from him yet.

"You're just as testy as Caleb," he said and laughed. "I only wanted to spend a few seconds with my Visionary. She's not very good at being an unbiased girl. The Watsons have barely seen her at all."

"And you won't see her without me. Walk on, Marcus," he growled that Jacobson signature growl. I felt a weird sense of pride.

Marcus laughed. "You gonna fight me right here in the hall?"

"Are you going to leave?" Rodney asked and pulled me behind him just a little.

"What do you say, little human?" He smiled, and it was evil. "Do you want to spend a little alone time with me?"

"I've spent enough alone time with you, I think," I spouted, remembering the kidnapping and the cell I was in. "Was all that really you, or were you just following orders?"

"All me, baby." He grinned. "I say we do a little round two, now that Sikes isn't here to spoil my fun."

"He was your uncle…don't you care at all that he died?"

He scoffed. "Sikes was out for himself, he always was. He tried to pretend that he wanted to help, but he didn't. He used me and my whole family to get what he wanted."

"And what was that?"

"You show me yours, I'll show you mine." He laughed. "Fair's fair." Rodney arched up at Marcus and he jumped back to avoid him. Then he scowled and started down the hall again. "Just because I want you dead doesn't mean we can't be friends, little human," he yelled and laughed.

"That guy…" Rodney said and fumed. "What a-"

"I'm fine. I am hungry though. Marcus is nothing new."

He tried the whole *ladies first* bit, but I wanted to wait as long as I could for Caleb. It didn't take much persuasion for Rodney to start piling his plate. I counted eight when he walked by. "Eight?" I said incredulously.

"I'm guarding the future of our race," he said and grinned. "A guy's got to keep his strength up."

I scoffed at him and laughed. I decided to go ahead and go through the line. Two banana pancakes were plenty and I picked up a cup of coffee as well and turned to face the room. Everybody's thoughts hit me at once. Some had heard about my 'jail break' from their signficants. They weren't sure what to make of me. They knew I was to be feared and respected, but the scales were out on which one would be the dominate response to me. I didn't want to be feared. So, I made my way toward them.

I saw the Jacobsons sitting all together and I knew it would be so easy to sit down and have a comfortable breakfast, but I needed to start letting these people see me for who I was.

I felt like the new kid at the lunchtime. Everyone eyeballed me, wondering if I'd pick their table to sit at since it was obvious I was looking for a place to park it.

A few looked at me like a judge and thought I was fashion challenged and plain. Some thought I looked like a typical American; like I knew everything and was completely spoiled. Some thought I was fascinating. A few looked at me hopefully, they wanted me to sit there, but I was on a mission. And I found it. Paulo, the councilman who sometimes spoke up when Donald was out of line, was sitting with his family and I saw a seat at the end. "Hi. Do you mind if I sit here?"

Paulo looked seriously confused, but waved his hand for me to proceed.

"Visionary," he addressed me. "I trust you slept well.

"I slept well, yes. And I know that you know I broke Caleb out of the cell. I also know that you know that my bedroom is charmed and that even though Caleb and I were together last night, we were both in withdrawal this morning."

His mouth was wide when I looked back to him. I smiled at him and the entire table who had stopped chewing to gawk at me.

"It's ok," I told them and laughed silently. "I just wanted to get it all out in the open. Now we start with a clean slate. I'm Maggie."

Some of them relaxed a little, but a couple of them couldn't seem to take their eyes away from my Visionary mark.

I took the woman's hand next to me. "Do you mind if I see your crest? I've only seen the Jacobson's." That was a small lie, but she didn't know that.

She turned her arm over and I saw that it was half of a rose bud outlined in black as they all were. The name around the edge said Paulo, and I smiled at him. "The rose is very pretty."

"Thank you," she answered in her accent and looked at Paulo funny before settling her gaze on me. "How's your breakfast?"

"Oh, it's great," I said casually and looked around. "So what's a dignitary luncheon?"

"It's the one day of the year where the council serves us," someone answered and earned a glare from Paulo. "I mean serves us lunch. Of course, they serve us every day."

"So you live here," I asked Paulo and then to his wife, "and you?"

"Yes," she answered softly. "We live here year round."

"And you have children?" I already knew she had two boys, but needed to make small talk."

"Yes," she answered again and looked over two teenagers sitting beside each other. I saw in her mind the guilt, the heartache, the misery. I didn't understand where that was coming from so I dug deeper. She missed her children, but why… I almost gasped when the answer appeared to me in her thoughts. The children weren't allowed to live there with them. Only the council member and their significant were permitted. These people only saw their own children once a year. I dug further, because I didn't understand her misery. If she chose that, then why be so upset about it?

It was the one rift between her husband and her. She had to be with him to survive, and vice versa, but he was just as dedicated to his people. Or so he thought. He thought that doing what the council had done for centuries was the best way he could serve his people. Gran was the only council member ever not to live in the palace. She's also been with the only one without a significant, but Donald has assured them that she would only cause trouble there.

See, that boiled my blood. If you're going to be such a stickler about the rules, then be one. But being so strict to a fault about the laws and then turning around and saying this one's alright to break because they didn't want the hassle, just made them all hypocrites.

I pushed back those feelings and focused. She was sad and so was he. Paulo felt like a failure to his family because of a stupid law that refused to let his children reside at the palace with them, he had let his children live with family. He made a choice to be a council member, knowing that every person who was had to make some sacrifices. But he was also a brave man as well. He knew that if it wasn't him, someone else would be chosen and they would be in as much pain as him. He felt he was strong, he felt he was able to withstand the task and all the consequences. But he was still wading in guilt, every day.

I looked around the room at the council members as they ate. All of their stories were the same. Split families broken for political bargains. It wasn't any of their faults, really. They were doing what they thought was right.

"I'm sorry, can you tell me where the original laws are written? I'd really like to read them over," I said and Paulo raised his eyebrow to me. "Well, if I'm going to be joining the council, I need to know the boundaries, right?"

He smiled at that, his thoughts confirming that the smile was genuine. "They are locked away in the library. I'll get someone to get them to you soon."

"The library?" I asked, remembering the little room I'd been in. "Is there a bigger one somewhere else that I don't know about?"

His eyebrow shot up further. "You've been in the library?"

Oops. Crap. Dang. "Um…"

"There is only one library. I've never even been to it, it's so old, unused and out of the way. But I'm sure I can get someone to pick up the scrolls for you."

"Scrolls?"

"Yes, scrolls." He smirked. "They didn't have Sharpies and fancy letterhead back then."

"Oh, yeah," I mumbled. "Yeah."

"Don't talk to the Visionary that way," Paulo's wife scolded in a hiss. He looked back at me differently.

"I'm so sorry, Visionary. You just seem so…"

"Normal?" I supplied and smiled. "It's because I am." I scoffed. "I'm not going to scorn you or make you go blind just for talking to me."

The table erupted in laughter. Hey, if they thought I was hilarious, that was peachy with me, but I didn't get my own joke apparently.

Paulo wiped his eyes and laughed through his explanation. "That's my ability, Visionary. Making people go blind! You hit the nail right on the head!"

He roared his laughter and I joined in even though I tried to fight it. Everyone in the room watched us with amusement. It was open season after that. Everyone was eager to ask me questions about being the Visionary, and about imprinting with Caleb. A few dreamy-eyed girls at the end of the table fell all over themselves through that story with their sighs and wistful looks, but all in all, it was a good meet and greet.

And that was how Caleb found me.

# Fifteen

"You seem to be a hit," he muttered from behind me. I'd been so wrapped up in conversation that I hadn't even realized he was there. I stood and accepted his arm around my waist.

"Thank you, Visionary, for so humbly humoring us," Paulo said, sensing my departure.

"No, no," I refuted, "I'm thankful to you all for letting me be myself. If you ever have something you want to talk about or ask or…anything, you can come to me."

Everyone looked around at each other and then Paulo nodded to me. "You are…a most extraordinary woman, if you don't mind my saying so."

I blushed and shook my head. "Thank you."

"Caleb," he said and stood to shake hands with him. "I couldn't be prouder of you or happier for you."

Caleb sucked on his lip for just a second before speaking. "Even though I'm supposed to be locked up right now?"

"Yes… Well, we heard the Visionary put on quite a show." He looked over to his wife. "But you know, I know that if my significant were in a cell, I'd do the same and accept my consequences. I'm getting pretty good at it," he said and sighed.

"Sir," I said softly. "Please make sure that someone gets me the scrolls. I really need to see them. There are things…" I chose my words carefully, not knowing how far his being my ally would go. "I'm hoping we can work on some things."

He looked intrigued and equally horrified at that idea, but nodded and bowed slightly. Then the whole table did the same, but no one kissed my hand and they kept their smiles in place, so I was mostly ok with it.

"You're a funny girl," Caleb said as we walked away, "but what on earth could have been that funny to them all?"

"Are you doubting my ability to entertain?" I laughed as we sat down with our family.

Then that same voice I'd heard before came back to me.

*You're making good progress. You really are a magnificent leader. But don't let your guard down. They won't stop until all hope is lost to their side.*

I looked behind me and scanned the faces. Why couldn't I find who was speaking? No one looked suspicious, but they were just hiding it well. I should be able to find the one who was freaking speaking into my mind!

Caleb hadn't heard the voice. He was still talking to his dad and would have surely turned in alarm if he'd heard what I heard. I turned back in my chair and heard him again.

*How's your father?*

He spoke low, like a warning instead of being social.

"What's wrong, Maggie?" Jen asked from across the table.

"I don't…know."

Caleb turned to me then, feeling my anxiety and hearing my thoughts. "What is it? What voice?"

"A guy. Someone here, he keeps speaking to me. He just asked me how my father…was…" I gasped as I remembered something. The time that I'd talked to Dad from Caleb's cell on the roof, he said I had a package there postmarked from Florida. I assumed it was Chad because there was no return address, but he would have definitely wanted me to have his new address. It wasn't from him… then I'd had that vision with that guy in front of Dad's house…oh, God, no…

Caleb took my hand, pulling me up, and Jen scrambled after us as he led me to the hall then right to the stairwell to the roof. We scrambled the many steps to the top and emerged out of breath, but not from exertion, from terror.

Caleb dialed my father's phone number and listened as I paced in front of him. Jen was wondering what was going on, since she wasn't in our thoughts she didn't know, but I couldn't bear to explain it out loud.

I heard my father's voice. "Hello? Caleb?" he said quickly.

"Jim," Caleb sighed and looked at me with a little smile, "here's Maggie."

"Dad," I said as I practically jerked the phone from Caleb's hand to hear the voice for myself.

"Hey, baby girl." He sounded fine, happy even. "How's everything going?"

"Good, um…I was just calling to check on you."

"Ah, I'm fine."

I breathed out a sigh. "That's good. How's Bish?" Jen's head jerked toward me, but I pretended I didn't see it.

"He's pretty darn good," he said and I heard the pride in his voice. "He's been on a few job interviews and it's looking really promising."

"That's good. Um…you didn't open that package I got, did you?"

I held my breath, praying he would say he had and it was a sweatshirt.

"Yeah, I did. There was nothing in it, just a blank sheet of paper."

Caleb and I looked at each other in confusion. "A blank sheet of paper?"

"Yeah. I've got it right…here." I heard him rustling papers. "Nothing, just…wait… There's words."

"What?"

"There are words appearing on the paper."

"Dad, what…"

He made a choked sound, like he was terrified. "Maggie, what's going on?"

"What do the words say, Dad?"

"They say…*you shouldn't have left your father behind.* Maggie, why- Ah!" he gasped and started breathing hard. "Maggie, something smells funny."

"What do you mean?" I said hysterically. "What does it smell like?" I saw Jen cover her mouth with her hand behind Caleb.

"It smells like…gas. Oh, no… They're trying to kill me, Maggie," he said with a calm that chilled my blood.

Caleb took the phone from me and started talking to my father. "Get out of the house, Jim! Now!"

He said something else about leaving, something about Bish. Jen came and hugged me to her, though she had no idea what was going on really, she just knew it was something bad and that I was upset. I clutched her like a lifeline as I tried to catch my breath. Caleb ordered and yelled around me, but the words escaped my comprehension. Then he hung up the phone and dialed a new number then started yelling at them, too.

When he got off the phone, he took me from Jen. He framed my face with his hands, his harsh breaths blowing over my face. "Breathe, Maggie," he ordered gruffly.

"I have to leave. I have to go," I wheezed and cracked through my plea.

"Breathe, baby," he said softer.

I sucked in a breath that choked me, but I got a few breaths in and calmed enough to listen to him. "He's fourteen hours away. You'd never make it there in time. I told him to get out of the house and get Bish. Uncle Max wasn't able to leave until today, so I called him and he's going to get your dad and make sure he's ok. He'll be fine." I whimpered, but Caleb wasn't done. "Do you hear me? He'll be fine."

A tear escaped the corner of my eye and I cursed it, but it was Caleb's undoing. He pulled me to his chest and wrapped his arms all the way around me, pressing me to him. He shushed me and murmured things to me to keep me calm and together. I was *this close* to a meltdown.

"Let's go inside," he said into my hair after some time. "You're shivering."

I was shivering, but it seemed silly to worry about being cold when your father could possibly be dead. But I let Caleb tow me inside, all the way down the bottom of the stairs as he explained to Jen what had happened. I needed to pull myself together, so I pulled Caleb to a stop.

"Yes," he agreed and looked at me sadly. "You can't let them know that we've caught on. I don't know what they'll do, or how they pulled that stunt, but we need to act normal."

I nodded. "You're right."

"I'll go so we don't all walk in together," Jen offered. She hugged me hard. "I'm so sorry, Maggie."

"Jim and Bish are fine," Caleb reminded her harshly.

"Of course they are," she said and smiled at me before making her way out of the heavy door and down the hallway. I sat down on the bottom step, no longer able to hold myself up on shaking legs.

"Here," Caleb said and sat next to me. He pulled me under his arm and ran his fingers over my cheek to keep his healing touch on me. "I'm so sorry, baby."

"This is too far," I said and heard my voice crack with anger. "This is too far, Caleb. It was bad enough messing with us, but my dad? He didn't do anything to them and had nothing to do with this."

"I know."

We sat there for a few minutes more and Caleb looked at me helplessly. "Are you all right enough to go back out? It's ok if you're not."

"No, let's go." I wiped under my eyes one more time and groaned. "Do I look all splotchy?"

He tried not to smile, but failed. He took my face in his hands and rubbed my cheeks with his thumbs. "No, you're not splotchy…whatever that means." He blew air across my face, focusing on my eyes. Any other time and I would have melted into a puddle at his feet. "There. Now you just look flushed, like you've been seriously kissed."

I nodded. "Ok."

"Maggie…" He looked down at something on the floor. "I wish there was something I could do. I should have known they might try something, but I honestly thought they'd be safe there without us."

"I know that," I told him. "You did do something. Your uncle's helping, at least you tried to do something. I was the one who couldn't stop being hysterical long enough to think."

He shook his head to argue with me, then said. "He's your dad. I'll go call Uncle Max in a little bit and make sure everything's fine. We need to get back in there though."

I nodded my head slowly and wrapped my arm around his for support. How was I supposed to pretend that everything was fine when my father could be dead this second and I had no idea either way?

When we came back in, Caleb's family saw us first. They looked like they'd been looking for us and when they saw us, they smiled and gave us a cursory glance before looking away, effectively dismissing our absence as making out just like Caleb had said. I hid my face in Caleb's shoulder to hide the tears that already wanted to come again.

The Watsons stood around the fireplace and watched us cross the room. I tried not to look at them. If they wanted to see if their plan had come into play yet, they were sorely out of luck. I wasn't playing along.

He took me to sit at the end of the table by Kyle and Lynne. We sat, but Kyle and Lynne were in their own little bubble together, oblivious to us or anyone else as they whispered into each other's face and ears. Lynne reached up to playfully slap Kyle's jaw and when she did, I saw it. On the inside of her right wrist was the tattoo with Kyle's name. They'd mutualized sometime last night. Which meant they'd ascended sometime last night, too. Everyone had freaked because I got a tattoo and I was human, but Lynne had one, so it must be something new to add to the imprints. And they didn't look much different to me, ascension wise.

They seemed so carefree and easygoing, could just be happy and together.

I envied them, because although my memory of that night was perfection in its truest sense, they could just be giddy and revel in it. Caleb and I were forced to be adults in a world of teenagers and it still chapped my hide.

And then I scolded myself for thinking about any of that when my father could be dead.

I turned to Caleb to find him watching me. He decided he'd have to do something drastic to take my mind off of things and Kyle had made himself the perfect scapegoat.

"Her bedroom's not charmed like Maggie's is?" he asked Kyle suddenly. Kyle jerked to look at him and then twisted his lips, knowing exactly what Caleb was talking about.

"Dude, come on," he hissed. "Don't make a big deal about it."

"But she has a tattoo!" Caleb said excitedly. "And she's human. It's a big deal."

"Let me see it, Lynne," I said, suddenly intrigued as to whether or not it possessed the infinity symbol. With her cheeks pinking by the second, she forked her arm over the table. Caleb and I both leaned over to look at it and saw that yes, the symbol was there.

"I didn't notice that last night," Kyle muttered and rubbed the infinity mark with his thumb. "It's what you guys have, right? How did I miss that?"

"I can probably think of a few reasons," Caleb said wryly.

"Dude!" Kyle hissed again and jerked Lynne's arm back, but it was too late.

Maria had seen it and was very excited…and loud. "Oh, my goodness! I want a tattoo, too! It's not fair."

The entire table jerked their gazes our way and immediately started in on Lynne and Kyle with 'ooh's and 'aah's and 'you scoundrel's and 'how did it happen's. Caleb beckoned Maria to him and patted his knee for her to sit. "Give me five, girl, 'cause you're just awesome."

She slapped his hand. "I am?" she beamed.

"Absolutely." He turned to me with Maria on his lap. "See? Now no one is looking at you now."

"You do realize that you completely threw Kyle under the bus," I told him. "Like threw him under and then put it in reverse."

He laughed and Maria did, too, but her thoughts were just happy to be included. She had no idea why being thrown under a bus would be funny. I had to adore her. I grabbed her hand and squeezed it. "Thanks for helping me get ready this morning."

"Oh, you're welcome. Anytime," she said all grown up like.

"You helped Maggie get ready?" Caleb asked her.

"Yep. I painted her fingernails. See!" She jerked my hand to his face.

"I see," he said with humor overflowing.

I didn't want to eavesdrop, but with everyone asking Kyle all those questions, his mind answered them whether his mouth did or not. He and Lynne had ascended, but not found out what their ability was, and then mutualized on the other side of the greenhouse. There was a patio there with chairs and loungers.

In Lynne's mind there were fireflies everywhere, the lights had a hazy glow around them, and the stars shined liked diamonds. I wondered if her memories were distorted like Bish's. Hers made her good memories seem extra dreamy and he made his bad memories seem extra horrifying with its unreal cartoony feel. It was strange that that was how I saw things, but I guess I would see them as the person saw them.

I tried to yank out and let them both be, but Kyle's memory of last night started to play, and in the interest of science, I stuck around. I was right.

Kyle's memory showed a few fireflies, and yes, the stars were showing, but it was more realistic. The chairs were sun-bleached and the lights had bugs swarming around them, the dreamy factor wasn't as dreamy. Satisfied with my findings, I backed out and shut everyone out. I needed to be in my own head.

I leaned against Caleb as he held Maria and laughed with his family as they picked on and razzed Kyle. I almost smiled.

Almost.

# Sixteen

"Alright, everyone," Paulo called and clapped to get their attention. "It's time for those of us who are going to serve to head to the kitchen as it gets closer to lunch time. Everyone else can enjoy their time by listening to the Namy clan's new opera."

I stood, knowing that the ones needing to serve included me, but when I heard murmurs around me, I looked up. Everyone looked aghast that I intended to serve anyone. Apparently, they hadn't expected me to help with the dignitary luncheon.

"I'm sure they didn't mean for you to help, Visionary," a woman near me said.

"They said all the council members were to serve."

I knew that I had to serve. I needed to do something to bring myself down off the pedestal they'd put me on and back to reality. I looked at Caleb and he nodded, hearing everything I'd thought.

*Plus, it'll take my mind off things, hopefully.*

*Probably.*

*Can you call your Uncle Ken?*

*Of course.*

I went into the kitchen and stared at the vast room. It would be intimidating to anyone, especially someone who had no idea how to cook. I gulped. Paulo looked my way and smiled. "Visionary, coming to see what we're cooking up, eh?"

"Sort of. Where do you want me?"

"We didn't expect you to help with this. I meant the council members, but you're not…" He seemed to be looking for words, and the ones popping through his head would have angered me, he knew. Then he remembered that I could read his thoughts and flushed before hurrying in his explanation. "You aren't expected to help. I can't imagine being served by the Visionary."

"Maybe that's exactly why I need to serve you," I said clearly.

His eyes opened more and he looked at me with a new respect. They always thought the Visionary was all about title and rank and respect, but I was the opposite of what they had expected. "As you wish."

"Thank you."

"Can you cook?" he asked carefully.

"Not a lick," I said and cleared my throat. "But I chop a mean potato."

He laughed and went to a big wooden box near the back door. "This is the root box. There are potatoes and onions in there and we need both chopped small for a few dishes we're making. The goulash is to die for."

"All right," I said and went to work finding a knife and cutting board. I refused to ask for help. You may call that stubborn, I call it independence.

After I found everything I needed I stood at the counter edge where I could see into the dining portion of the big ballroom. Marla saw me watching her and sauntered my way. I ignored her until she was right next to me.

"Maggie," she said sweetly.

"Marla," I said dryly in return.

"So, how are things going?"

"Peachy."

"Such a snide comment from such a respectable dignitary."

I put my knife down with a clang on the metal counter. "Do you have something to say other than goading? I'm a little busy here."

"I just wanted to see how everyone was doing. I know this week can be tiring." She leaned in a little and spoke softly. "And with everything the council is pulling, I can't imagine you're having too much fun."

"If you hadn't threatened me, my family, and everything I stand for the first day I got here, I might believe you."

She laughed, the sound reeling in my ears. The knife shook in my hand. "Oh, that? I'm just trying to look after my family. Sikes never had our family in his thoughts, only himself," she said bitterly.

"And now you're on the same path."

"No, I'm not," she replied carefully and looked around to see if anyone was watching us. "I'm on the path that's proactive. Sikes' research was intriguing, but he used it selfishly because he'd gotten what he wanted and didn't want anyone else to have what he had."

I figured out that she was talking about the forced imprint. "He was trying to save you from the same fate as him and Ruth. It wasn't right and I'm not just talking about morals. It hurt him to have done that to her, can't you see that he was really just trying to save the rest of you from living with the guilt he lived with?"

Her face turned blood red with anger. "Auntie Ruth has been letting her lips loose with lies."

I recognized my mistake too late. "I'm just assuming from what he said to me when he kidnapped me. Your uncle is the one with loose lips."

"Right," she said condescendingly. "Well, that's ok. I know just how to deal with people with loose lips, don't I? Just ask Sikes."

Then she walked off back to her family. I looked to see that Ruth wasn't with them. I needed to find a way to remove her from the family. She was tied to Marla by blood, but Sikes was gone, she should be freed. I'd find a way, but for now, I focused on my potatoes.

~~~

I followed Paulo's instructions to add the onions and potatoes to the pots. Now I had a legitimate excuse to look like I'd been crying. I was really surprised that Donald hadn't said a word about my helping. He seemed mad about something and I could guess what. I probably embarrassed him in the cells. Oh, well.

Once that was done, I helped Gran set the tables. I wouldn't have thought opera was my thing, but as I listened to the softness and quick sharpness of her voice as it maneuvered around his baritone, I was awed. It was beautiful. It wasn't like I imagined at all and everyone else must have agreed with me because they all stood around and watched them, enraptured.

Caleb came back. I realized he'd been gone for quite some time. He saw me and immediately slammed his mind shut. I panicked. Oh, no. My father was dead.

*No! I'm sure he's fine. I just couldn't get Uncle Max on the phone. I'll try again in a little bit.*

I nodded and went back to lining up the ridiculous amounts of silverware and hearing Gran explain, once again, that forks go on the left.

Caleb walked to Lynne and Jen, who were watching a heated game of chess between Rodney and Kyle. He started talking to them and looked back at me a couple of times. I started to go over, because his mind was still closed off to me, but Gran grabbed my hand and took me back to the kitchen. "You can go necking with him later," she said and cackled.

I wanted to tell her no and go to Caleb, but he apparently had a reason for why he shut his mind. I trusted him, so I stayed put and prayed that he wasn't keeping anything from me.

We put the crystal on the table and I started pouring the punch that Gran had made. Marla came and took it from me when my pitcher was empty. "Here, I'll help. I make a seriously good punch."
~~~

I let her take it, though the good girl act wasn't fooling me. She was definitely up to something. They called everyone to come and sit and they all piled in eagerly. The goulash they had made smelled like something right out of the Wolfgang Puck cookbook.

I spent the next hour and a half of my life serving drinks, bringing bowls of soup and baskets of fresh rolls with scoops of cinnamon butter to anyone who dared to ask me. I tried to smile and show them they didn't have to be afraid, and it seemed to be working. To be served by the one you were *supposed* to bow to was humbling and eye opening.

I made jokes about being a waitress and being made for serving the dignitary lunch. They laughed and oohed when I carried the bowls stacked down my arm like I used to do at the 25 Hour Skillet.

Then it was finally my turn to sit. I was exhausted. Or rather, I felt like I should be. My imprinted body could withstand a lot more now, but the memory my body had of doing work like that was playing tricks with my mind and making me feel like I should be achy and tired.

When I sat next to Caleb, I already had a bowl in my hand, but didn't have a glass. I said screw it and began to eat. Eventually I saw Marla going around refilling glasses. What was she doing?

She eventually came to our table and saw I had no glass. She left and came back with one and a pitcher full as well. She smiled as she set my glass down for me and began to fill more glasses with the red liquid. Caleb gave me the *What the* look and I shrugged. She was apparently trying to play the angel card with everyone.

Oh, well. I scarfed my bowl and carefully sipped the punch. I'd never been a big fan of punch before. It always tasted so hokey to me, but this was really good. A good mixture of sweet and tangy and fizz.

I took the last roll from the basket and started to butter it, but my knife slipped from my buttery bread, clanking loudly with my glass. "Sorry," I muttered.

"Are you ok?" Jen asked from across us.

"Yeah."

"Your eyes look funny," she mused.

"I had to cut up onions," I told her.

"You had to what?" she asked and gave me a funny look. I looked over at Caleb and he was looking at me strangely, too.

"I said, I had to chop onions," I said, but it sounded like my tongue was triple its size and my words were muffled in my mouth. That was suddenly the funniest thing ever that this world had seen. I giggled and my knife slipped from my hand to my plate, once again clanking loudly. The sound seemed to travel around the room like music.

I tried to bite my bread, but it completely missed my mouth, smearing a dab of butter on the side of my face. Caleb laughed nervously as he took his thumb and wiped it off for me. I leaned in and kissed him. It seemed like the perfectly acceptable thing to do when he was being sweet and sexy, wiping my mouth for me.

But when he pushed me back and looked into my face, I bristled. "Oh, you don't want to kiss me now?" I shrieked.

"Of course I do," he soothed and shushed me. "What's wrong? Is this about your dad?" he whispered.

"No, this is about you not wanting me! Why? What did I do?" I groaned and heard him shush me again. "Why are you shushing me?" I shrieked again.

"Because you're yelling, babe," he said and looked around the room. I looked around, too, and the lady next to me was wearing glasses. I realized it was Gran. Her glasses looked huge! They were clown glasses! I laughed so hard I doubled over and fell off the back of the bench to the hard floor. I giggled more as Caleb scrambled to help me up.

"What's going on?" I heard someone say.

Someone else said, "Something happened."

"Hey, it's a party…kind of. Lighten up, people!" I yelled back and then leaned on Caleb as the room began to spin like the Gravitron at the county fair.

"Maggie," Caleb said and patted my cheek. I didn't know why he was doing that. I was looking right at him. "Maggie," he said louder and held my face. "Say something, baby."

I tried to say, "What's wrong with you?", but it was a mumbled, jumbled mess of words. Then I felt a sickness hit my stomach and the fun was over. I no longer thought things were funny. I was about to hurl goulash all over my significant.

I groaned and leaned on him more. I felt him lift me under my knees and back, holding me against him, and I seemed to black out, for how long I didn't know. Then I was all of a sudden awake, and the shouting had already started. "Marla spiked Maggie's drink and you're telling me to calm down! She could have killed her and still might! You can't just sit back and do nothing this time."

"Where would she even get alcohol in the palace?" Paulo, I think, was saying. "We don't keep that poison here."

"Marla apparently brought it with her!" Rachel shrieked, just as I had and it was like fingernails scraping my head. "Paulo, councilors, this is too much evidence for you to let slide. Maggie is-"

"There is *no* evidence!" Donald roared at her.

"Don't you speak to my wife that way," Peter said and I heard Rachel calming him, which meant he was probably about to bash Donald's face in. I wanted to giggle at that, too, but my body was numb in a sickening way.

"Forgive me, Rachel," Donald said. "What I was saying was that no one saw her spike anything. Maggie could have taken the alcohol on her own. She was human, after all."

"No," Caleb growled at him. "I told Maggie about what alcohol does to us. She wouldn't have done that, especially in the middle of a dinner with everyone around."

"I would never do something like this," Marla said and sniffed, further away from the rest of them. "I was just trying to be nice to her, show her that I could be humble, too."

"Well," Donald interrupted, "innocent until proven guilty works best in this matter, I think. Marla can't be blamed for something plainly on hearsay, and we won't know that Maggie didn't do this to herself until she wakes, and even then, she could lie. She is quite the little manipulator."

"Donald!" Paulo yelled. "That is enough. Just because she can't hear you doesn't mean that you can be so disrespectful."

"And she can hear you," Caleb said. "She's awake, she just can't move."

I was awake. So this wasn't some dream. I was just lying there and could hear them and they were all just standing around looking at me like the freak show I was.

"Yes," he said to me softly, laughing sadly "Where can I take her?" he asked someone. "Her room won't work since it's been charmed," he barked angrily, cutting someone off

"Take her to my room," Gran volunteered. It sounded like she was really upset. I wondered why. "Come on."

I felt myself being carried. His steps were extra loud and jarring, the swaying was extra big, like he was trying to make me sick.

"No," Caleb said. "You're just drunk."

"Drunk?" I slurred. "I've never been drunk before."

"And you shouldn't be drunk now," Peter said beside us, startling me. I felt myself being lowered to a bed. I sagged into the comfort of it. "Keep touching her," Peter said quickly.

"Yes, don't take your hands off of her at all," Rachel ordered and I felt her rub my hair as Caleb's warmth settled in beside me. "This new life hasn't been very good to you so far, has it?"

"I'm ok," I tried to say, but even I couldn't make out the words. My head swam with the fishes. "Can we stop the rocking?"

Caleb once again did that little sad laugh. Like it was funny, but it also wasn't. "We're not rocking, babe, just you."

"Keep your hands on her," Peter reminded. "If the alcohol gets even a few seconds without your healing counteracting it, it'll be too late."

"I got it. You couldn't make me leave anyway." He sighed and then jerked his head. "Hey, Dad? Can you go call Uncle Max for me?"

"Of course. What for?"

The reminder that Dad was in danger, or worse, brought on a hysteria that was worse than the first time I heard it. I cried with big, heaping sobs into Caleb's neck. I could hear the rumble of his voice vibrating his neck and chest as he explained to his parents about my dad. I heard Peter scold Caleb for not saying something sooner. Caleb said back that there was nothing his dad could do to stop it any more than Caleb or I could.

Then he left to go make the call and I felt someone rubbing my back on my other side. I cried myself into a strange sleep, where half of the things were out of reach completely and the other half were hazy and unfocused. Time was of no consequence at all and I had no idea how long we lay there like that. I heard people come and go, not making out who they were. I felt hands on me at all times, Caleb's or someone else's, didn't matter. The pounding of my blood in my ears was the only real sound I could make out.

~~~

When I finally woke up for real, I could tell that I was myself again. I was also going to throw up. I scrambled up from the bed, scaring Caleb because he thought I'd been asleep. I made it to Gran's nice white toilet just in time for the goulash to make a reappearance. And Caleb was standing behind me the whole time with his hand on my back.

"Uuugh," I groaned. "Get out."

"Nope," he answered and squatted to be down with me. "Are you done?" he asked, the concern and sweetness totally all wrong with the situation. Shouldn't he be running and shivering with disgust?

"Yes." I gulped. "No." I threw up some more. I heaved so much that my stomach muscles were sore like I'd had a workout. I eventually stopped long enough to breathe. I leaned my head against my arm and felt Caleb leave me. Good, now that it was all over he was leaving.

But, no, he was just bringing me a warm washcloth. I wiped my mouth and face with it. Then he put a glass of water in my hand, making sure I had a good grasp before leaving it. I remembered everything from what had happened. Well, I assumed I did.
~~~

"So let me get this straight," I started and coughed before sipping the glass of water he'd handed me. "Marla put something, some kind of alcohol, into my drink at lunch and I acted like a complete fool in front of everyone that I had worked so hard to show that I was a down to earth and sincere person."

"Pretty much," he said and pulled me to stand. "Oh, and you forgot the part where you almost died," he said angrily. "I've never thought about strangling a girl before, but I swear to you if I see her-"

"You'll do nothing because she keeps her family around her like a bunch of bodyguards," Kyle supplied from the doorway. "I just opened the door," he said, "don't worry. You're little upchucking act was private, I promise."

"Wow," I said in annoyance. "Could you yell a little louder?"

He laughed, which pissed me off with the quickness. I glared at him and he actually took a step back.

"You better get out of here before she turns you into toast," Caleb told him, and though I heard the humor in his voice, his voice wasn't as annoying. Kyle saluted us and grinned as he made his way back into the room. I stood and used a swish of whoever's mouthwash was on the sink.

I came out of the bathroom and stopped dead. Almost Caleb's entire family was in the room. They had all saw me run for the bathroom and possibly heard me hurl through the door. Could this day get much worse?

Then everyone started to talk at once. Wait…no, they were thinking. I tried to turn it off, tried to focus, but that just made it worse. My mind overloaded and I fell into Caleb's arms as I went down for the count again.

# Seventeen

When I woke this time, I was on the floor and everyone was gone, save Caleb, Gran and Peter.

I sighed and covered my face.

Gran spoke first. "You just can't get a break, can you, girl?"

"Why did I do that?" I asked muffled through my hands. "Why would I overload? I know how to handle myself now."

Peter answered me. "Your senses are all messed up because your body is working extra hard to fix the damage the alcohol did."

What could I say to that? But I did remember that Peter had called Uncle Max. "How's my dad? Did Uncle Max make it to him on time?"

"First, you need to shut your mind, Maggie." He looked at me closely. "You've got to give yourself time to heal before you do anything else." I nodded. "All right, I called Max and he didn't answer, but Caleb had a voicemail from him saying that he went to the house and got your father and Bish. I have no idea where he plans to send them, he didn't say, just that he had them. All right?"

"Ok," I sighed in relief. "Ok."

"All right, you two," Gran said and stood, her knees cracking. "We've got to head in to the gold room for the dance. Y'all need to get your butts in that bed and sleep this off. I want my bed back tonight."

I tried to protest, but Caleb was already lifting me. He carried me back to the bed and we lay on top of the covers. "But I'm not tired," I lied, when in truth, I could see myself sleeping for a day or two. "And I don't want to miss the dance."

I had plans for that dance. I wanted to schmooze and laugh and get to know people.

"That'll have to wait 'til another day," Gran said and stuck her arm through Peter's. "When's the last time you tossed your old Ma on the dance floor?"

"It's been too long, Momma." He smiled as he said it. I'd always heard him call her Gran. "Come on, then."

"You kids rest up. I'll be back for my bed later."

"Gran," Caleb said and cleared his throat. "We could switch rooms, you know. That way we wouldn't have to worry about Maggie being in withdrawal in the morning."

She looked at me and then back to him. "She's not gonna be in any mood or condition to mutualize with you tonight, Mister."

"Gran," he sighed and gave her a look that only a grandson could give an overbearing grandmother. "Come on, that's not what I'm talking about."

"Uhuh," she replied unconvinced. "Regardless, they've already made it clear that we are not to switch rooms. They want to be sure that you don't mutualize and have already stopped by to make sure that I understood the rules. We need to choose our battles. We can't fight them on everything."

"Oh," he said and I heard his disappointment. "Ok, I guess."

"Sorry, honey," she said as she left and shut the door behind her.

He looked down at me. "I was talking about withdrawals, not mutualizing. You know that, right? I wouldn't try to do that to you when you're…like this."

I nodded and pressed closer. "I know." I was so sleepy that my eyes fought me.

"It's ok. Sleep," he ordered.

"Are you going to sleep?"

"Nah," he said and picked up a remote off the dresser. He pressed a button and the armoire doors opened to reveal a flat screen. "The summer Olympics are on."

"You going to watch the swimmers?" I murmured into his neck.

"Yeah," he said and chuckled as he kissed my forehead. "I'm gonna watch the swimmers."

I drifted off thinking how lucky I was to have such a down to earth guy.

We were woken by Gran later, practically shooing us from the room. Caleb carried me to my bed and this time, he did sleep.

~~~

The next morning was a repeat of the previous morning, minus Caleb in his underwear. We woke, it sucked to be in pain and agony even though we were right next to each other, Caleb dragged me to the hall and we sighed in relief.

I saw that he had slept in his clothes and his scruffy chin was back. I felt bad. He seemed to always be taking care of me and not himself. But I felt tons better, no traces of the alcohol was left in my system, so my mind was clear and it went straight to my father.
~~~

Caleb, hearing my thoughts, said, "Listen, I'm going to go change and then call Uncle Max again."

"Thank you. Any idea what's planned for today?"

"Nuhuh, I wasn't really paying attention yesterday," he said and smirked.

"Yeah, I guess not." I wrinkled my nose. "Any chance that everyone is just going to forget what happened yesterday?"

"Nope." He kissed the end of my nose. "But they'll be nice about it or I'll deal with them."

I smiled a little. "Ok, please go call Uncle Ken."

"Done." He left, yawning and rubbing his hair back and forth.

I went back inside and took another scalding shower, wrapped myself in a towel, then came out to find Jen and Maria waiting for me. Jen smiled.

"The Jacobson day to cook is today. Mom and Gran have been in the kitchen all morning."

Maria bounced up. "But we didn't have to go because we were going to help you get dressed."

"As much as I appreciate – really appreciate – you guys helping me, I can dress myself."

"They won't have it," Jen said. "They have a need to make you feel important, yet incompetent at the same time."

"Ok," I sighed in defeat. "What am I wearing today?"

Maria squealed and ran to the closet. "Gran's not here so I can dress you today."

I shot a scared look at Jen, but she waved me off and mouthed a 'no way'.

After I was dressed, we met Rodney in the hall and he poured on the sympathy. He was fighting mad at Marla and had no doubt of what had happened. He said he came see us yesterday in Gran's room, but we were asleep for hours. I assured him I was fine and dreaded the reception I was going to receive.

But I remembered something that I needed him to help me with. I pulled his arm to stop him. "Hey, can you do another guard detail for someone else?"

"Who? What?"

"Ruth." He looked puzzled, his mind blaring obscenities at watching a Watson. "Something Marla said to me made me think she might hurt her and I barely see her out of her room. She told me some stuff about the Watsons that'll get her in trouble."

"Ooooh," he said with crescendo. "Ok, sure. I'll try to keep my eye out for her."

"Good. Thank you."

We moseyed down to the ballroom and I paused in the doorway. He grinned at my self-consciousness and I let him take my hand as he led me to the breakfast table. I waited for the onslaught of negativity, of the people thinking I was silly and immature and chuckling behind my back at the show I'd given them yesterday.

But that wasn't what I found.

People were begging to come and find out how I was. They were worried about me. Worried…about me. Rachel found me and pulled me to her, wrapping her arms around me. She leaned back and looked me over.

"You're better today," she observed.

"Yes, lots better."

"Good. Don't worry about anything today. Peter and Caleb won't let anyone mess with you. Alright, dear?" I nodded. "I better get back to breakfast."

"Aren't I supposed to help?" I asked.

"No, honey. You just rest."

"But I want to help. I feel fine." She eyed me and decided on whether or not to fight me one it. "Rachel, come on. I can't act like this hurt me. I need them to see that I can handle things."

She nodded. "You're right," she sighed. "Come on." She looked back at me with an odd expression though. "Let me handle the bacon, though."

I laughed and let her put her arm around me as we went into the kitchen. Rodney followed us in and stood next to me.

"Honey child, I need help with these eggs," Gran called. "It's about time you got your lazy bones up and at 'em. Now crack these eggs and then put a sprinkle of pepper on 'em."

"Sure," I said, totally amused at how Gran never gave that Visionary status of mine a second of thought. She spoke her mind and nothing was changing that fact.

"Can I help?" Rodney asked.

I nodded. I cracked and he whipped and sprinkled pepper until we were done. Then I grabbed a pot of coffee and started toward the dining hall. I took a deep breath and turned to face the room. Paulo's wife was the first one to walk up. Everyone else was trying to act like they were eating and not watching me.

I assured her I was fine and thanks to Caleb, I was one hundred percent up to par. Rodney had his own pot, but was just kind of walking around with it. I started making the rounds with the hot brew. Everyone was very concerned and not one person thought anything but sympathy and anger toward the one who did that to me. And surprisingly, most of them agreed that Marla was to blame, but no one wanted to point the finger that way for fear of Donald.

Even more surprising was how much I learned that morning. Donald was the one everyone was afraid of. I thought Sikes had been some kind of evil genius, but that had been child's play. Donald was pulling everyone's strings. Even though

Marla was the one who'd hurt me, everyone assumed Donald, somehow on the sly where he wasn't connected, had put her up to it.

In my opinion, their little plan backfired. Instead of everyone thinking I was a raging wino, they felt sorry for me. I spoke to almost every single member of the Virtuoso that morning. I tried to steer the conversation to neutral topics and we wound up talking about where they were from, what school they went to, what company their family operated.

By the time I was finished and made my way back to the Jacobsons, it was almost lunch time and they were gearing up for another round of serving. I sat down with Rodney for a second to catch my breath and suck down a glass of sweet tea.

"Hey," I said and realized that Caleb had never come back down.

*Caleb...Caleb, where are you?*

He didn't respond and I instantly panicked. He'd said he was going to change and then call his uncle.

"What's the matter?" Rodney asked beside me as he scooted his plate away.

"Where's Caleb?" I said more to myself than him.

"Oh, he came by my room this morning. Said he was sneaking out to go to this Italian motorcycle shop."

"What?" I said in disbelief. He wouldn't have left me like that, without a word, while my father was possibly dead and the day after I almost died of alcohol poisoning by my enemy.

"Yeah. I thought it was a little weird myself, I mean with everything that happened last night, but he said you were fine and that he would only be a little while. He said to keep an eye on you until he got back."

I didn't really know what to say to that. So I just stood and went back into the kitchen. He followed me and asked me if I was ok. I said I was, but I was definitely confused. I decided to just chop something, so I asked Gran what needed to be done. She said we were having some kind of Greek salad and that I could handle the olives. I tried not to be insulted that the only job she'd give me was opening olive jars. I guess it was no secret that I was a disaster in the kitchen.

"So," I asked Jen, "did you see Caleb this morning?"

"Yeah," she answered. "He came by and asked me to keep an eye on you."

What? What was he doing?

"Ok," I dragged out in sarcasm.

"He said he had to run an errand," she said and shrugged as she cut tomatoes.

Run an errand… Ok, I needed to step back a little. I was about to become serious-clingy-girl. I took a deep breath. He could go to a frigging motorcycle shop if he wanted to, right? He was a man with his own money and I was here with his family and lots of protection. It was totally fine.

At least that was what I tried to tell myself. So I kept busy and I helped with everything they would let me help with. Then we served lunch, with Rodney shadowing me, and eventually it was time for the afternoon event.

Today was an indoor soccer game. Boys were playing first, so I sat off to the side with Jen and watched…and sulked a little. Music began to play from the overhead speakers. The Police's *King of Pain* of all things. Rodney wanted to play, I could see it.

"Go on," I told him. "I'll sit right here and won't move a muscle."

"You're sure?" he said excitedly.

"Of course. Go."

"Alright." He started to go and then said, "I'll get someone to come and sit with you."

"You don't have to-" I started, but he was already gone.

A few minutes later a guy I'd talked to briefly before came up to us. He was the same guy who'd done the three-legged race with Jen. He was tall and slim, but very handsome with blonde hair. He had a bashful smile as he bowed to me slightly. "Visionary," he said and then turned to Jen and it was a completely different story. "Jenna," he practically hummed.

My lips pursed as I watched her.

*Oh, great.*

"Hi, Jonathon. How are you?" she said politely.

"I'm great," he said and beamed at her. "We didn't get much of a chance to talk earlier. How is everyone?"

"Good," she answered. "How's school coming?"

"I finally got my law degree," he said and shook his head. "Been working hard to buy my first house."

"That's nice," she said and blushed at the mention of his house.

Houses were a big deal with their race. Houses were their engagement rings\wedding presents and for him to be considering his own place meant he'd given up on waiting for his significant. Jen understood the implications.

Jonathon, however, was only focused on one thing and his outer and inner monologue was all I could hear.

*Wow, she looks so good.*

"That Maria has turned out to be a little beauty, huh?" he said nervously.

*Ah, such an idiot. She wants nothing to do with you, man.*

"Yeah," Jen said and tucked her hair behind her ear. "She's a mess."

*Ah, I love it when she does that.*

"I bet. Um…would you like a drink? I can get you a glass of tea or something?"

Jen stalled, her thoughts wild.

*Why not? It's not like it'll hurt anything. Maybe it'll take my mind off of Bish if nothing else.*

"Sure, I'd like that."

He grinned in delight. "Great. Be right back." He practically ran to do her bidding.

I stood laughing and Jen nudged my arm as we leaned against the tabletop together. "Shut up," she said through a sad giggle.

He returned with two glasses and sweetly handed one to me as well. I thanked him and started to give them some space. Jen caught on and also caught my sleeve.

*Don't you dare leave me with him.*

I bit my lip to stop the smile. We watched the match that Jonathon had no interest in as he leaned next to Jen. He spent the whole hour trying to come up with points of interest solely to speak to her.

He'd been infatuated with her since he was little. They were the same age and grew up together. Once they reached teenage age, and Jen filled out nicely, he was hooked. He never broke any dating rules, but he would if she just said the word.

When it was the girl's turn to play, I was pumped. I had an anger and a frustration that needed to be worked out today. Jen didn't want to play, but she wanted to get rid of Jonathon so she was on my team, along with Marla.

It seemed weird to me to play in our regular clothes, though we all played barefoot. I was in a dress for goodness sake, but no one else was weird about it. They strapped these yellow sashes on us and blue on the opposing team.

We took our sides and got ready. You had to play with your hands behind your back at all times in their rules, so I linked my fingers behind my back and tried not to roll my eyes at the music choices. So far, we'd heard Michael Jackson's *The Way You Make Me Feel,* U2's *Sunday Bloody Sunday, and* Tom Petty's *Free Fallin'.* These people were seriously stuck in the nineties for real.

The whistle blew – What was up with that whistle? – and we started off. I closed off my mind. I didn't want to be a cheater for reading their next moves right out of their heads. I went after the ball and was knocked from my left side. I caught myself on my knees and looked up to see what had happened. Marla bounced away happily and looked back at me.

'Oops,' she mouthed and laughed.

Oh, it was on now. I got up and went after her.

"We're on the same team, you know," I said loudly as I finally got the ball and kicked it to Jen.

"Are we?" she said sarcastically. "I thought we were mortal enemies."

"Have it your way," I said and rammed her with my shoulder as I scooted between her and someone on the other team. I heard her grunt and fume behind me, but I didn't look back. A girl from the Petrona clan had the ball and was switching it from foot to foot, but not moving a whole lot toward the goal. I swooped in from behind her and stole it. I kicked it once hard and it zipped right into the goal. I wondered if someone had used their ability to make me win that shot. It seemed really clean and tight for someone who didn't even play soccer.

We heard the whistle and were just about to go again when I saw Caleb by the door. My breath caught and I found myself running to him.

# Eighteen

He met me half way as I slowed to a walk. "Hey," he said quickly. "I know you're confused, I can feel it, but come with me."

"What's going on?" Jen asked from behind me and Caleb shook his head.

"Come on," he told us and gripped my hand tightly. I blew a calming breath at the contact, but wondered what he was hiding from me as he still had his mind closed off.

"This is what I'm hiding," he said and threw my bedroom door open, only to drag Jen and me in quickly and shut the door.

"What the-" I cut myself off as I saw Caleb's secret. "Dad?"

"Hey, there," he said and seemed glad that I looked happy to see him.

"Of course I'm happy to see you," I said and hugged him hard around his middle even though I couldn't read his thoughts. "I was so worried."

"Ah, I'm fine. Max showed up and we hopped the first plane out. Caleb met us at the airport." He leaned me back to see my face. "I'm fine. No crying, now," he said sweetly.

"I'm not," I lied and sniffed. "I'm just glad to see you. I really missed you, Dad."

"I really missed you, baby girl." He hugged me hard this time and I opened my eyes to see Bish behind him. He smiled at me, but his eyes glanced nervously over to Jen as well.

I let go of Dad and went to Bish, only to be lifted into a massive bear hug. "You're collecting enemies left and right, aren't you?"

"It seems that way." I choked on a sob. "I'm so sorry."

"What for? You didn't do it," he reasoned as he set my feet back to the floor.

"But they went after you to get to me."

"And if I'd been home when they dropped off their little present, we'd be having a very different conversation. So what? They just thought they could rattle you, but they can't, because you're not weak like they think you are."

I twisted my mouth to the side, not wanting to disagree. I was just so happy to have them both here and alive and fine. I couldn't hear Jen and Bish's thoughts, but I assumed that they needed some sort of hello. They both stared at each other wistfully and surprisingly unabashed. I stepped back a little, but Bish didn't release my arm.

"Hey," he said, his voice holding none its usual gruffness. He seemed lighter and brighter now that he could see her. But there was a strain in his neck, a tightness about him.

"Hey." She licked her bottom lip. "I'm...really glad you're all right. And you, too, Mister Masters."

"Me, too," Dad joked.

Bish looked at me before looking back at her. "You look so great."

She blushed and it made her even prettier. "Thank you. We've been uh, playing soccer." She rubbed her hair self-consciously. "I'm probably a mess."

"Nah," Bish said and it sounded like a sigh.

"Well," I said to thwart the awkwardness, "I have no idea what to do with you guys, but I'm so glad that you're here. I know the council won't be happy about it."

Dad spoke up first. "Caleb told us all about it on the drive. He's going to try to explain to them the situation. We'll be fine, don't worry about us. I'll sit around this room the whole time if I have to, but Caleb here seemed mighty worried to get back to you with a quickness. Are you ok?"

Caleb. In my haste to greet my father and make sure they were all right, I'd forgotten Caleb. I turned to find him leaning his back against the door, just watching us and waiting. He smiled when my eyes met his. I made a quick path to him and took his hand. I dragged him with me to the bathroom and closed the door. Pushing him against it, I devoured his mouth with gratefulness and love. I couldn't tell what he was thinking in the charmed room, but he kissed me back and held me so tightly around my waist that breathing was not feasible, so I was happy for now.

When he switched places with me and pressed me against the door instead, I was even happier. His hand pressed my lower back into him and his other hand rested against the door to brace himself. He pulled back a little, leaving his forehead against mine.

"I'm not complaining, not even a little, but what was that for?"

"For everything," I answered. "You took care of everything yesterday to make sure that my dad made it out safely, you held me all night long while you healed me, then you lied to Rodney about going to a motorcycle shop so that you could personally be there to get my dad for me."

He smiled. "I had to make sure he got here all right. I knew how much it meant to you, so I did it myself."

"I know. That's what that kiss was for. Because you love me so much that you'd do anything for me." I touched his cheek, laughing at the scruffiness. "I have never been so grateful of anything in my life than I am for you."

He smiled, showing teeth and all of his emotions. He kissed my palm, holding his lips there for emphasis. "I love you," he whispered.

"I love you." I licked my lips. "Can I ask one thing though?"

"Shoot."

"Why couldn't you tell me where you were going? Why did you have to lie to Rodney?"

"Because if they knew I was bringing humans here, they would have locked down the palace, and that wouldn't have been good for anybody."

"Oh," I sighed and clamped my eyes shut at the thought of being stuck here without him. "That's a good reason, I guess."

"I'm sorry. I know you probably thought I was a jerk for leaving-"

"You just did the sweetest thing ever for me. You risked not only trouble, but you're already on thin ice with the council. It doesn't matter what I thought, don't be sorry." I hugged him around his neck. "You are racking up so many points right now."

He laughed and squeezed me with affection. "That's what I was going for."

I shook my head at him, kissed him once more before opening the door and facing my father. He had a wry look on his face. It was then that I noticed how good he looked. He'd been taking better care of himself, I could tell.

"All right, first things first," Caleb said, all business. "I have to find Dad and get him up to speed. Sorry," he said to Dad and Bish, "but you'll have to sit tight until we get this straightened out."

"You brought us from one danger zone right to another?" Bish grumbled.

"Bish," I scolded. "He just snuck off to go and get you. Be nice."

"All right," he admonished with a little frown.

"Maggie and I will go and get everything straight," Caleb said and he took my hand. I knew what that meant; I was coming with him and he wasn't letting go.

"I'll…stay," Jen offered reluctantly, "with Jim and Bish, until you guys get back. Tell Maria to stay with Mom," she told Caleb. He nodded and we started to leave. We opened the door and were met by Jonathon. He'd been waiting in the hall for Jen.

"Jonathon?" she said and Bish's face went from passive to pissed.

"Who's this?" Bish asked, not even caring that he looked irrational, plus the fact that he wasn't even supposed to be here.

"Jonathon," Jonathon said and crossed his arms, arching an eyebrow with curiosity. "And who are you?"

"Bish, Maggie's brother." Bish crossed his arms as well.

"I hate to ask, but what's going on?" Jonathon said.

"This is my father and brother. They were in danger so we brought them here," I answered. He bowed and shook his head.

"It's not my place to question the Visionary." He straightened and looked at Jen. "Always a pleasure. Hope to see you tonight, Jenna?"

She nodded and tried to shoo him politely, but Bish's growl stopped us all. He looked at us all and then went into the bathroom, slamming the door. I bit my lip. I could imagine what he was thinking, poor guy.

"I'll go," Jonathon said awkwardly as Jen tried to shut the door, but it was too late.

"What's this?" Donald boomed and threw my door open. "Humans? In the palace?" He looked at me in accusation. "You've done it now," he said and laughed. "You've just ended your little charade. This won't stand with our people."

He turned and sauntered off, to tattle to the council I was sure. Crap!

I slammed the door and leaned against it. "We just cannot get a break, not even for one day. What the hell?"

"Maggie!" Dad scolded my language.

"I'm sorry, Dad, but what the hell?" I said louder.

He rolled his eyes and sat on the settee like he was exhausted.

"Ok, well…there went that plan," I said, rubbing my eyes in irritation. "Screw it." I looked up at Caleb. "Let's just go out there, all together."

"Maggie," Dad said carefully, "I'm not sure now's the best time to throw a Hail Mary."

"No, she's right," Caleb replied, "let's go. Let's just look like we never planned to keep them hidden, that Donald just beat us to the punch."

I nodded, but Dad stood. "Hold up. You two are acting like they are going to throw you in the brig or something?" That wasn't far off. Caleb and I shared a look. "So we shouldn't have come? That's what you're saying? I thought these were your kind, your people. Why would you be so scared of them?"

"They just have rules," Caleb explained and sucked on his lip for just a second. "No human has ever set foot in the palace before. I just broke a centuries old law."

"But Maggie is human," he argued.

"No, sir, she's not," Caleb admonished softly. My father's eyes grew weary.

"Dad, you're dealing with a…government almost. You have to think about it like that. The original council made all these laws and these people have followed them for a very long time. They aren't a bad people, but they've been a little misguided, and change after so long is not easy to swallow. We haven't even really started to break any of that down yet. Just don't judge them yet, ok?"

He held up his hands and shook his head. He wasn't happy, but felt there was nothing he could say. That would have to do. Bish emerged from the bathroom. "Are we really going to be stuck in this room?"

"No," I answered. "But you have to be quiet for a while. When we got out there, you can't bark off your sarcasm and be…yourself."

"Oh, come on," he complained.

"I'm serious, Bish. You can't defend me. That's Caleb's job and he knows how much he can say. They will just see you speaking up as disrespect. Please, Bish."

"Fine," he grumbled. "You don't want my help, fine."

Caleb opened the door. "Well, let's go before Donald sends the guards down here." He took my hand and led us down the hall.

"Guards?" I heard my dad mutter from behind us. I looked back to see Dad was in between Jen and Bish. I took a deep breath as we entered the room. Donald was causing a ruckus with the council members in a corner while everyone else wondered what was going on.

Everyone stopped and gasped. No one moved a muscle, just watched us as we entered and made our way to the center. I decided it was time for them to see me as the Visionary, for real. I gripped Caleb's hand tighter, closed my eyes, and began to show them everything. I saw the energy ribbons in the air and knew that the visions played out above me for all to see.

I showed them how Caleb and I met, how sweet and loving his family was to me, how I was scared and so very human in the beginning. How Marcus had messed with me in my dreams and then kidnapped me from the beach. I showed them all the things that the Watsons did to me at the compound and in the well, then my rescue. I showed them us in California when Marcus cut my hair, when the Watsons scared people into trying to steal my blood for them. I showed them Marla coming to the club and seeing us in the alley, and then what happened when we went home to Caleb's and were met by the guys on motorcycles. Then Caleb getting shot before we had to defend ourselves and us killing them. Then Sikes and the Watsons holding everyone at Uncle Ken's and scaring little Maria with the fire. Then one of the Watsons stabbing Sikes and killing him before begging for mercy. Our flight here, what Marla said to me at the entrance when we came in, what the council said to me when I tried to stop them from putting Caleb in a cell, what happened with my father with the note and the gas. And lastly, what Caleb had gone through to make sure my dad and Bish got here safely. Then we were back in the present and everyone stood, in stunned catatonics.

I stepped forward a little, but stopped. I realized I'd left the part about my being Visionary out. I'd tried to show them a couple of times, but something always stopped me. Too late now, I had to finish this. "Now you see why I had to bring them here. My dad and brother have nothing to do with this, but the Watsons are refusing to let them be. I left him behind in Tennessee, but they won't leave him alone. I'm sorry, I'm not trying to stomp on your laws or traditions, but I didn't know what else to do."

"He knows about us?" A woman stepped forward. "He knows about our kind?"

"I told him," Peter said loudly as him and Rachel moved to stand beside us. "With the unique situation, I thought it was best. The imprints had been dormant for a long time and for Caleb to imprint with a human had to mean something."

"How could the Watsons do this?" someone yelled. "How could they do this?"

"She wasn't the Visionary then," someone else reasoned.

"Yes, she was. Didn't you see?"

They all started yelling at once, and though it sounded like they were angry with us, they weren't. They were appalled at the Watsons. I watched Marla and saw her gulp as her plan crumbled. She looked at Donald, who glared at her and rolled his eyes.

She ran forward, pushing people out of the way to stand near us. "That was all Sikes," she yelled. "If you saw, I tried to help them in the alley that night."

"But you said she was standing in your way," someone said. They stepped forward a little and I saw that it was Jonathon. "You said you planned to raise your family back to power."

"I was mad, ok? That didn't mean I meant to hurt her. We've done nothing but be nice and calm since we got here!" she shrieked.

"It was you who poisoned her!" Paulo's wife said and gripped her chest with her horror. "You tried to kill our Visionary, right here in front of us all."

"No, I didn't!" She looked back at Donald. "Donald, help!"

His face took on a different expression as I watched him. He pinched his chin and looked around the room as chaos ensued. Everyone was yelling back and forth, and though Marla was shrieking, you couldn't hear her over the others.

Donald nodded his head to Gaston, who stepped forward and a clap of thunder rang out through the room. So, that was his ability. Marla was right, their powers stunk. What could you do with thunder?

"All right!" Donald boomed and held his hands up. "Alright. Now, I know what Marla did wasn't right, but no laws were broken-"

"No laws were broken? And was this man dealt with for killing the Champion of his clan?" the woman pointed to the man who had stabbed Sikes.

"Well, I have taken over honorary Champion duties until another one can be appointed," Donald informed with an air of regality.

"Donald," Peter addressed formerly, "breaking rules are you? The Champion can't be a council member, remember?"

"Well, there's no one else," he said in defense.

"It doesn't matter. The law is the law. There are plenty of eligible men who can take your place on the council if you wish to step down and assume the Champion role."

"No! Never!" Donald yelled, his face the color of tomatoes.

"Then you must appoint someone to be the Champion of your clan," Peter told him, looking thoroughly intrigued with where things had gone.

"There's no one to handle that job, either," Donald grumbled.

"Well, I'm afraid that you've disqualified yourself," Peter continued and I started to see the light in people's eyes as they got his meaning. "By breaking the law of only holding one office at a time, and admitting it in front of other council members, you are hereby disqualified as a council member and the Watson clan must appoint a new member to represent them."

"Watch yourself, Peter," he threatened.

Peter just laughed. "You did this to yourself. You can't be a hypocrite and a leader." Donald lunged as if to run for Peter, but several other members stopped him as Peter went on. "Now, we must deal with appointing a new council member before moving on with Maggie's father and brother."

"I suggest myself as council member," Marla said and smiled, smoothing her hair as if that alone redeemed her. She gave Donald a snippy look as he stalked passed her.

"Not on your life," Marcus sneered.

A man who put a hand on Marcus' shoulder spoke next. I assumed he was his father. "I appoint Haddock Watson as council member. All in favor, say aye."

"Aye," the Watsons said behind Marla and she boiled. Marcus waited until everyone else had voted and then said, "Aye."

"Marcus, you little traitor!" Marla yelled.

"Some things are bigger than you, sis," he growled and she crossed her arms like a sullen child.

"Great," Paulo announced. "Haddock, come forward."

A man stepped forward from the back of the group. I'd never seen him before and he looked as if he was very good at blending in. He looked right at me, even as he ascended the stairs to the council table. I couldn't read his thoughts, of course, but his eyes had something familiar in them and I felt instantly intrigued. He sat and finally removed his gaze from me. Caleb put his arm around my waist and leaned into me. "Here we go," he whispered.

"Alright," Paulo started and motioned for the other council members to join him. Gran squeezed my arm she went by. "Now, Visionary, I'm sorry, but once again this matter concerns you therefore you are not eligible to vote." I nodded my understanding to him and he went on. "Now, we know that there have never been humans in the palace before as it's our sacred place to live, work, and convene. However…"

"Paulo, no. It's doesn't matter!" Donald said from off to the side.

"It does, actually. We can't pick and choose which laws to follow." Paulo cleared his throat. "There is no specific law against a human being here. This is what the law reads." He slipped on a pair of small reading glasses from the table and squinted at a page in a large, red leather book that I hadn't even noticed was there. "There shall be no one, not of our kind or knowledge, allowed through the entranceway of our people. This is a sacred journey of pride and acknowledgement of the way and keeping of our people. Now." He took his reading glasses off. "The entranceway of our people refers to the stairwell through the cottage which was carved by the hands of our ancestors. A burden they took with pride and acknowledgment of the sacrifice for the greater good, for us to have a place free from persecution and fear of being ourselves. We were all here and I know that you did not bring the humans through the entranceway, Caleb, we would have seen." Caleb nodded and I heard the thoughts in his mind. These people and their loopholes.

"No, sir. I brought them in through the south entrance, near the greenhouse, and we entered through the roof."

"Then I see no law broken. With that being said, there is a law against telling humans what we are," he said and it seemed that he didn't even want to say the words.

"That was all me," I blurted. "I couldn't lose them and I-"

"Maggie," Peter said and looked at me. He smiled. "It's alright."

I shook my head. "You don't have to."

"Yes, I do." He looked back at Paulo. "I was the one who told Jim about our kind. I was the one who told him what I was and what had happened to Maggie."

"But I was the one who told Bish, my brother," I insisted, determined that Peter not take all the blame.

"Thank you for your honesty, Visionary, but if you had told your father as well there would be no problem." I squinted in confusion before remembering the law right before he spoke it. "This Visionary is granted clemency. Peter, however, is not." He looked at Peter sadly. "You know what happens."

"No," Caleb said as he read Paulo's thoughts through me. Peter had to step down as Champion for punishment.

"No, don't," I said, though it was no use. Peter had already acknowledged the law and got down on one knee.

"I resign as Champion of the Jacobsons, and as punishment, I know I'm not allowed to appoint my successor."

"Jacobsons," Paulo said loudly. "Who will you appoint as your new leader?"

*It's all falling into place, Maggie. You're doing great.*

I held my breath and tried to block the voice out, then heard the resounding thoughts around us. Caleb stiffened right before Gran yelled clearly, and with as much conviction as I'd ever heard, "Caleb."

# Nineteen

"Caleb!" Rodney yelled.

"Caleb," Jen followed along with Uncle Max and everyone else. Caleb stood in horror. How could he take something from his father like that? How could he just accept something that his father loved and found so much pride in?

"Caleb," Peter said, but he wasn't voting, he was calling his son. Caleb's gazed obediently jerked to Peter's. "It's all right, son."

"How can it be all right?"

"Everything happens for a reason. It was meant to be this way; this day, this reason, this cause, this way."

"I can't, Dad."

"Yes, you can," Peter told him harder. "Caleb, did you really think that you imprinted on the Visionary of our people and that you would sit back on the sidelines?"

"No…no, I didn't think that, I just…"

"I'm still here. We're still here as a family. You just call the shots now," Peter said and grinned. "It's what you always wanted when you were little anyway."

Caleb didn't laugh at the joke and I bit my lip as I listened to Caleb's inner tirade with himself. I needed to do something, so I rubbed my hand against his back. He looked over at me instantly.

*Is this real? Are we sleeping somewhere and I just haven't figured it out yet?*

I shook my head. *Your family believes in you, just like I do. Who do you think they would have chosen if they'd waited until later to choose? I always knew it would be you one day.*

He smiled a twisted smile. *Really? Or are you just saying that now?*

*Really. You pushed me when I fought being the Visionary, now I'm pushing you. Do it, babe. Your dad's right, you were so made for this.*

*You're going to make me kiss you in front of all these people.*

I giggled silently. He turned to the council. My eyes shot around nervously when I realized that Caleb wasn't embarrassed about that conversation with his dad in front of all those people. They didn't hide anything from anybody; they were like one huge family, ups and downs and all.

"I accept," Caleb's voice told the council in his deep rumble that meant he was serious and full of all kinds of emotion.

"Give him the object, Peter," Paulo told him and waited.

Peter walked from Rachel's grasp and came to Caleb. There was some unspoken boundary that even I realized so I stepped back to give them a minute to themselves, and shut my mind. Peter put his hand on Caleb's shoulder and spoke something low to him. Caleb nodded and held out his palm. Peter put something small, but apparently significant, into Caleb's waiting palm. I could see the emotion sweep over him and he slipped it into his pocket without another word.

"It is done," Paulo announced. "The rights to the Jacobsons now rest in your hands, Caleb." Caleb nodded once and then jumped a little when his family started to clap. He looked at them and smiled bashfully before beckoning me back to him with outstretched fingers.

"Now," Paulo began again and I wondered if he was now the designated spokesperson. "We must address the issue of what to do with the Visionary's father and brother."

I squeezed Caleb's hand and started to speak, though I wasn't sure what to say, when Dad spoke behind me.

"I've sat here quietly the whole time." Everyone looked over at him with interest. "I watched the horrible things some of you have done to my daughter." I sucked air through my teeth. I'd forgotten when I showed them all the things that happened to me that Dad was in the room. He'd seen everything as well. "She told me some, but some I didn't know about, and I'm furious. I don't understand how you can all sit there and go on and on about your laws and rules and regulations when all I want to do is punch that dark-haired boy in the face for what he did to my girl." Marcus looked on humorlessly at us. "Now, I know I'm looking at this from a human perspective, so I'll try to tone it down, but I think it's a little silly for you all to be so worried about my son and me. You all have abilities and skills that I will never have. And you're scared of me? Really?"

Paulo cleared his throat and started to speak, but stopped. He tried again, but stopped. Finally he found his voice.

"Do you promise to adhere to the rules as long as you're in our palace and won't cause any trouble?"

"Yes," my father answered though, his mind said he felt like this was Kindergarten.

"Do you promise never to breathe a word of our kind to another human being?"

"Of course. They wouldn't believe me anyway."

Paulo nodded once. "And you?" He looked at Bish. "The same?"

"Yep," was Bish's clipped answer.

He looked at the other council members and they nodded. "Then I say everything is settled. Meeting adjourned." He closed the big, red leather book with a loud bang that reminded me of a gavel, and made his way down from the table.

"That's it?" Dad said. "They make such a fuss and then cave just like that?"

"Dad," I replied in disbelief. "Take a victory where it comes, ok?"

"Whatever, I'm just saying." He put his hands in his pockets. He looked very uncomfortable. "What the heck am I supposed to do here while y'all rule the world, huh?" He scrunched his brow. "I feel like I crashed a wedding."

I laughed and suggested, "You can be happy that you're alive."

"Ok," he said and softened a little. "Ok, you're right."

Music started behind us. I looked over to see the invisible band had been started up. Dad's eyes watched the instruments play themselves with fear and fascination. People started to dance to relieve the tension in the room. It was a folk dance where they dance with a group in a circle.

It looked pretty easy to follow. Everyone just followed the person next to them.

"You want to dance, Jenna?"

I squeezed my eyes before turning to make sure that Jonathon was still alive. He was quite alive and his hand was open, willing Jen to accept his invitation. Bish looked away and put his hands on his head. My heart ached for him. I had to figure a way to stop this thing between them or make them see that it wasn't worth it to live in worry. I'd work my fingers to the bone to try to stop that vision.

"Come on, Bish," I said and gripped his arm, my fingers not even meeting each other all the way around. "Dance with me?"

"I feel sick," he said in a groan of agony. I watched as Jen turned a guilty expression to Bish's back before taking Jonathon's arm and letting him lead her. When she touched him, Jonathon half expected them to imprint and was disappointed. He thought he felt a real connection with her, but it was nothing compared to Bish and Jen's. I turned back to Bish as he spoke. "It felt so good to see her again, like my body just…was whole or something. But now…. I just hurt."

"I know, and I'm sorry. I wish there was something I could do," I said and he gave me an odd look.

"You know something. What do you know?"

Bish was oddly open and raw. He was never this way and I hated to refuse him when he was so willing to be that way. "I think you're both in withdrawal…for each other. The imprint that would happen if you touched wants you two to be together. You haven't been able to stop thinking about her, right? But it's different. It's like you have no control over it."

"Yes," he sighed. "It's like she's…in my head, in my skin. I can't do anything anymore without having her there with me. Sometimes it feels like she's right there. And when I saw her in your room, it took every ounce of my control not to grab her to me." He grimaced. "I hate this, Maggie."

"No, you don't," I said.

"Yes, I do. If my wanting her hurts her that much, if she wants nothing to do with me and is so upset at the thought of being with me, then maybe I should go."

"She wants you, Bish, but she's scared."

"I didn't mean to scare her," he answered and glanced over at her. When he saw her, he looked away like it was painful.

"No, she's scared of the consequences. She thinks about you all the time. I know," I told him and gave him a look. "I'm in her head. I'm in everyone's head. She hurts, too. Her body feels strange, too, when she thinks about you. She's only doing what she thinks is right. And don't say it," I stopped his thought, or his pity party. "She's yours, right?"

"Gah, yes," he groaned.

"Then fight for her. Show her that it's worth it to leap."

He sighed and his mind seemed to clear some. He stood straighter. "Ok." He nodded. "I know that she's worried about Maria, about her being left alone, but I have complete faith in you." He looked at me and slung his am over my shoulder as we walked out into the hall. "You've changed. You've changed so much in such a short time. From what I've seen, I'm not sure there's much that you can't do."

I bit my lip hard. "Thanks." I saw Marcus strolling leisurely down the hall and I knew an altercation was coming. Marcus would not be able to shut his mouth. "And Caleb…" Bish said and made an annoyed noise, "he let that guy get away with all the crap he did to you."

"Well, Caleb tried to choke him when we got here, but everyone stopped him. They are really strict on the rules, especially if others can see you."

"Huh," he said and smiled. "Well, no one's around right now." He turned, just as Marcus started to spout off something smart, and clocked him right in the mouth. He shook his fist as I gawked at his quick thinking move.

He shrugged. "What? I guess *I haven't* changed that much."

I laughed into my fist and accepted his arm as we started back down the hall. Maria ran out to meet us, though. "Where are you…going?" She stopped when she saw Marcus on the ground, out cold. Then she shook her head and carried on. "I wanted to dance with you!"

"With me?" I asked.

"No, silly. You," she said to Bish and held her hand out with childlike assurance. "All the other boys are taken. Please?"

He flashed her a prince charming smile and bowed as he took her hand. "Alright, we'll dance, but you have to teach me how."

"Sure!" They stepped over Marcus to go back onto the ballroom. I went around him and we left him to 'slumber' while we went back inside. It wasn't an intimate dance, like I said, it was a circle, so you only touched the person's arm next to you.

Rachel and Peter were next to Gran and Caleb, who'd been obviously pulled out by her given by his playful scowl. I watched them for a while. Bish was being a seriously sweet guy, letting Maria teach him how to do the moves and laughing with her. I caught Jen looking at them several times with a blindsided look. She didn't want to think about possibilities or consequences, so she just looked on blankly.

Eventually, someone came up and tapped my shoulder gently. I turned to see the Watson who had been appointed the new council member.

"Haddock, right?" I asked.

"That's right," his deep, rich voice said. "And you're Maggie," he said knowingly.

"Yep. And thank you for not calling me Visionary."

He nodded once at that. "Care to take a spin with me?"

"Sure," I said. I decided I needed to look diplomatic, so I let him. He wasn't wearing gloves, which I had noticed that most of the Watsons were, and he must've had my blood as well, because I was completely blind to his mind.

We latched onto a circle. I wasn't sure which way to go and fumbled my steps a bit. "Just follow me, Maggie," he said and I felt a strange calm, like I could trust him not to lead me astray. So I let him lead me and soon, I was stepping with the rest of them. And it was so much fun.

Laughter could be heard all around and when the music finally stopped, I was a little winded. Haddock smiled at me in a strange way, but not creepy. "Thanks for that," I told him.

"It really was my pleasure," he said and bowed. "I look forward to many more in the years to come."

"Sure," I replied and smiled.

Something struck me as very weird with him. I turned to find Caleb and almost ran into Marla and a man. She was smiling and looking very proud of herself. The man, who wasn't a Watson, but I couldn't hear his thoughts either, just stared at me.

"What?" I barked, done with even pretending to be nice to her.

"I have someone I want you to meet, but first, I'd like to take this somewhere private."

"I'm not going anywhere with you," I said.

"Bring your precious Caleb, I don't care, but you need to hear what *we* have to say." She gripped the older man's arm, indicating that he was important. I weighed my options.

"Ok, fine. Let's go to the roof."

"Perfect!" she purred and smiled. "We'll meet you there, while you grab your boy toy."

I rolled my eyes at her and went to find Caleb. I found him with a young girl, one of Paulo's clan members I believed, and she was obviously half in love already.

I giggled to myself as I sidled up to Caleb. "Hey."

"Hey, babe," he said roughly and made a noise in his throat. "This is, uh..."

"Jacquelyn," the girl said, hurt that he'd forgotten her name so quickly.

"Yes, Jacquelyn, sorry. She's Paulo's daughter." Aha. "Jacquelyn, this is my fiancé, Maggie, the Visionary."

"Hi," the girl said softly. "I was just asking Caleb what had changed since the last time we were here together." She smiled at him and her eyelashes seemed to bat themselves.

"Oh?" I asked and felt Caleb tense beside me. "How old are you, Jacquelyn?"

"I'm nineteen, though I know I don't look it." She smiled again. "Anyway, so the last reunification, Caleb showed me the roof. It was so…dreamy up there at night."

Ok, so I wasn't giggling inside anymore. "Oh?" I repeated. So he'd shown another the girl the roof. *Our roof* that had been so romantic. So what, right? So what if I wanted to jab a cocktail shrimp down her throat? I cleared my own throat to keep from saying the words out loud.

*Babe, it's not like that. She was crying, she was sad about something. I never even really got it out of her what she was crying about. It was last year. I took her to the roof to get some air. We did* not *go to the greenhouse. Do you hear me? That's yours and mine.*

I shook my head a 'no'. *It's fine. I'm not upset. It's just so weird to hear other girls talk about you, that's all.* I rubbed my chest. *My imprint isn't too happy with you taking other girls to the roof.*

*I promise you it wasn't like that.*

*I know that.* I looked back to Jacquelyn, who was eying us with disgust as she realized we were speaking without her involved. She was remembering the night she tricked Caleb into taking her on the roof. She had been fake crying in the hall and said she needed some air when he stopped to see what was wrong. Naturally, he took her to the only place with air, the roof. She tried to touch him several times, but he eventually just scooted on out of there and left her to her air.

She was trying to make me jealous with her insinuations, but why?

"Ok, well it was nice to meet you," I said and took Caleb's hand. "Marla's waiting for us. She has something she wants us to know so we'd better go."

She looked longingly at Caleb. "You know I always thought you and I would imprint. It was like…I don't know, a feeling. I was so sure of it. So when I heard about you two, naturally, I was…upset."

"I'm sorry," Caleb told her.

"Maybe if you'd just given me a real chance instead of always being a good little boy, I could have been the one-" she started.

"Nope, I'm going to stop you right there," Caleb said and pulled me to him. He spoke gently, but firmly. "Everything is happening for a reason. It may not seem like it at first, but all this was supposed to happen. I'm sorry, I hope you find your significant one day, but I won't listen to you wish away the fact that I found mine."

She shrugged and turned away. I was kind of speechless about the whole thing. I figured I'd run across some girls who had their eye on Caleb, especially after all those stories about him running from the girls, but to actually meet one and hear her still be so bitter about it, was shocking. I would hope his people would be happy for him.

"Let's just…forget this whole conversation," Caleb suggested, with puppy dog eyes to boot.

I laughed sadly and leaned my head back. "Oh, my gosh, that's such a good idea." I looked back up and blew a breath from my lips. "All right, come on. Let's see what the witch wants."

The cool air felt like absolute heaven on my face as Caleb opened the door to the roof. I was ready for a few minutes of just rest and normalcy, but it looked like that would have to wait.

"Ok, what, Marla?" I said as soon as the door closed behind us.

"I'll get straight to the introductions," she said and smiled at the man. "Maggie, meet your father."

# Twenty

"I'm sorry, what?" I croaked and looked at the man who looked as foreign to me as any stranger.

"I said this is your father."

"How do you know that my father isn't my father and this man is actually my father?" I said and it made sense in my head, but came out weird. She must have gotten the gist because she smirked and went on.

"Because we made it our job to find out these things." She started to pace along the bricks, her fingers glancing along the surface of the short stone wall. "You see, when we used your blood we found out that it was Ace blood." She waited for the shock to set it, and it did. What… "So we set out to find what had happened and why you had mixed blood. We knew it had to be because an Ace had slept with you mother, a human," she shivered and made a small gagging noise, "and so we just started searching. We've been searching ever since Sikes had you in the compound. This is David of the Reinhardt clan of Tennessee. And he is your father."

Caleb leaned against me, or maybe I was falling onto him. "Show me the proof?"

"Tell her," Marla barked at him. He flinched and looked at me.

"I had an affair at your house with your mother while your dad was at work. I knew she got pregnant, so I called off the affair."

"You knew she was pregnant?" I asked and it hit me just then that I hadn't been able to read any of his thoughts. "Wait a minute. Why can't I hear your thoughts? You took her blood?" I accused and he stepped away a little.

"No," Marla answered for him. "You can't hear his thoughts because he made you. You have his blood running through your veins and you can't use your ability on yourself. It makes sense that you wouldn't be able to read him."

"But I could read my mother's thoughts."

"But she wasn't an Ace," she dragged out. Ok, that made sense and it pissed me off. My hands were shaking as I looked at that man. That man couldn't be my father. He was rail thin with scraggily, brown hair on top of his egg-shaped head with a pointy chin. He was weak and looked nothing like me as he cowered near Marla.

"I can't believe this," I said. "I just can't. Why would you tell me this now?"

"Well, I hadn't planned on telling you at all, but you brought Daddy dearest here, and the possibility of the drama and the heartache I could cause was too much to pass up." I just stared at her with a hatred that I didn't know I was capable of. "Ask him something," Marla sang. "He'll make you believe it, because it's true."

I thought about the vision I'd had of my mother and him. "Tell me what you used to say to my mom, when you'd…leave her," I said the words around my gag.

He sighed and his lips thinned. "I'd say, same time tomorrow."

That was it for me. I turned into Caleb with angry tears stinging my eyes. He held me and I could feel the heat from his glare over my shoulder at the one who made me cry.

His voice was harsh. "You're a real piece of work, you know that?"

"I'm here now, though," my father was saying with little conviction. No, scratch that, double scratch that. I was not going to call him my father. My father was downstairs. This douche bag was just a sperm donor. Caleb choked on his laughter at my thought as I turned to look at David, the sperm donor.

"I have a father."

"I just…feel bad." He reached out to give me an awkward sideways hug, and I didn't pull back. He had gloves on, but a little piece of skin from his glove to his sleeve was exposed and it touched mine. I jerked back with a hiss. Not from a vision…but an offense mark. I gasped at the horror of my father wanting to cause me harm, but it all blew up from there when Caleb reared back and punched the sperm donor's jaw so hard that I heard the crack as he fell back against the stone.

Twice in the same hour, two of the men in my life had knocked the lights out of two scumbags who had done me wrong.

"Are you crazy?" Marla shrieked at him.

"Nope," Caleb said and looked down at the man who groaned and held his battered face. "You want another one of those? You come and mess with my girl again."

Then he took my hand and led me into the stairwell.

I was reeling. I was proud and frightened and pissed and fragile all at once. I felt like I was about to overload again. Caleb stopped midway down the stairs and looked at me. He took my arm in his hand and did a half growl, half sigh at the offense mark sitting there. His touch began to take the dark mark away and soon it was just a bad memory.

"Just…" he started, "I know that this is crazy. I mean the implications of what they said alone…"

"I know." I shook my head. "They're saying I was an Ace before I met you."

It was his turn to shake his head. "We need to tell Dad and Gran, and see what they think."

"Yeah, but first we need to occupy my father and Bish. They can't find out."

He nodded and asked me silently if I was ok enough to go down. I smiled at him, somehow able to even after everything. We emerged in the ballroom to see a full on party. Music was blaring from the speakers and everyone was doing a hundred things at once.

My dad was involved in a horseshoe match with Peter and Rachel. Rachel was cheating her butt off. I laughed as my dad scratched his head and picked his shoe up once again in confusion. When he turned his back, Peter and Rachel laughed and giggled. I could have sat there and watched that all night.

Bish was tossing a football back and forth with someone. My steps faltered when I realized it was Jonathon. Then I understood again when Bish shot the ball to him and Jonathon curled his lip in pain and shook his hand out when he caught it. Jen and Maria were watching the tossing massacre with Gran, who laughed and egged them on. Ok, everyone seemed to be pretty occupied, so we went to Gran first.

He tried to find a little bit of something to tell Gran, and his mind ran through the scenario. He had a thought. If only we'd met Marla and that guy in my bedroom, we'd never have known something was up with him because there would have been no offense mark. He was grateful for the knowledge that my father apparently meant me harm, but hated how we had to get it.

Caleb asked if Gran could come with us for a minute, but that peaked Jen's interest…which peaked Bish's interest and he gave up his game to come to us.

Then an idea hit me, causing me to gasp. Bish and Jen looked at me concerned, but Caleb had heard my thought. He squinted, thinking it over, and then shrugged. It might work.

"Come on," I said to Jen and Bish. "Gran, can you keep Maria here for just a minute?"

"Sure, honey."

Bish frowned. "What's this about, Maggie?"

"Yeah," Jen agreed, "what he said."

"We'll explain it all, just not here." I led the way to my room. Once we entered, I stay turned toward the door to gather my thoughts. What Caleb said had given me the idea. If we'd had the 'meeting' in here instead, we'd have never known that my real father was a scumbag because no offense mark would show…because my room is charmed.

Then why wouldn't it work so that Jen and Bish could have a few minutes together, and actually touch after longing to do so for so long, and not worry about imprinting?

I turned and saw a very uncomfortable Jen and an intrigued Bish.

"I repeat," Bish said, "what's this about?"

"Ok, hear me out," I said and raised my palms towards them. "The council charmed my room, so that Caleb and I wouldn't be able to…" I stopped and looked at Bish. Hmm, not going to bring up mutualizing to that one. "Um, to have any abilities in here. So neither my abilities nor Caleb's work, and we can't have our healing touch either, and we've been in withdrawal two mornings already because of it."

"Ok," Bish dragged, clearly not understanding, but Jen did. She gave me her best nosy sister-in-law glare.

"Maggie, no."

"Jen, yes." I stepped forward and gripped her hand in mine. "I've been watching, and from talking to you both, you are in withdrawal for him already. Your bodies understand that there should be an imprint connecting you and something is keeping it from being. Now, while this won't help with that part, because your touch won't heal, you won't imprint in here either. You can just have a few minutes to be together."

She looked at him, and boy did he get it now. He looked ready to pounce, but she shook her head.

"I can't, Maggie." Her gaze went to his as if magnets were involved. "Bish…it won't solve anything."

"But it won't hurt anything, either," he said humbly and begged her with his eyes. "I won't hurt you. I'll stay away from you if that's what you really want, but I need you to know that it's not what *I* want. Every second I live begs to be with you."

She sighed a painful noise. "I…" She looked at me again.

"If we can't figure this out, and stop the vision, then this may be your only chance to touch each other. These few days, in this room."

"It'll hurt too much when it's over," Jen reasoned. "Caleb," she implored his help. "You wouldn't want to only touch Maggie once and never again would you? It would hurt too much, be too much of a reminder of what you couldn't have?"

He rubbed the back of his neck in awkwardness at having this discussion with his sister. "I would've touched her had I'd known it was my only time to. It would've been worth it."

That was it. The dam in Bish broke and he made his steps to her. Her breaths were loud as she backed up to the wall. Just before he reached her she finally spoke.

"Don't," she breathed, her arm outstretched, but we all could hear the lie in that word.

He collided with her in a crash of everything that had been building up between them. He didn't peck and gather her in his arms like some butterfly, he went straight for the kill. He groaned as he pulled her to him and practically swallowed her small frame whole with his huge body. She was no longer fighting as she clung to his hair with one hand, while the other was trapped between them. But their mouths… Their mouths were gentle and full of love as they kissed, but when Jen sighed his name, it was time to go.

I pulled Caleb out of the room. He had already closed his eyes and was pinching the bridge of his nose.

"Oh, my goodness! It worked!" I said in excitement. It was a small gift, a small battle in the middle of a war, but even that felt so huge with everything else going on. Bish and Jen were some of the best people I knew and it hurt me for them to be in so much pain.

Caleb was looking at me. "As gross as that was…thank you."

"I got the idea from you," I told him.

"But your brain put it together, and it was you that made it happen. I don't think I've seen Bish that…" he searched for the word.

"Soft?" I supplied.

"Yeah," he grunted. "I always thought he would be mean and rough, but when he looks at my sister…" He grimaced. "Ok, enough of this. Let's go, Sherlock. More mysteries to solve."

"Yeah, like how to occupy my dad while we talk to yours. Bish is definitely occupied," I said and laughed at Caleb's expression. "So, now to come up with…something," I stopped with wide eyes. In the middle of the palace ballroom, my father was teaching The Shuffle to a group of people who gathered around him. I turned my head to the side at the sight. People in cocktail dresses and heels…line dancing. Hmm.

"Ok," I said, "Dad's occupied. Where's yours?"

"He's there, with Gran." He pointed and waved them over. He also grabbed Rodrigo, the guy who charmed my room, and got him to do the same for us so we could speak freely. Gran took us to the sentencing room. I shivered when we went inside, but Caleb got down to business. He thankfully hashed everything out so I didn't have to and explained everything from my mom showing up at the house, to now with the sperm donor on the roof.

Peter rubbed his chin between his thumb and fingers, his eyes unfocused and thinking. Gran had her hands in her lap, showing her tattoo, and she just sat there, blowing a breath every now and then.

After a while, I couldn't take the silence anymore. "Please, say something."

"You were an Ace all along," Peter said incredulously. "It all just worked out that way? The consequences piling on top of each other? Him having an affair with her, you going to meet Kyle and instead imprinting with Caleb, then being the Visionary? No," he shook his head, "no, too much coincidence. I don't believe Marla or this man."

"He knew things," I reminded him. "I don't want it to be true anymore than you do. I was perfectly fine to just forget I ever found out the truth." I took a breath as the words clouded in my throat. "My dad is my father, that won't change. I had no intentions of looking for my real father."

"Come here, pretty girl," Gran beckoned. I went with a sigh. I sat on the tabletop next to her and she put her arm over my shoulder. "Listen, I know it's hard sometimes, but the truth is always best. Even if it doesn't seem like it makes sense, even if it seems pointless." She looked at Peter. "I know you thought Peter was crazy earlier when he said he was the one who told your dad when he could have just let the council assume it was you and you'd have been granted clemency and all's well. But the truth is important, the truth is what makes us free people. No guilt or shame holding us back. That's why I speak my mind right then and there, that way nobody can say that I'm hiding or holding back anything." She squeezed my shoulder. "You may not have wanted to know about your father, but it's good to know the truth. Then you have all the facts and know that your decision is based on something real."

Caleb and I both looked up at each other at the same time with the same thought. It was time to tell them about Grandpa Ray.

*No, Caleb. She doesn't need to know. She's just trying to make me feel better, she'll regret saying all that if you tell her about your grandpa.*

*I think I have to.*

He looked at them both. These are the two people it would hurt the most; Raymond's wife and his son. "Dad…Gran, we found out something. Um, when Ruth was taking Maggie's blood, they talked. She talked about Sikes and some of the things he had done."

Caleb told them about Sikes forcing the imprint on Ruth. Peter stood and paced, running his hands through his hair at that, but when Caleb got to the part we didn't want to say, he slowed his voice and stood in front of Gran.

"Gran. We had a suspicion about Sikes. So we asked Ruth and she answered our question. Grandpa…"

"No," Gran snipped and stood. "No, my Raymond died of a heart attack. It was my fault, my cross to bear all these years."

"No, Gran. Sikes went into Grandpa's dream and-"

"No! Not another word." She covered her ears and shook her head. "Not another word."

Peter took Caleb by the arms and was the only one willing to pry the information out of Caleb. "He killed him in an echo?" Peter asked and turned his head as if anticipating a blow. When Caleb answered, Peter jerked like he'd been hit.

He went to his mother, who was hysterical in the corner. She shook her head and said over and over again, "No, no, no." She let him pull her into his embrace and then let loose a sob that had me crying and shaking along with them, but this was Caleb's hurt, not mine. I didn't even look at his face as I wrapped my arms around him and tried to take away even an ounce of the hurt.

Judging by his grip, he was accepting my offer. So I reached on my tiptoes to reach more of him and let him lift me, pressing his face into my neck. I tried not to hear the agonizing cries of the broken woman and her broken son.

# Twenty One

I was not in the mood for any more partying and neither was the Jacobson family. Peter had finally gathered himself enough to tell Caleb that he would have a meeting later with the family in one of the second floor rooms. It would look too suspicious to call everyone together without the rest of the clans. So, we ate a dinner that I wasn't hungry for. Gran was sullen and everyone noticed because Gran was just not a sullen lady. Caleb sat next to her at dinner and he kept glancing over, probably a million times, to make sure that she was still in one piece.

She eventually said she was tired and going to bed. She hugged Caleb so hard and long that it made me ache for her all over again. Then she hugged me and I felt like I should say something. She'd been so good to me and always had something witty and smart to say.

"Gran, I'm so sorry," I said muffled into her shoulder. "I wish I could hurt them for what they did to you."

"Sikes is gone, honey," she leaned back, "but the Watsons are just a cruel people. I've never known a more selfish and cruel bunch of folks. Just be careful. I don't want anything to happen to you."

"I'll be fine. I just wish I knew what to do. Waiting for signs and visions doesn't make me feel very productive."

"You can't put fate on a schedule, girl," she said saucily. Caleb chuckled behind her. "You've gotta understand that everything…was meant to be this way," she said slowly.

"I'm supposed to be making you feel better," I told her, "not the other way around."

"Oh, don't you worry about this old gal. I'm gonna keep on kicking like I always do."

We watched her go and I felt terrible. Dad came up and asked where Bish was. I'd almost forgotten where he was. I assured him Bish was fine, that he and Jen were just talking somewhere. Dad was seriously blowing my mind.

Dad was having a blast. And he was a hit! Everyone loved him and was fawning all over him. It was like he was made to be one of them.

Caleb and I walked to my room as everyone started to think about bedtime. I knocked softly on my door and, when I heard nothing, I peeked my head into the room. I didn't see anyone and I was a little disappointed. I hoped that Bish and Jen would enjoy their little bit of time and make the most of it, but it looked like they'd both left.

Caleb shut the door behind me as I went to remove my shoes at the foot of my bed and heard a snore. Bish's snore. The bed was empty so I went to the sofa over near the armoire and there they were. They both were still in their clothes from before, but their shoes were kicked off on the floor. Bish was flat on his back and Jen was curled into his side, her hands resting on his chest. He had one arm behind his head and one around her back. Their faces rested against each other's.

I twisted my earring in contemplation as I looked at them. Caleb's arm came around my shoulder, as easy as breathing. "Hey, let's just let them sleep in here. Your dad can take the bed."

"Where are we going to sleep?"

"Well-"

The door behind us burst open and Rodney was breathing heavy as he struggled to get out his words. "Your…your dad…"

"My dad what?" I asked, but couldn't be polite if something was wrong. "Rodney, either spit it out or get out of the room so I can read your mind!"

He took a deep breath and blurted, "Your dad just imprinted."

My breath stopped along with time. What did he just say?

Caleb and I took off running. We arrived on the scene like spectators who had witnessed an accident. I wanted to look, but also didn't. I wasn't sure what I'd find or see.

My dad was wringing his hands, a blonde beauty stood next to him as he listened to Peter and Paulo explain about the imprints, about how they never happen in front of other people, and the fact that Dad was a human and he just got here was all amazing.

The woman, who wasn't as old as my dad, was beaming in a shy way and she watched my dad with eyes that said he was all she could ask for. I saw it as my dad's eyes glanced from her to Peter and back. He'd loved my mom once, but he had never been so enraptured like that before.

I didn't know if I had the energy to wade through the onslaught of emotions, but I was happy for him. And the fact that he was a human and imprinted in front of everyone may have been the push these people needed to get over their human aversion. It had been a long, emotionally draining day and to end it this way was just barely believable.

In fact, I wasn't up for the puppy love I knew was in their brains, so I just shut everyone out but Caleb.

*Good idea. Are you ok?*

*Yeah, I'm just shocked. I would have thought someone younger would have imprinted. And I'm afraid that someone might be angry. Like Dad stole their chance to imprint with whoever that is over there.*

*No, they won't think that. If anything, this will force them to see that the imprints will come back if they'll just pay attention to the change that has to come. That's all they want is the imprints. This will change everything, Maggie.*

He was sincere, and even in awe. I hoped he was right.

"Maggie," Dad called and I looked up to see him watching me. He smiled a little and came my way. The woman came with him, of course. "Maggie, I, uh..."

"I heard," I said. It seemed it was all I could say.

"Hi, Fiona," Caleb supplied and shook her hand politely.

"Caleb, hello," she said and laughed this embarrassed little breathy laugh. "I'd never thought I'd feel this strange. I thought I'd be ecstatic...and I am," she said hurriedly and smiled at Dad, "but this is also very embarrassing. I feel like I've just realized that I forgot my shirt or something."

Dad's eyes drifted to her chest on instinct of talking about shirts and he flushed before looking away quickly.

"This happened right here in front of everyone?" Caleb asked her and it sounded as though he almost didn't believe it.

"I know," she said and laid her hand on my dad's arm. They both sighed a little and I could have fallen over from the sweetness of them. "It's strange. I mean, I'm 34, I never thought I'd imprint. I'd given up on that and we were dancing and he was showing me this twirl thing and...it just happened." They looked at each other. "It just happened."

Dad smirked. My eyes bulged. What? My dad does not smirk. "It's alright. Maggie told me all about what happened with Caleb when they imprinted. I understand. It's a little strange to be put on display like this, but it's ok." Then he turned his attention back to me and seemed to remember that I was there. "Oh, I'm sorry. Maggie, this is Fiona. Fiona...this is my daughter, Maggie."

"Yes," she said, "the Visionary, I know. So nice to actually meet you," she stumbled over her words and fidgeted her fingers nervously. "I wish I'd met you before these circumstances. I'll just be upfront and honest, I have no idea what to do with you. Should I bow? Should I kiss your fingers? Or should I continue to stand here awkwardly and hope that you don't smite me for imprinting on your father?"

Caleb and Dad were silent. I pressed my lips together. It didn't help. I burst out laughing and tried to cover it with my hand, but it was no use. Dad was the next to follow. Fiona was last, as if she didn't know if we were laughing *at* her or *with* her. So I threw her a bone and hugged her. She was going to be my freaking step-mother!

"Fiona, I'm not going to smite you," I joked as I leaned back and hugged Dad to me. "Dad, I'm…so happy for you," I whispered to him.

"Me, too," he answered. "I thought I was going to have to live in the shadow of your mom for the rest of my life."

"Dad," I groaned. "That's the saddest thing I've ever heard."

"It was," he said and chuckled. "I'm ok, though. Don't worry about your old man."

"I still can't believe this happened. Do you realize that you're the only forty year old that has ever imprinted?"

"Hey!" he said and laughed. "You could have kept that number between us," he joked.

"Oh, it's fine," Fiona said sweetly. "Older is better with wine and men."

I was still reeling. I decided to let the noise of the room in so I could feel out the mood. I wanted to see if people really were upset about it or willing to maybe be more open to change as long as they got what they wanted in return; the imprints.

The mood of the room slammed into me and I held back my smile. Yes, there was jealousy, yes, there was longing, yes, there was even a little anger, but the general thought was people wondering what the Jacobsons, and now my family, were doing right. And they were walking the line of throwing everything out the window that they'd always known if the imprints would come back.

Dad's thoughts were finally in understanding. He finally got my crazy need for Caleb, that it wasn't just hormones and teenagers. Fiona was humbled and literally jumping in her skin. All she wanted to do was get my dad out of there and be alone, to feel for real what it was like to have a significant, without a couple hundred people staring at you.

"Hey, we're gonna go to bed," I told them, since my dad seemed to be waiting for me before he'd do anything else. "I'm so tired. We had so much stuff go on today, and I'm sure you're both ready to be away from all these people." They both nodded and slyly glanced at each other. "But, uh…Bish and Jen are in my room."

Dad blinked. "Bish and Jen are in your room…what?"

"Sleeping," I answered wryly. He released his breath. "They fell asleep on the couch and we left them there, so..."

"Ok, well." He didn't know where to go or what to say without being presumptuous.

"My room is on the second floor," she offered and smiled. "We can just get over the awkwardness now, I guess. If we don't sleep together, we'll regret it in the morning."

"Yes, I know." He clucked his tongue. "Ok, let's go. Goodnight, Maggie. I'll…see you in the morning."

"Night, Dad," I said in amusement.

"Wow," Caleb leaned down and said.

"Yeah, wow," I said through my yawn.

"Come on. I have the perfect spot." He went into the kitchen quickly and then to Rachel and told her that Jen had fallen asleep in my room. He asked could she keep Maria with her tonight. She was, of course, delighted. We left the Bish part out since no one knew about them and no one knew about the vision I had of them, either.

"Are we sleeping in your room?" I asked as he towed me down the hall.

"I assume my room is charmed as well," he answered and pushed my back to the wall by my room. "Stay."

I complied with another yawn as he went inside and came back out with a pillow and blanket.

"Are we camping?" I joked.

"Yep," he said and grinned as he led us.

Once we reached the stairwell, I knew exactly where he was taking me. I smiled as we climbed the stairs. Once we got to the balcony, where two unpleasant instances had occurred today, I noticed that Caleb went a little faster.

He held my hand and helped me over the ridges of the rooftop. We reached the greenhouse and he set to work on getting it all straightened out. He opened the skylight and then laid the blanket and pillow out before beckoning me to him. I lay down with him, reveling in his warmth.

"We could have just slept in your room," I said as he pulled the edge of the blanket over us.

"I'm not spending another night somewhere where you'll be hurting by morning." He kissed my forehead. "It goes against everything in my body to do so."

I nodded and agreed. "You don't think Fiona's room is charmed?"

"Nah," he said and pulled something that crinkled out of the pillowcase. "I don't think they'd have made him charm all the rooms, just the ones where they thought they'd have a problem."

"A problem," I scoffed and snuggled closer as I smiled at what he was holding. A package of Oreos. He twisted a cookie and held it out for me to lick it. I laughed as I did and then let him put that half of it in my mouth, his fingers touching my lips. I chewed and then he held another one out for me. I licked it and then he finished it, his chews noisy and cute as it crunched.

"So, was that all you did when you snuck out? Get my dad?" I asked.

His mind closed and he popped the blanket where my butt was with his hand. "Stop trying to figure out if I've bought you a house yet."

I smiled up at him. "I wasn't," I said innocently. "Just curious. You were gone a long time."

"It's really hard to make plans and do research for houses when there's no phones, no internet, and no cell service," he said. "But don't worry. I've got a plan that will work out."

"Not even a hint?"

"Not even a hint," he said, amused.

"And what about the wedding?" Caleb's heart jumped under my head and I bit my lip. "You're the Champion now, so who's gonna perform the ceremony?"

"Oh…" He'd almost forgotten already that he was the Champion now. "Dad still will, I guess. Not sure what protocol is for that type of situation, but I'll fight to have Dad do it. He wants to. I know it."

"Yeah. So your dad knew when he told my father about your kind that he could possibly be removed from being the Champion and he still did it?"

"Of course." He rolled a little to put me under him. "You're not just marrying me, you're marrying my family. My dad has loved you since he set eyes on you." He laughed and leaned further down. "He would do anything you ask him to, you're just too modest to even think about asking him."

"Hmm," I grumbled. "Well, I want your dad to marry us, too, so I'll just tell everyone to screw off if they have a problem with it."

Caleb laughed, his chest shaking against mine. "You're so funny. But you're right. If you can't use the Visionary card on something like that, then what can you?"

"Exactly."

"Besides, you're too cute to say no to." He grinned, his hair falling around his forehead and around his ears. He ran his fingers through my hair and around my ear, and then rubbed my earlobe in between his fingers gently. "You're so soft…and amazing. I think you can pretty much do whatever you want to. Just stop being so sweetly naive and start believing that you're as amazing as I think you are."

"You're the sweetest guy for saying that," I rebutted in a whisper and exhaled all my worries.

"I'm not sweet, I'm being truthful." He kissed my lips and hovered there. "You're strong," he kissed my cheek, "and you're so gonna rock at this running our people thing." He smirked before taking my lips again…and taking his time. He was in no hurry as his movements were almost slow motion. His lips moved from my lips to my neck. I leaned my head back and silently begged him never to stop doing that.

When we rolled so that he was under me, I did the same to him. His neck, though strong and hard from his muscles, was also soft with his smooth skin. His hands moved to my face and took control. He pulled me to his lips. I rested in the 'U' shape of his legs and lifted his shirt a bit to feel his ribs. I counted the hard hills of his abs and he laughed into our kiss and jerked from the tickle.

He was such a…master of kissery. He barked out a laugh at my thought and we giggled together. The thought was swirling in both of our minds, and I think we both knew we needed it. We needed to be as close as we could be tonight. So, when he rolled and put me under him, his arms holding mine above my head, I knew just what was coming.

I let him open the gates of our minds and when the tingles started to zing through my body, I reached up to kiss him and held on with my legs wrapped around his. I can't say it was better than the last time, but it was just as beautiful and I learned so many new things about him from the mutualizing of our minds. He loved watching roller derbies, after everything that happened he still wanted to move to Arizona and be a teacher, and he wanted nothing more right now than to take me away from the palace for good.

I felt his hand moving up the back of my thigh, but his real hands were still holding mine down. In my mind I wrapped my arms around his neck and held on to him as the mutualizing came to an end and the energy ribbons bounced around us before illuminating and expanding in a burst. I remembered to breathe this time, and it was loud and ragged. As he settled back down to me with his face in my neck, I felt his harsh breaths against my skin before he rolled to his side and pulled me against him. Our hearts banged against each other and it set a rhythm to remember how to breathe properly. He lifted my chin with a finger and kissed my lips. "I really needed that," he said gruffly.

"Me, too," I said and laughed softly. "Maybe more than you."

"Sweetheart," he chided, making my heart skid. "You'll never need me more than I need you." I didn't argue out loud, though my mind made it clear that he was insane if he thought that was true.

His sigh was filled with happiness and exhaustion as he tucked me under his chin. I pressed my fingers to his heart as we closed our eyes.

I wanted to stay like that all night, but the reason for the camp out began to hit us. We couldn't cure sleep and it was late, and the stars were practically a nightlight.

He pulled my head down to rest on him and weaved his hands through my hair. As we drifted off, Caleb's mind was running with thoughts of his Grandpa and Gran. Mine was full of Bish and Dad, and their lady troubles.

A long day, indeed.

~~~

Our peaceful little sleep was interrupted by someone yanking our blanket off. I jerked up, expecting to see Marla and Marcus, but there was no one. I was confused and thought that maybe I imagined it, so I started to lie back down, but instead my body got up from the pallet. I tried to move, tried to do anything, but I wasn't in control of myself. I started walking away from the pallet, and Caleb, so I yelled for him.

"Caleb!"

He jolted up immediately and scrambled after me as he saw me leaving.

"What happened? Did someone come get…" He drifted off as he read my thoughts. He jumped in front of me and grabbed my shoulders to stop me. But my arms tossed him to the wall on my left. I gasped in horror as he slammed into it and slid to the stone walkway.

"Caleb!"

"I'm alright," he groaned and got up again. He came back to me, but didn't touch me. "What is this?"

"I don't know," I shrieked in frustration. "It's like something in me is in control."

He wanted to help me over the rooftops, but didn't want to touch me again. But my body didn't lumber over the ridges, it powered through with a purpose that I didn't understand. When we reached the stairwell, we made our way down. The gas sconces were the only light and noise, but when we reached the bottom, my body turned and went down another hallway.

Then, as if I was watching a vision, everything changed. The brick and stone were more colorful, the gas sconces on the wall were lanterns now, and there was a girl in front of us. She was walking in her white, long-sleeve nightgown and appeared to be leading the way. I had control of my body now and clung to Caleb, who sighed at my being released.

He pulled us to a stop and the girl turned. I thought she was looking at us, like she was a ghost, but then she screamed and ran the other way. We turned behind us and saw a man chasing her with a torch in his hands to light his way. Caleb pulled me behind him as he pressed us to the wall, but the man didn't give us a second glance.
~~~

Then I felt the cold settle on me. This was a vision! I looked at Caleb and he understood.

We followed her.

They ran all the way through the halls, tunnels and stairwells until they came to the spiral staircase. I slowed remembering this room. The library that Rodney had taken me to show me the Visionary records.

She ran the stairs with a knowledge that made me think she'd done so many times. He gave chase, but stopped when she made it inside. He yelled.

"I warned you!"

Then the man stalked off passed Caleb and me without another word. He looked familiar, but I didn't know who he was. I was confused as to what we were seeing. Then we heard the girl crying. If she couldn't see us, then it didn't matter if we went to see her, right?

We climbed the steps and once we reached the threshold, we stopped. She was lying on the floor, crying and rubbing at her arms and stomach. She was in such agony, but it was more than just physical. It looked like she was in withdrawal.

She finally got up and went to the wall. She took the feather, dipped it into the inkwell, and began to write her small, dainty words.

She was the Visionary.

But they had told me the previous Visionary hadn't been imprinted with anyone, that it was a weakness and a luxury that the Visionary couldn't afford. So we watched her silently. Caleb held my waist tight as if to save me at any moment. Then we were quickly jerked from that vision to another.

It was the girl again, the Visionary. She was at the table with the council members and looked very put together and regal. Once again, no one saw us, even though we sorely stood out in our clothes in the room full of well-dressed people. From the look of their clothes, this was long ago.

The girl's eyes stayed locked onto something behind us as a council member stood and made an announcement.

I looked back and saw nothing, but just as I was about to turn I saw the boy. He was staring back at her with the same wistful expression. I looked between the two and tried to piece it together. When the man who was speaking banged his goblet on the table, she jolted upright again and looked at him. She raised her glass as everyone else was already doing and toasted to long life and prosperity.

But the girl just seemed dead inside.

Then that vision flashed to another. She was inching her way down a dark hallway. It winded and twisted and I remembered it as being the way to the cells. I cringed into Caleb's side and watched as she crept slowly passed a sleeping guard, who was leaning back against the wall.

A man spoke from one of the cells, "Ashlyn."

She gasped happily and ran to him, but before she reached him, the guard grabbed her from behind. The man in the cell and her reached their fingers, for just one touch…but it was no use. She was so small and tiny, and though I could feel her power radiate from her, she was helpless in her fear and anguish.

The man hissed and jerked back before grabbing her sleeved arm and slinging her toward the doorway. I saw the offense mark across her neck and she screamed in agony before crumpling to the floor. The agony was for her would-be significant.

The knowledge of what was going on hit me all at once. She was the Visionary. She had been known as the Visionary since she was seventeen. She'd always known the boy, or man I should say, Richard, from the reunifications, but had never spoken to him. When she was twenty three, she just seemed to be so taken by him, so drawn, and he in turn couldn't keep his eyes off of her all night. They eventually found a second to speak in the hallway and right as he was about to brush a curl from her face, the man who had chased her in the vision was there.

He was none too happy and barked for the boy to go. He bowed to Ashlyn and went, but had no intentions of staying away. The man came into the light of the lantern and I caught my breath at the resemblance of Donald and Sikes to that man. He growled at the girl.

"Did I or did I not forbid you to touch any man?"

"I am the Visionary, yet you let me do nothing of what I'm supposed to do. You don't let me share my visions, you don't let me speak to anyone. It's like I'm an ornament instead of a person."

"Don't speak to me that way," he growled. "I am your mentor!"

"And I am your Visionary! You have to let me do what I'm supposed to. I'll go mad if you don't!"

He reared back as if to hit her and even Caleb leaned forward as if to stop him, but the man stopped himself. He instead nodded his head at someone and they took her down the hall, careful not to touch her skin. "No! Please," she begged. "The only time you let me come out is the reunification. Please!"

"Maybe you should have thought about that before you misbehaved."

They dragged her back to her room in the library and left her there, sobbing on the floor.

More visions came. The man, Richard, tried to visit her several times. When they started to understand that they would imprint if they could just touch, they began to sneak. But every time they almost touched, someone was there to stop them and eventually they threw Richard in the cells to keep him from trying. So she began to try to reach him instead.

Then Caleb and I were standing in her room again. The library walls were full of words now, just like they were when I was there the other day. She had her back to us and she was writing on a clean piece of wall. The bed was unmade and down from the wall. There were several trays of food and drink by the door, untouched. Her feet were almost black from dirt and soot, and when she turned around, we understood. She'd gone mad, exactly like she said.

She was a little older and I saw in her mind that Richard was still in the cells, even after all those years. All the things she was supposed to do and teach her people and she'd been denied the right. The Watson council member kept her locked up and away from everyone. The other council members had their suspicions, but no one wanted to be the one to accuse him of such a thing, to ruin his reputation if it were true.

Ashlyn had scratched her hands and arms until they bled and scabbed over and over. Her hair was pulled out and missing in some spots. Her neck, where her Visionary mark was supposed to be, was burned and had a nasty wound. When I saw in her mind how she'd burned it off with a cast iron spoon she'd made hot by the fire, I lost it. I began to cry and turned into Caleb's shoulder.

It was too much. This was what I was? This was what was inside of me? She was a broken shell of a woman who'd lived through something no one should have to, but she didn't believe in herself. She didn't even try to use her power against them when they came at her. She could have easily fought them off, she could have made them listen, but she was weak in her fear.

And because of that, she went mad from being away from her significant, though they never got to touch, and from the fact that her ability was useless without an audience to see it.

The first thing that came to my mind was Bish and Jen. They'd go mad just like her if they didn't touch and imprint. I ached for them. I ached for Ashlyn and Richard. It wasn't right. The imprints were a beautiful and joyous thing and for it to be made into something closer to a burden and a curse by the Watsons, even as far back as then, was unforgiveable.

It didn't escape my notice how the situations of my circumstances mirrored hers, except for details that were ironically opposite. We both met our significant, but I met mine at seventeen and imprinted, whereas she met hers at a normal imprint age of twenty three. I was a human and she was not. I imprinted before anyone else even knew, so no one could have stopped us. Even my Visionary ability didn't work without Caleb's touch. And it all made sense now.

Whatever is was that controls the Visionary knew the mistakes that were made the first time, they just misjudged the evils' determination to stop it. So it fixed all of those issues with me.

I looked up at Caleb, who was as sick as I was about what he'd seen. I vowed right then to myself, to Caleb, to Ashlyn and whoever else who gave a darn to listen to my thoughts, that I would not be weak. I would not let them control me and make me some novelty instead of doing what I came here to do. I would never, ever, *ever* let them keep my significant away from me. I would make the hard decisions and sacrifices and I would figure out a way for Bish and Jen to be together in the beautiful way they deserved instead of waiting for disaster.

And the Watsons? There was nothing else to do. They had to go.

# Twenty Two

We found ourselves standing in the Visionary's library and we were back in reality.

"This is the library?" Caleb asked and looked around. "I've never been up here."

I nodded. "Rodney brought me here the night I went and broke you out of the cell." I smiled sadly before crumpling with a sob again.

He came and wrapped me up. "Baby, she showed you that so you wouldn't make her mistakes," he said gently. "She wasn't trying to scare you."

"I know. I just can't get over what they did to her. I mean, they literally kept them from touching each other. Can you imagine…" Caleb grunted and pulled me tighter.

"No," he breathed. "I can't."

"And I feel so cold and strange when I have my visions. I can't imagine not being able to have someone see. It really would make me crazy."

I sniffed and took a deep breath before blowing it out. Caleb wiped under my eyes with his thumbs. "Let's get out of here," he ordered gruffly. "I don't want you in this prison."

I followed him as he led us all the way back to the main hallway. I wanted to go to Bish and Jen. I wanted to tell them both to stop being idiots and just be happy that they found each other in a palace where hundreds of people were waiting to find just what they had. I wanted to tell them to have faith in me and don't doubt. But I couldn't. I knew they had to see it for themselves. To be pushed into it was the same as being pushed not to do it. I wouldn't take their choice, as stupid as I thought their aversion was.

Caleb took me back to the roof, but neither of us slept. We just stayed there until morning and when the sun crested over the rooftop, we decided it was time to face the day. We both looked awful. Caleb was dragging and I saw in his mind that I looked droopy and tired.

Oh, well. I followed Caleb to his room and he gathered all of his stuff. He took it down to my room. Whether we were going to use my room or not, he wanted all of our stuff together. After what we saw last night, he no longer worried about my safety from some stupid Watson prank, he feared for my life.

We entered my room slowly, so as not to disturb Bish and Jen, but they were up. They were sitting next to each other on the bed, their arms and legs touching. Jen was laughing at something he was saying, but they stopped when they saw us.

"What happened?" Bish barked and came to me, gripping my shoulders in his hands. "What's the matter?"

"Nothing," I answered sarcastically. "What?" I asked when he just continued to stare at me.

"You just look terrible."

"Thanks."

"No, I mean it. What's the matter?" he said in his big brother voice.

"I can't tell you," I said through a sigh, but when I saw his face, I went on. "I mean, I can't as in I won't. We've had…quite a night and I'm tired and I just can't rehash it all right now, ok?"

"Ok," he answered carefully. I remembered the one good part of the night. "There is something I'll tell you though." I smiled a little. "Dad," I shook my head, "Dad imprinted."

"What?" Jen breathed, but it was loud and telling in the room.

I nodded to her. Caleb explained further. "He imprinted with Fiona, in the ballroom…in front of the entire room."

"No," she gasped and covered her chest with her hand. "Oh, my." She came to stand next to Bish in front of us. "I wonder what it means."

"It means that the imprints are coming back," I said. "But we have a lot of work to do. Caleb and I learned a lot last night. This is going to be so hard."

"What do you mean?"

"Later," Caleb told her and took my hand, bringing it up to his chest. "And we have to talk with both of you. We learned something about you two, too."

"About us?" Jen said and stepped back.

"Yeah."

"But, there is no us…outside of this room," she said and looked at Bish. "You understood that, right?"

"Yes," he answered and the hope there died. He'd understood, but still hoped. "I know." He walked to her and held her face gently as he kissed her once. "I'm going to go find Dad."

"Probably not a good idea to walk around by yourself," Caleb supplied.

"I can handle it, I think," he said and just as he opened the door, he was grabbed by a little determined fist. She pulled him out of the room and slammed him to the wall. We all ran out to see what was going on. Jacquelyn, the girl who had been so upset about Caleb and I imprinting, was planting a kiss on Bish that would make red roses blush.

"What the hell are you doing, Jacquelyn!" Jen yelled and grabbed the girl's arm. She stumbled back a little and looked at Bish, who was stunned into silence.

She cursed loudly and stomped her foot. "He's the only human left! I thought if I touched him, he'd imprint with me since imprinting humans seemed to be the running theme."

"Well," I tried to explain, "you have to be a little attracted to the person beforehand. He'd never even met you before you kissed him."

"And I think a simple touch on his arm would have sufficed," Jen grumbled.

"What do you know?" Jacquelyn yelled and then her eyes remembered who I was by the mark on my neck. "I mean, Visionary, you have your significant so I don't see how you can judge someone who's just trying to find hers."

"That's true, I guess," I conceded to appease her. "But you're not even of imprint age yet."

She shrugged and went to go, brushing my arm as she went. I saw a scene of her past and I braced myself for something unpleasant. This vision was grimy and I could almost taste a salty feel on the air.

She'd been spending an awful lot of her time skipping classes and lying to her family. She flunked her first year of college already and had quite a bit of extracurricular activity that involved guys. Lots of guys. I almost threw up in my mouth as I scrambled to be free of the vision.

"How did you do that?" she screeched.

"I'm the Visionary," I said, and boy was I sick of saying it. I walked on down the hall with Caleb, Bish, and Jen following me. It was time. It was time for everyone to see the vision I had when I became the Visionary and it was time they knew what had been done to their last Visionary.

We came into the ballroom and I immediately sought out Dad. I heard his thoughts as he poured coffee. "There he is, Bish," I told him.

Bish looked at him and his mind warred with him. He wanted to see him, but felt guilty for being envious. "Just go," I said. "You'll be fine."

He gave me a twisted, sidelong glance and then made his way to Dad and his new leading lady. Dad still seemed awkward, but in an excited way. Caleb said he was going to find his dad so we could once again spill an ugly heaping of bad news on people.

Jen stayed with me and watched as Bish got up close and personal to the newest imprinted couple. I looped my arm through hers and sighed with her in sympathy. I'd seen firsthand, and felt it, what it was like to be kept away from the one thing your body thought it needed most. She closed her eyes tightly when Fiona's fingers discreetly reached out to brush my dad's.

"Jen," I started softly. "I need to tell you something."

"I love him," she blurted and then looked at me. Her eyes brimmed with wet sorrow. "I do, I love him. It's not just Maria that I'm worried about. If we imprint and your vision comes true, he'll die, too. Don't you understand that? I can't let that happen."

"But you may not have a choice," I implored. "I really need to say something to you and I need you to listen to me and not try to just brush it away."

"If it's about trying to get me to touch Bish, then save it." She pulled away gently. "I'm sorry, I know you just want to help and I'm…so grateful for what you did for me. Caleb was right," she smiled, "one night was so worth it. But I can't hurt him. Anymore of this and it will hurt us both. I have to stop this."

Then she turned and walked right to Jonathon. He smiled in surprise at her and swung his arm out for her to pass him in line for breakfast. I peeked at Bish, wondering if he saw. He did.

Great.

I swiftly bolted to him in as ladylike a way as I could and stopped him from pounding Jonathon into dust. "Bish," I said and put a hand on his chest to stop him. "Think about it. You're just overly upset because your body is mad that she's with him."

"You're daggum right it is!"

"It's just the imprint. It makes you feel over protective. Jen is just hurting and trying to figure it out. If you make a scene right now, you're going to be moving backward, not forward."

He sighed in a grumble. "So I'm supposed to just sit around and watch her do things to piss me off on purpose and pretend it doesn't bother me?"

"For now? Yes. Please. I will figure this out for you, but right now we have some seriously messed up stuff going down and that has to be dealt with first."

He lifted his hands to the back of his head and closed his eyes. "Fine. I won't touch pretty boy."

"Thank you."

"I'm going to…uh…" His eyes fastened on Maria. He smiled. I looked over to see, too. Maria was throwing grapes into the air and catching them in her mouth. Then giggling to herself as no one else was at the table with her. Bish left without another word and walked right to her. I watched and could hear their conversation in their mind.

"Hey, Maria. You're pretty good at that, kid," he said.

"I know," she spouted. "This boy at school taught me. But then he pulled my ponytail on the playground the next day, so I'm not really friends with him anymore."

"Why did he pull your ponytail?"

"Momma says boys are mean when they like you," she whispered in a disgusted voice. "But I think Momma's been misinformed."

Bish barked out a laugh and I covered my mouth so mine didn't slip through and people thought I was nuts for talking to myself.

"Well, your mom is right, sort of. Boys are mean sometimes when they like a girl, but they are also nice when they like a girl, too."

"So you like my momma? That's why you're so nice to her?" she asked nonchalantly.

"I do like your momma. Is that ok?"

"Yeah, totally! Maybe you should be mean to her," she mused and threw another grape into the air, catching it easily, "then I bet she'd really like you."

"Maybe," Bish told her with a sad smile.

*It seems to be working so well for her*

I jumped out of Bish's mind and looked for Caleb. We needed to show everyone the visions I'd had. We had to put an end to this once and for all. For some reason, the visions had stopped themselves from coming or something always seemed to come up. I didn't understand why, but I couldn't let that happen again.

Caleb and Rodney were discussing something by the door. Rodney was saying that he'd been following Ruth and she was in trouble. Caleb looked my way, but I was already coming to them.

"Come on," Rodney said and led the way. "I was suspicious because she never came down for supper last night, so this morning I went to check on her because you seemed so concerned about her before. But when I got to her room, it was empty. Like empty as in, her stuff was gone, too."

"What?" I asked horrified. What did they do to her?

We took the stairs two at a time and he directed us to a door. We opened it to find it empty.

"Where is she?" I asked him in a flurry. "Where is she!"

"Calm down," Caleb soothed and looked around before taking me into the hall. "We'll find her."

"How?" I asked in my hysteria.

"Well, she's the only Watson that you could hear thoughts for. Look for her." Caleb was calm and looking at me with certainty. I took a deep breath and held it for a few seconds before blowing it out slow and long. I could find people I focused on, I'd done it before.

I remembered helping the guy from the ice cream place in California and his mother. And just like that, there they were in front of my eyes. She was shopping for him, trying to get him to let her buy him a button shirt. He laughed and shook his head, and then he pointed to a 'Cabs Here!' t-shirt instead. She rolled her eyes and took the shirt to the counter. He smiled as he put his arm around her shoulder and squeezed her. They were still in California, they never went home, and they were wonderfully happy and fine. Both worked at the diner together and they had a crappy little apartment that they loved.

I pulled back, feeling guilty for eavesdropping, but also getting caught up in something else when I was on a mission. Caleb looked at me with his favorite line sitting on the tip of his tongue. "Don't say it," I told him.

"What? You are amazing."

I sighed, really not feeling amazing right then. I focused on Ruth, how she told us all of her family's secrets that she could and tried to help us. I felt something. Something ticked its way into the side of my brain and I turned my head as if to focus. I let all my senses go and just felt for her.

"Maggie?" I heard and shushed whoever it was. "Maggie, where are you going?"

"What?" I opened my eyes to find my feet moving.

"Is it happening again?" Caleb asked, referring to our night of visions.

"No," I answered and stopped. "I'm in control, I just…I don't know. Let's just see where this goes, ok?"

"After you," he said, and he and Rodney followed me. We went all the way to the roof, as my feet seemed to know the way. To where, I didn't know yet. We passed the greenhouse and Rodney saw the blanket and pillow there.

"Been sleeping up here, huh? You little rule breaker."

"Why do you automatically assume it was me?" Caleb said. I listened to them as my feet treaded softly over the rooftop. "Could've been Kyle. He's the one who always got us into trouble."

"Because Kyle's not that romantic," Rodney goaded in a dreamy voice and I heard scuffling, like they were play fighting.

Boys.

We came to the edge of the roof and it seemed to stop. But my feet didn't. I gasped right as I felt Caleb's arm go around my waist from behind and catch me. I turned my face to find his there and bumped his nose against my cheek.

"Why don't you let my feet take over," he said breathlessly. "She's apparently in town if it's leading you out this way."

"Ok," I sighed. "How do we get down?"

He released me, but not before making sure Rodney had a hold on me, just in case, and went to the wall right under a low roof, the last rooftop of the palace. He reached around the edge, over the huge drop from the rooftop to the town below, and felt along the wall. His hand came back with a rope and he pulled it until I heard the squeak of the lift he was summoning. Great. Of course the way down had to be a frigging wooden elevator over a huge plunge to our deaths.

Caleb chuckled at my thought and gave me a look. "You are not scared of heights."

"No, I'm scared of meeting my doom on the top of a church steeple. Why would they put this here like this?"

"This place was built centuries ago," Caleb explained. "They needed secret routes in and out, and they didn't have elevators back then."

Rodney laughed, but I ignored them both as Caleb held the rope and opened the gate to the death machine. He stepped inside, and then Rodney and they both looked at me expectantly. I rolled my eyes as I climbed inside. When Caleb started to lower us, we jerked and I squeaked, clinging to Caleb like the scared, pathetic girl I was.

He just smiled and Rodney took over the pulley. With Caleb's arm around me I looked out at the city as we got closer to the bottom. It really was spectacular. It was a shame we couldn't come here for a real vacation.

"We will one day," Caleb promised. "London is one of my favorite cities."

"I'd like that a lot," I said sincerely. He kissed the side of my neck as we watched the busyness beneath us.

"You're going to let me spoil you and not even gripe?" Caleb joked in my ear.

"It's not spoiling me when I'm your wife," I said and smiled as I turned to look at him. He looked at me for a moment before pressing his face to mine, cheek and forehead touching. It was a strange thing to do, I guess. He'd done that since almost the first day I met him. And I loved it so much, I was soaking up the cinnamon.

We finally reached the bottom and when we stepped off the lift, we were back into a little alcove of hills. It hid us from the city bustle just a little bit away. "Now what?" I asked.

"Now, we figure out where Ruth is and then get a cab."

"Ok," I said and focused. I felt it stronger now. We were closer. When it came, I felt all of her emotions as she wondered where she would live, where she would go, how she would get there with no money.

What does she mean? Ah…they denounced her from the clan.

# Twenty Three

"Come on," Caleb said and tugged my hand to get me moving. Rodney ran ahead the couple of blocks to the street and stopped a cab. We climbed in and they smushed me into the middle. Caleb told the driver to just drive around until we gave him an address. He nodded and started down the narrow streets.

I focused so that I could see something around her, any signs or landmarks to tell me where she was. I could see a church, but the name wasn't in view. She was sitting on the steps there, holding her wrist to her chest, and she seemed to be waiting for something or someone.

Caleb must have recognized the church from my mind because he told the driver where to go and he went. Within a few minutes, we pulled up in front of a large church and got out quickly. Caleb pulled some money out of his wallet and paid the driver before jogging to catch up.

I approached Ruth gently. She should be furious with me. I was the reason she got denounced and now had nowhere to go. All she had with her was one suitcase. Her wrist was still clutched to her chest and she jerked when she saw someone approaching.

"Maggie?" she said with wide eyes. "What are you doing here?"

"I asked Rodney to follow you around, because I was scared that Marla might do something to you. When he found out you were gone, he got me and we came to find you."

"How did you find me?"

"I can find anyone if I know who I'm looking for."

She gulped. "Perks of the Visionary, I guess," she muttered.

"Something like that." I squatted to be in front of her and continued softly. "What happened?"

"Can't you just drag it out of my brain?" she spouted and sniffed.

"Yes, but I'd rather you tell me."

She stayed silent and looked at the cobblestone walkway.

*Why is she so hostile with you? Is she upset that she told you?*

I looked up at Caleb to answer his question. *They did something to her, Caleb. I should have made a point to keep a better eye on her.*

*We've been more than a little busy, baby.*

*Yeah.* I sighed. *And she paid the price for my being busy.*

"Ruth," I prompted.

"They found out what I told you," she said and sniffed her annoyance once more. "They found out the loophole that I used and they denounced me for being a traitor."

"I'm sorry," I said sincerely. "That was my fault. I let something slip when I was talking to Marla. I'm so sorry."

"Now what am I supposed to do?" she almost yelled. "They may not have been good to me, or good for me, but they've been my family for so long that they are all I know!" She sniffed again and flicked her eyes to mine. "I haven't seen my real family since Sikes took me. It's not like I can just go home again. And I don't have money to get there anyway."

"Ruth, I'm sorry. Tell me what I can do."

"There's nothing you can do," she replied and winced as she shifted her body. I saw the little flash in her mind as she remembered the dark-haired man standing over her and slicing through her tattoo.

I grabbed her arm gently, and she didn't stop me. I pulled her wrist away from her chest to see a towel wrapped around it. I unwrapped the towel, swallowing when I saw blood, and then stifled my scream when I found what I'd seen in her mind.

They had taken a knife and slashed two lines across her wrist tattoo in the shape of an awkward 'X'.

"Marcus did this to you?" I said in disbelief as I remembered the dark haired person over her.

"No. Marcus didn't do this, Donald did."

The actual memory as she remembered it came to me and I saw it now; the broader shoulders, the tall and stout man coming out of the shadows, growling that she had disgraced them and was no longer welcome in their family. Ruth had thought they'd kill her, but Donald said for them to send her down the lift at the back of the palace and let her fend for herself was a more fitting punishment for a traitor.

That she deserved to live in the human world where she came from and die in it, too. Now, she was waiting at the church on the steps, hoping that someone there could send her to a shelter or something.

When I came back to myself I couldn't remember a time I'd ever felt so guilty.

"Ruth," I tried, but the words wouldn't come. I shook my head. I felt Caleb squat behind me and rest a hand on my back.

"Ruth, where's your family?" he asked.

"I don't know. I looked them up once, but they moved away. There's no telling where they are now."

"Ok, listen." Caleb leaned forward and touched her arm.

I watched my Caleb take over and put the massive Band-Aid on things, like he was so good at. He was amazing in a way that still seemed to shine new light on him every day.

He told her he'd send her wherever she wanted to go. She argued that she couldn't take his family's money, and he argued back that it was his own money and she absolutely would take it. I kind of felt like Caleb might be trying to pay off my mistakes, but he shot me a look for that thought. Rodney sat quietly off to the side as Caleb and Ruth worked out the final details. He'd put her up in a motel here, since she wasn't interested in going back to Tennessee. She would try to get a job and make a new life for herself. There really was nothing else to do.

I still felt terrible and found myself staying pretty quiet. Then we all stood as Ruth prepared to get into her cab to a new life. "None of this will really matter, you know," she said and crossed her arms as if cold.

"Why?" I said, but heard her thought. "Oh, I hadn't thought about Marla's blood being in you."

"Yes, she can find me, or pretty much use me, anytime she wants as long as I'm bound to their bloodline."

I thought. I plundered my brain for a solution, but it was Rodney who had the idea. I turned to him. "That's brilliant."

He looked puzzled, but then lit with the revelation. "No, I was just throwing ideas around in my head."

"It's the only way," I answered and looked at Ruth. "Do you remember how she gave those people my blood? Do you know how to do that?"

"Yes," she sang in hesitation.

"Here. Does one of you have a pocketknife?" I asked, dread clogging my throat.

"No," Caleb answered tightly. "No, we do not and even if we did, no."

"I do," Rodney answered, pulled a little back knife from his pocket and flipped it open as he smiled wryly. "All cowboys carry a knife."

"Awesome." I took a breath and held my hand out. "Cut me."

"Wait, what?" he said, his tune changing completely.

"No," Caleb told him and looked back at me. "Come on, Maggie. You're not going to make him cut you."

"Caleb, come on, I have to." I licked my lips. "Will you do it?"

"Absolutely not," he barked and then sighed. "Look, Maggie, my body won't let me do it. It'll be hard enough to stand here while someone else does it to you."

"Oh," I replied and then looked at Ruth.

She pursed her lips. "So, let me make sure I'm understanding you. You want me to take some of your blood, because your blood will be the last blood I took, so it'll be the one I'm bound to, right?"

"Yes."

"But can't you just control me then? It'll be you instead of her?"

"Yes, but I won't."

She came to me slowly. She held her hand out to Rodney for the knife without taking her eyes from mine. "There's extra blood vials in my bag, Caleb."

He huffed, but got one for her after rummaging through her bag and grumbling in his mind. He handed it to her and gave her a silent message with his stare.

She took my hand in hers and turned it over. She sliced my palm without waiting for me have to think about it. I winced and watched as she let my blood drip into the vial. As soon as she released my hand, Caleb took it instead and immediately began to heal me.

When the burn ended, he looked around, but knew he wasn't going to find anything to wipe my blood on. So he took the corner of his perfectly good shirt and wiped all traces of my injury away. I looked up at him from under my lashes. His eyes stayed on me as he spoke. "Rodney, can you get Ruth a cab?"

"Mmhmm," he hummed and went to the street. I turned to Ruth to apologize once more, but she was crying. I felt even worse.

"I'm so sorry-" I tried, but she stopped me.

"You set me free."

"What?"

"You set me free. I'm not upset with you," she assured me and took my hands. She looked at the hand where she'd just cut me and then back to my eyes. "If you hadn't done what you did, whatever it was, to let Marla know that I had betrayed them, then I'd still be bound to them and still be under their thumbs." She held the vial with my blood in her grasp as though it was most precious. "This will change everything for me."

I didn't know what to say, so I just hugged her to me.

What strange turns and twists our relationship had made. First, she helped kidnap me and take my blood against my will, and then she took my blood again, kind of sort of against my will, but completely made it clear she was on my side. Now she'd taken my blood again, but this time it was a gift.

She squeezed me and then picked up her one suitcase. She smiled, gladly taking the credit card that Caleb gave her from his wallet, and went to the cab that Rodney was holding for her. Caleb hugged me from behind as we watched her go.

"Come on, guys," Rodney beckoned with a swing of his arm. "Let's walk. I'm in no hurry to get back to the palace."

"Good idea," Caleb said and left his arm slung over my shoulder. "We're already out. Let's grab some lunch before the hike back up." He smiled down at me. "We know where all the good places are."

"I don't doubt that," I said, remembering that he knew all of those places in California and Tennessee. "Are they going to know your name, too?"

"Nah. It's been too long," he scoffed as he held open the door for me. As soon as we walked through the door and Caleb waved to the lady behind the counter, she beamed and lifted her hands in the air.

"You Jacobson boys no come see me!"

I rolled my eyes in humor. Gosh, Caleb knew every person on the planet.

He jerked his head to the side for me to look. Inside the deli glass was every kind of cinnamon roll, croissant and danish known to man. I bit my lip and he laughed at me.

We finished our lunch, and freshly made cinnamon honey buns, and walked slowly and leisurely around the small shops and streets. Caleb jerked me into this little jewelry shop where everything was handmade. We looked at the intricate and extravagant designs of the rings and necklaces. Rodney looked at belt buckles. I smiled at him and shook my head. We didn't buy anything, but moved on to the next store. I did let Caleb buy me a scarf there, a gorgeous black and silver thin scarf. I left it wrapped loosely from my neck and looked around the tall buildings as we dallied and tried to find excuses not to go back.

Then we walked down the streets back to the well-hidden lift. I wanted to shop more or sightsee, but we needed to get back and I wasn't really in the mood for much else with the nagging that was growing within me. I needed to show everyone my vision so that they would know what happened and why things had to change, but every time I tried, something stopped me. I had to figure it out.

"Beam me up, Scotty," Rodney said grinning and stood back to let Caleb do all the work since he was the one who brought us down.

Caleb yanked and pulled on the pulley, his muscles straining and stretching. The tattoo on his upper arm danced as he used the muscles. I bit my lip as I watched him.

We emerged from the lift and I felt good. We found Ruth and stopped her from being tortured forever by the Watsons. Now, if we could just kick their butts over the edge of the balcony, things would be easier for everyone.

Caleb stopped to use the phone since it was our last chance at cell service. Rodney went on inside after I thanked him for helping us. Caleb called his office for the tutoring service to see how things were going. It had been weeks since he'd been in any of the facilities and he missed it. He loved the work. Teaching and being around kids all day was definitely something he could see himself doing.

The lady who answered the phone told him that all was well, but he was missed. He hung up and then texted Vic a quick lie, 'We're still in California. Come see you soon.' Then he handed the phone to me. I quirked a brow at him in question and he quirked one right back at me in jest. "I know you want to call Beck."

I grinned and dialed her number, but before she could answer, I heard the thoughts of others. I peeked around the edge of the greenhouse to see Donald, Paulo, and Haddock.

Busted again.

Caleb pulled me to his side, slipping his phone into his back pocket. "Councilors. And Donald," he addressed, making sure Donald understood that we no longer saw him as our authority. He was Champion of his clan now, and Haddock was the councilor.

"Caleb and…Visionary," Donald said in a menacing voice. "The roof is off limits."

Caleb answered. "I was just letting Maggie call her friend so she wouldn't be worried about her."

"Our Visionary needs to learn that some things are more important than friends and keeping up with the latest human gossip. She is not a human any longer. You can't continue to humor her human past, Caleb."

I huffed a breath, but Caleb went on.

"And you're not a councilor any longer, so I wonder what it is you're doing up here. You're not my Champion, so this doesn't concern you anymore."

"I'm the one who told the council that you'd taken our Visionary from her duties."

I bristled again. "And what duties are those?"

"To learn to become one of us and to discuss your coming to live at the palace."

"That won't be happening," I told him.

"Foolish child," he growled low.

"Donald," Paulo scolded. "Caleb is right, after all. You're not a member of the council and though you told us where to find them, this no longer concerns you. Haddock and I can take it from here."

Donald turned slowly to look at Paulo. I had an overwhelming urge hit me to touch Donald's skin. It was more like an afterthought because my body was already moving. When I touched his arm, the vision of him scolding Marla and Marcus for letting me manipulate Ruth played out. After he got through all the details of having her denounced, he ordered Marcus to slit her tattoo to shame her, but Marcus refused. He cowered into the wall and shook his head 'no'.

Donald, enraged, moved to the ones holding Ruth down and did it himself. He threw the knife down with a clank and made his way to the door. He stopped in front of Marla and Marcus. He moved swiftly and punched Marcus in the stomach. Marcus doubled over in a silent scream as he fell to his knees. Then he reached up and grabbed Marla's jaw with his hand. She shook and then was still. More still than was humanly possible. He'd frozen her with his ability, but not with ice. It was like she was stone, but wasn't.

"I will turn you all to stone and leave you in a cell if you fail me again."

Then he stalked out and Marla gasped as she crumpled beside her brother. Marcus pulled her to him in a move uncharacteristic for him. He hugged her as they both glared at the path that Donald had just made.

I came back to myself and jerked back as the spot where I touched Donald stung and shocked me. He hissed too and reared back. We locked our eyes, him knowing that I had seen it all. Paulo was aghast at the mark on my hand and automatically went to accuse Donald of wanting to cause me harm, but Donald was clever.

"She gave me an offense mark," Donald said, as if hurt, and covered his arm. He turned his eyes to Paulo and then back to me. "Why would you want to hurt me?"

"I don't want to hurt you, you hurt me!"

"Ok," Paulo soothed us, "all right. Let's just all take a step back. I'm sure this is just a misunderstanding." He flipped his gaze to Caleb. "Now, Caleb. You know you can't come up here, let alone bring the Visionary up here. It's dangerous."

"Yeah, we might get crapped on by a pigeon," Caleb rebutted sarcastically, "Come on, Paulo, there's nothing up here. We just needed to get away for minute, that's all."

"I'm afraid that that's the exact opposite of what you need." He sighed as if delivering sad news to a dying patient. "We've decided that the Visionary needs to spread herself out a little bit. She needs to be more than just your significant, she needs to be the Visionary for all."

"I've been trying," I argued. "I've made sure to speak to other clans and even sit with them at lunch. You know that. I sat with your family."

"I know, and while it was a good effort, it needs to be more. So," he clapped his hands together and smiled as if thoroughly proud of himself, "we've orchestrated a ball in your honor. Many balls, in fact. Every night for the rest of our stay here, you'll be escorted by a different member of each clan. We've already gotten your room prepared with everything you need."

"You were in my room?"

"Winifred was," he corrected. "She picked out all of the dresses."

Dresses…and I saw in his mind exactly what they had in store. Each clan supplied a necklace. I chose a necklace each night, not knowing who it belonged to, and whoever was the lucky winner was my escort for that night. That way there could be no biases and no cheating. It would be fair and everyone had to adhere to the rules.

The catch was that the Jacobsons weren't allowed to put any necklaces in the pot. This was my punishment for wanting to be with Caleb so much, my freaking significant and fiancé.

Caleb got the full understanding of the rules, too, and hummed a noise of annoyance. "This is ridiculous. You can't expect me to sit back and watch as every guy in the place fights for a dance with my significant. You all act as though you don't know how the imprints work!" he bellowed. "You know that my body will rebel against this."

"Yes, and it's very good practice for you," Paulo stated. "You need to learn to share her, however uncomfortable that may be."

"Would you share your wife?" Caleb growled.

"No, I wouldn't," Paulo growled back, "but I'm not married to the Visionary either."

"This is bull." Caleb grabbed my arm, gently even in his anger, and started to take me to the door.

"You will adhere to the rules, Caleb," we heard from behind us. We turned to find Haddock, stoic as ever. "It's important that you do this."

Haddock had been awfully quiet throughout it all. I cocked my head at him, but he just looked at me. I switched my gaze to Donald, who seemed ever so happy with the turnout of things. Then to Paulo, who was watching us all as if a fight would break out any second.

"We will follow the rules," I told them and brought Caleb with me as I opened the door with a bang.

"Like hell we'll follow the rules," Caleb rumbled as we made our way. He pulled me to a stop. "I'm not going to sit there while they pawn you off to the highest bidder!"

"They've got something up their sleeve," I told him in a whisper. "I know it. This is our chance to figure it all out and end this with the Watsons for good."

"All the more reason not to do it. I'm not going to knowingly put you in danger."

We could have stood there all night and argued, so I took his hand and led the way to my room. When we got there and I flipped on the light, I was stunned. There were gorgeous dresses lining the walls on racks. One dress, a cream one that made me sigh at its gorgeousness, was laid out on my bed. And near the armoire was a table lined with jewelry.

I turned away from it all and pulled Caleb down to kiss me. He sighed at first, but soon kissed me like I wanted. He probably thought I was trying to distract him with kisses, but I wasn't.

I pulled back a little and leaned my head against his. "Thank you for what you did for Ruth."

"She helped us," he reasoned through a ragged breath. "It was the right thing to do." He let out a long, telling breath. "Ok, fine. I know that you have to do this, but I don't have to like it and I'm not going to pretend like I do."

"Deal," I said in gratitude. "I'll get Rodney to sit with you."

"You mean hold my arms so that I don't pummel anyone," he half joked.

"Yep," I answered. This time he was the one who kissed me. I wrapped my arms around his neck, thankful that he was there and mine.

# Twenty Four

After Caleb left to get dressed, I took a long, hot bath, because I had a lot of time to kill. Caleb needed to go and see his father. I was left to my own devices, so I soaked in the ostentatious tub with bubbles up to my neck until the water turned cold.

After that, I did my hair and makeup before coming to stand over the dress on the bed. That Gran had awesome taste and this dress was no exception. I slipped it on. I just had a feeling that no one was coming to help me dress today. It fit like it was made for me. When I zipped up the side, I tried to ignore the designer label, but Dolce was Dolce.

The dress was beautiful, but long and heavy feeling. I'd never been a fan of long dresses and apparently, the beauty of the gown had no effect on that fact. It rubbed my legs and ankles in a way that I knew was going to affect me all night.

I looked the dressing table over. Yes, the dressing table. The room the council had stuck me in was extravagant beyond belief and reason. As were the necklaces that lay before me. To choose, to choose… It wasn't easy. I had no idea who gave what necklace and the necklace of my choice held my fate for the night's escort. I was going to be stuck with some other guy for the whole night because of one of those beautiful necklaces. And, of course, Jacobsons weren't allowed to offer necklaces to me. I had to 'spread the courtesy' they'd said. Though I belonged to the Jacobsons, I shouldn't show favor to that clan. And the necklaces; it seemed wrong that the council was using something so beautiful and elegant to so blatantly piss Caleb off.

I pondered the events of the week so far and collected everything so I could put myself together and try to be ready for what had to be tonight. Tonight was the night and the Watsons were going down. So I started off with Caleb.

Caleb's blowup hadn't helped things. I couldn't blame him one bit though. As a matter of fact, I was bursting with pride as he let the council have it about all the hypocrisy they were spewing our way. Of course, them carting him off to the 'dungeon' wasn't exactly how we planned things either.

And my subsequent jailbreak and threatening of the guards was just the cherry on top of this crazy sundae.

I had no idea what I was doing. The way everyone looked at me and spoke to me; everyone was afraid to look me in the eye or touch me for fear that I'd read something about their past. Or future. Power is an odd thing. It's destructive, it's addictive, it's idiotic at times, but it's also strangely beautiful how the chaos just flows around it. The beat of the human heart thrives for it, but not this heart.

I was ready to be done with this week. I wanted to marry my Caleb. And despite the fact that the council tried to call our bluff and marry us the first day, luckily Peter was a quick thinker. I wanted to marry him, but not because someone told me I *had* to. I know I was so against marriage before, but I couldn't even remember why. And the age thing? Blah. It meant nothing now. I was so ready to be everything for the man I loved and it wasn't just to escape the Visionary stuff. I just genuinely looked forward to learning how to be a couple, on our own, with no distractions, with Caleb.

Gosh, the look of pride on Peter's face…watching Caleb turn red and defend my honor…Caleb's powerful arms twitching and moving to protect me… Even now, I could feel the ache in my chest, of both pride and want. The councils' stupid rules and traditions had me away from Caleb too much and I was already feeling the withdrawal again.

I steeled myself, raised my chin, swiped the tear that escaped, and chastised myself for letting it. I picked the keychain up from the dresser and rubbed the cool, smooth surface of the obsidian. I was the Visionary, I was everything they said I was and more, I could feel it, and I was about to use their words against them. They were about to see that things were going to change. I was not to be put on display and worshipped and passed around like some trinket or commodity. I was me and I had my family behind me.

Defiance of the way things are is the only way to embrace what's coming. The council had been worshipped and revered too long for a bunch of coots with nothing to do but get manicures and live underground. And the Aces needed to learn that complacency was acceptance, even if you wanted to believe otherwise.

And we were not going to accept it anymore.

So, I put the keychain down and chose my necklace. It was beautiful and matched my dress so perfectly with its cream leaves, intricate gold filigree and moonstone. I wondered who it belonged to and who I would be stuck with for the night. I slipped it on, placing the gold shawl around my neck to cover it as instructed. I checked my mascara for smears and then opened my door to reveal my guard, Rodney.

"Are you ready to go, milady?" he jested.

"No," I said as I took his arm and let him guide me. "No, absolutely not."

"Don't worry. I'll keep one hand on Caleb at all times," he said. So he knew exactly what tonight was about. "He won't like it tonight, but he'll be ok. He just has to learn to share," he said and winked.

"Ha ha. This is a stupid tradition - I'm sorry, I'm not trying to offend - it just is. What is the purpose of this? The council doesn't even know me. How do they know how I would react to other clans? I planned to be sociable, as I have been since we got here," I sulked. "They didn't have to go to extremes and make out like this was the only way to spread me around."

"I don't know, Maggie. We haven't had a Visionary in any of our times before. We're all going on what the council says is customary."

"I know," I said pointedly. "That's what scares me most."

"We're here," he stated the obvious and stopped at the doors. "You'll be great. Just be the sweet, chatty girl I know you are and dazzle them with a smile. I guarantee you'll have them eating out of your little Visionary palm."

"Thanks," I said sincerely. "Really. Doing all this without Caleb feels wrong, but with you here, it makes it bearable at least."

"It is my honor and pleasure." I grimaced at the Visionary worship and he caught it. "Maggie. It is my honor and pleasure, *Maggie*. You're family and Caleb is like a brother to me. I'd do anything for him, including," he opened the big double doors to a room full of anxious people, "escorting his girl to another guy," he said wryly and smiled.

I looked out over the sea of faces. Even the married Aces wanted a night with the Visionary. It was status and bragging rights, and a glance at the coots table told me they were enjoying the show. Though I tried not to, I glanced at Caleb. I almost lost it as my heart jumped violently. Rodney pulled his arm around me and though I knew it would break 'protocol', I hugged him. I heard a few gasps, but didn't even look their way as my eyes stayed locked on my significant.

"Thank you. Would you please go to him now?"

He nodded and smiled as he made his way to the Jacobson huddle. They were all pretty ticked from the looks of things and their thoughts. Caleb had explained it all and they were ready for a fight if the night called for one. They were finally done with being a sideline family. Then I heard the most beautiful sound in my mind.

*You look so…agonizingly…beautiful.*

*You look pretty good yourself, slick.*

*I am so sorry I brought you here.*

*It's not forever. They're just trying to push your buttons. They all envy the Jacobsons, whether they'll admit it or not.*

*But it's not fair to you. You're already withdrawing, I can feel it, and I'm not even allowed to touch you tonight.*

I could see his color rising. His father put a hand on his shoulder and Rodney put a hand on the other. Even Kyle stepped up to flank him. They were showing us once again that they were behind us. We just had to ride out the councils' rules and so called 'traditions' until we could change them for everyone, not just for ourselves. We had to save the race, not just our family. And the race was so consumed by tradition that it would be a hard case to sell. They'd all turn against us if we didn't do this right. So…we'd play by their rules. For now.

*I'm ok and ready to do this.*

*I'm not.*

I smiled. *I love you, Caleb Jacobson.*

*I love you, Maggie Jacobson. And don't you dare forget it.*

I smiled again at his use of his family name for me, and held in my chuckle at the protective vibe I was getting from him. I was surprised every person in this room couldn't see it floating around him. It really was stupid for them to make some ritual like this. They know the significant's nature, to be possessive and protective. So why go to so much trouble to push me on others, knowing that our bodies would rebel against it?

I turned to the eager crowd. The first man I looked for was my father. My *real* father. I didn't see him anywhere. Bish was standing with the Jacobsons, but my dad was with Paulo's clan because that's where his significant was from. It settled on it then that my father was not part of my clan. Rachel had told me in California that when you imprint you follow your husband to his clan and they rarely even saw their other families anymore. I wondered in terror if that was how it would be for Dad and me now that he was in her family.

But her clan was very happy and proud. They smiled at my dad and Fiona with a true sense of joy. At least there was that.

I looked out at the rest of the room. All the men were lined up front, their women behind them. I assumed they were waiting for me to reveal my necklace so they could claim their prize. So I undid the shawl and let it slide off the side. The groans of disappointment were evident, but one other voice rang out clear and true.

A Watson.

He came forward, all smiles and evil grins. He looked extremely pleased by my discomfort. I decided right then and there that if I was going to be stuck in this, that I would be a player in it as well. So I smiled, too, and curtseyed to him. He faltered and almost tripped over himself, making me press my lips together to stop the laugh. When he reached, me I held my hand out with a sweet smile.

"Shall we?" I said, dripping with sugar.

"Of course, Visionary," he said smoothly, but was clearly taken off guard by my actions, or intentions, but he smiled back and took me to the dance floor. When we stopped on the green granite circle in the middle, he glanced to Marla, who nodded. He looked back at me with a renewed vigor to his task.

Good, I thought. Two can play this game.

I was surprised when they played actual music instead of the instruments playing themselves. Some John Mayer ballad played over the speakers and the man began to lead me. He had white gloves on, which had not escaped my notice, to match the white shirt of his tux. But I knew the gloves were to keep him from putting an offense mark on me.

"What's your name?" I asked to start.

"Walker," he said and smirked. "And you're Maggie." He grinned and then I remembered where I'd seen him before. He was one of the ones who helped Sikes guard me at the well. "I know all about you."

"Do you now?" I dragged out. "Doubtful."

"I know you love honey buns, you hate to be the center of attention, and you don't like me much."

I smiled. "All of that could have been concluded pretty easily since it's blaringly obvious."

He laughed at my response. "Probably. I also know that you want things to change here." I glanced over at Caleb and saw that nothing had changed with him. He was still glaring. As if the man knew it, his right hand slid an inch lower on my back. I used my mind to jerk his hand back up to my upper back and he balked in confusion.

"Thought I couldn't do that because you have my blood in you?" His face said that I was right. "It just keeps me from seeing your thoughts and your future. Your hand is an object that I can move, so that doesn't matter." He gulped a little loudly. "Marla sent you off to war without the proper knowledge of the enemy, huh?" I goaded.

"This isn't a game," he said in a low voice.

"You're right, it's not. So what are you and Marla planning for me tonight? Why don't you just tell me and then we can move on."

"Nice try," he said and dipped me back a little. It was so sudden that I jerked in surprise. He grinned and leaned me back up. When he did, I twirled out of his arm and stood back.

I smiled. "You're right about change. I think we need to change the rules of tonight as well." I walked over to the first boy I saw that wasn't a Jacobson or Watson and asked him to dance. He was elated, in an almost creepy way, and let me take him to the dance floor. He couldn't dance well, however. I kept my eyes from the council so their scowls would be their little secret, though I knew they were there.

After the song ended, I grabbed another partner and let him twirl me, and twirl me, and twirl me. He was an expert dancer and seemed to be fond of the twirling rhythms of Salsa. I laughed as he guided me and showed our feet how to wind between each other's. I looked back at Caleb, and though he wanted to look mad, he was smiling, watching me.

Rodney thumped Caleb's chest with his fist before making his way to me. "May I have this dance?"

"Of course," I answered and smiled at the man who was being relieved. "Thank you. You're seriously good at that."

"Thank you, Visionary, for giving me the opportunity to show you."

I nodded and turned to Rodney. He smirked and took my hands and waist formally. We moved back and forth gently. Rodney looked behind us and started to laugh softly.

*Caleb is seriously love struck.*

"Me, too," I replied and looked at Caleb over Rodney's shoulder. He was still just watching me while Kyle was going on about the crappy music in Caleb's ear. "Your cousin is pretty great, you know."

"Yep. I cannot wait," he said and laughed a little. "It's almost worse now that I saw the vision. Now every girl I see I wonder if she's the one."

"So knowing is worse than not knowing?"

"In ways, but I'm glad that I know." He looked way different in his tux. His hair was combed over to the side instead of his normal unruliness. "What?" he said when he caught me looking.

"You Jacobsons…you're just a good looking bunch."

"Really?" he said, his ego inflating by the second, given by his cocky grin.

"Yes, really. My friend Beck came to California with us and we went swimming. She almost fainted when Peter came on the beach in just his trunks."

He laughed. "Well, that guy's built like a beef factory. It's understandable."

"A beef factory?" I asked through my laugh. "You miss the ranch, don't you."

"I sure do. I'll have to buy myself my own ranch after I meet the little lady. We'll make us a cozy homestead, right there in Tennessee, with bacon and beef running wild in the fields!" he said in flourish.

I laughed again and then turned when Caleb put his hand on my arm. I turned to find his cleverly disguised amused face. "What's going on here?"

"Nuttin'," Rodney drawled playfully. "Just tryin' to steal your girl is all."

"Well then I better have her," he said and grinned as he put his hands on my hips. "She's not available to be stolen."

"I think you're missing the point of stealing, cuz," Rodney goaded as he saluted and went to the food table.

Caleb smiled, but didn't look his way. We swayed together, knowing we weren't supposed to be dancing tonight, and I happened to catch Marla sneering at us over Caleb's shoulder. I looked at her. She looked back. Then she smiled. It was a smile that was layered with many things: giddiness, cruelty, malice, hatred, and even a little bit of envy. All of it pissed me off, and just as Caleb looked back at her over his shoulder, she pursed her lips as if to send him a kiss. Then I saw her face whip to the side as if she'd been slapped.

She turned and glared at me. I bit my lip. I'd done that with my ability and anger. I looked back to Caleb, who was watching me with amusement. "She deserved it," he said and crushed me back to him.

The song that was playing above us was *You and Me* by Lifehouse, and he pressed his face into my hair and softly sang the words to me. ***And I don't know why I can't keep my eyes off of you.***

I could have died…or cried…or sighed. I wasn't sure what I wanted to do more. He looked down at me, all the way to my toes, and slowly back up. "You look so good." He pressed his face into my hair again. He groaned his words, "I could eat you up."

My heart skidded and he leaned back to smirk slightly. I barely had caught my breath when he brought one hand up to lay against my heart. "Caleb," I sighed, "you can't do that kind of stuff in here."

"And why not?"

"Because I need to be ladylike and proper and you're making me want to drag you to my room."

He leaned his head against mine and groaned. "Did you go to a school that tells you exactly what to say to drive a guy insane?"

"Maybe," I said playfully, thinking that I needed to mingle with the others more before the night was over, though I could have stayed right there.

He leaned down and kissed my cheek. He hovered and then dragged my lips to his in a slow and agonizing assault that left me sighing and clinging to his tux front. "One for the road," he said when he finally let me go. "Now go mingle."

He smirked at my inability to say anything. I lifted my hand to my hair, my star bracelet jingling in my ear. Then I looked for my next victim. Bish was standing there watching Jen, who had been grabbed by Jonathon to get some punch with him. They weren't allowed to dance together. Only imprinted significants could dance…and me. So I chose Bish, though technically he probably couldn't be considered as mingling.

"Hey, you," I said. He turned to me and tried to smile. "Come on," I beckoned with an open hand.

He went willingly, but we were stopped by Maria. She gripped Bish's hand and looked up at him. "Can it be my turn now?"

"You betcha," he said and looked at me. "Sorry."

I shook my head. "Don't be." I smiled as I watched them. She had her hands on his arms and watched their feet. Everyone watched them with smiles. Jen watched, too, and gulped as she did so. Jonathon was holding in an eye roll. He thought Bish was trying to use Maria against Jen as a cheap shot. Little did he know.

Walker took that opportunity to snag me again. He took my arm and began walking toward the door with me. "I would like to discuss some things with you, if you'd like to go somewhere more private."

"Alone with you? Hmm."

"I'll make it worth your while," he promised, but made it sound like an innuendo.

I thought about it. This was it, whatever he had planned was about to be executed. I flicked my gaze around the room casually to see that Marla, Marcus, nor Donald was present any longer. Caleb could follow us without the guy knowing. I had to do something. "Ok, let's go."

*Caleb, follow us. He said he has something to tell me.*

*I know. I've been listening. I'm behind you. Be careful.*

"Follow me this way," Walker said and held his arm out for me. I took it and let him lead me down the hall. Once we reached the end, he opened the door to the stairwell leading to the roof. I faltered for a second, but then went on. As soon as I turned, I felt him wrap his arms around me from behind and press a cloth to my mouth. I screamed, but that was the wrong thing to do. When I inhaled to scream, the poison went right into me…and I went right to sleep.

~

I woke with a start with my heart going nuts in my chest. I remembered everything perfectly. I had been drugged and was now tied to one of the greenhouse posts to sit upright. I looked at the rope and yanked against it, but when I did, I got a shock. I gasped, which prompted someone's laughter. I looked up to see the man who'd taken me.

"You like those charmed ropes?" he said and grinned.

I wondered where Caleb was. He was following me…but then I screamed as my eyes found him. That's why my heart was beating so fast. It had been alerting me that he was in danger.

They must have been waiting for us to leave, and for Caleb to follow us. Dang it, of course they know he'd never let me go by myself. And they had beaten him to a bloody pulp.

He was awake, and watching me from the corner of his eye. One of his eyes was swollen shut and the other was barely a slit to see from.

*I'm fine.*

*You're not fine!*

*They jumped me. You're right, they knew I'd follow you. And that's not all.*

He jerked his head to the other side of the greenhouse and there was Kyle and Lynne. They were both tied up opposite each other and both still knocked out with whatever they had given me. How long had we'd been gone already?

*A long time. At least an hour. I've been...awake.*

That caused the sob in my throat to release. He shook his head for me to stop, but I couldn't. Before I could say anything else, a shadow crossed over me and I looked up, blinking against the harsh lamps above, to see Donald.

"Visionary, what a predicament you've gotten yourself into."

"Don't you speak to her," Caleb growled at him, my ever-ready hero.

"Caleb, you're in no position to command things of me, boy!" He laughed. "The Jacobson prince, now the Jacobson Champion." He shook his head and put his hands on his hips. "Really, times have changed for us to lower our standards so drastically."

"What do Kyle and Lynne have to do with this?" I asked to keep him from continuing his rant.

"Nothing. I just hate it that they imprinted. And I needed some leverage."

"Leverage for what?"

"Leverage for you to agree to come live in the palace and let me control you." He smiled. "You see, these people actually think you have something to offer them and they would blindly follow you if only you'd grow a little backbone to scare them into it. Instead, I want you to come here and keep your mouth shut. Nothing needs to change, nothing needs to be fixed. I am my family's new Champion and Haddock is the councilor. We still reign control over everyone as we always have. With you locked away, they'll think we're following your lead. Think about it," he leaned down to be eye level with me, "you'll be pampered and taken care of. You never have to lift a finger here. You'll be spoiled beyond your wildest dreams."

"I have a significant to spoil me," I argued.

"I knew you'd say that."

"Plus, I saw where you kept the last Visionary. She wasn't being very well taken care of, now was she?"

"I didn't know you were going to say that," he said dryly. "Sneaking around the palace? Marcus wasn't doing a very good job at watching you, was he?"

"You've been pulling all the strings this whole time. Marla, Marcus…"

"Of course I have. And you can add Sikes to that list as well. He thought no one would find out about his little experiment with his wife, but I knew. I told him to get going on another experiment. You. He refused, so I used Marla and Marcus for a little persuasion. He didn't know that they were helping me and they didn't know that I had him either. It was pretty enjoyable to watch."

"This whole time…" No, I stopped that thought. I would not feel sorry for Marcus or Marla. "You can take your little deal and shove it right up-"

"I knew you wouldn't just accept my offer so easily, so I brought Lynne and Kyle to sway your vote." He walked over to them and patted Kyle's face until he woke. He immediately called Lynne's name in his groggy disorientation, but when he saw Donald over Lynne, he jolted from anger, then he jolted from the shock he received from the ropes. He breathed out in anger and confusion, but when he turned and saw us, he got this look of hopelessness. He winced at Caleb and turned back to Lynne.

Donald had Lynne's face in his hands and she was definitely awake now. I bit my lip at her scared thoughts. But when Donald pulled a box cutter blade from the tabletop next to him, I no longer stayed silent and still. I used my mind to knock the blade from his hand…but I received another shock from the ropes when I did it and it seemed to drain me.

He laughed as he picked up the blade. I tried again and again, using my power to push him away from Lynne, but every time I tried, my ability seemed to weaken.

Finally, I was spent, used up, and all I could do was watch in horror as Donald put the blade to Lynne's cheek. Kyle was yelling and cursing at him, but Caleb pulled the little bit of power I had and used it to force Donald's hand down. His gloved hand shook as he fought it, but Caleb managed to get one of the lines of the rope cut before he finally slumped against his own ropes as well and groaned in defeat.

Donald was done smiling. He looked at Kyle, who was giving him the look of death. "Now, you can watch your human significant bleed and scream while you can do nothing. But don't worry; I won't kill her, or you. No, I'm going to leave you here long enough so that you can't heal her face. And then I want you to live forever looking at that scar and remembering how you sat there and watched it happen."

Then he sliced Lynne's cheek in one swipe. She tried not to scream, but she failed, and Kyle's rage-filled roars were even louder.

I yanked against my ropes, the painful consequences be darned. Kyle was doing the same, although cursing loudly in his thoughts from the pain. Donald saw Kyle and pursed his lips in annoyance before having my date, Walker, come. He punched Kyle so hard that his head snapped to the side and he fell over as much as he could with being tied up.

He and Donald starting talking in hushed voices. I glanced at Caleb to see he was barely hanging on and my heart ached for him. I pushed down the ache to focus on getting us out of this. I felt my hands being maneuvered and a 'Shh' in my ear. Rodney.

But he wasn't the only new guest to the party. Marla, Marcus, Gaston, and even a couple of others came over the rooftop.

As Rodney wiggled my hands free, I kept them behind me so no one would know I was free. Then Rodney attempted to creep over to Caleb. He was pretty hidden by the shrubs, but someone would see if they were looking.

I tried to focus their attention on me as they plotted in a huddle.

"Ok, I guess I'll consider your offer to stay here," I told Donald.

He laughed. That turned into a cackle. "Oh, my dear, that deal has passed."

"But you just said-" I tried to stall even as I heard the squeak of a chair being moved swiftly and saw the rest of the Watsons coming across the patio.

"That was before I knew you knew about the previous Visionary. And you've seen the Visionary records." He tsked. "I can't let you stay here now. I'll just have to kill you and your significant."

I peeked to see Caleb's hands were free and I held back no more. Haddock was the only Watson missing so I let my ability blaze to the angriest part of me and let it loose. The greenhouse glass didn't rattle and the windows didn't shake. No, they *shattered.*

Every window in the building, floor to ceiling, burst in an angry shower all at once. It was like an explosion and glass rained down all around us. I saw my enemies running away, and I refused to let them. I controlled it all, and knew exactly what do. I forced the bigger shards to head for my targets. They sliced through legs, arms, and backs as the cowards ran. Marcus whined and groaned while Marla shrieked. Walker cried out as a shard sliced his face and neck.

But Donald was determined. He walked through the assault right for me, only pausing when I got him with a shard. When he'd almost reached me, I saw Caleb jump for him. He grabbed his head from behind and Donald went as still as ever.

Caleb was borrowing Donald's ability and using it against him. Everyone else just watched as Donald froze and even seemed to stop breathing. He could have been a wax figure as Caleb's hands fell away and Donald was left to stand there. Marla screamed in rage, stood all bloodied and wild, and ran right for Caleb.

He swayed on his feet, but stopped her with borrowing my ability. I didn't see Walker come up behind him until almost too late. I knocked Walker back into the post so hard that the frame of the greenhouse shook. We really needed to get out of there.

Rodney emerged from behind me, saying pretty much the same thing to me, that the greenhouse was done for.

I ran to Caleb, putting my hands under his shirt to heal him, and evaluated the situation as Caleb sighed and let my touch make him new again. Marla was in Caleb's ability's grasp. Walker was unconscious. Donald was a statue, Marcus was crying on the ground and the rest of them stared in silent horror. Most of them weren't imprinted so they didn't possess much power as a whole and the ones who did didn't have good ones.

Caleb pushed Marla with his mind so she'd fall back toward them. She ran back to a woman who could have only been her mother. I didn't understand why she let them control her daughter that way. Rodney took my other side and we waited for a move to be made as the glass crunched under our feet.

Caleb, seeing the opposition in some of them, took it upon himself to demonstrate that he was not sitting quietly while they tried to destroy us. He lifted his hand and let the flame come. The man who'd held little Maria against her will in Uncle Ken's house just a few days ago cursed and came forward to stop Caleb from borrowing his ability, but someone stopped him with a hand on his chest.

"We get it," Marla said. "You took down Donald, that's all that matters. He's been controlling us all for years."

"You made your own decisions," I told them and glanced at Marcus, who was glaring at me. "In fact, Donald was just a guy who handed out orders. You all were the henchman!"

"He threatened to have us denounced!" Gaston said and begged. "You have to believe us. We only did what we did to save our own necks."

"It still doesn't make it right," I said and waited for him to argue. He didn't.

The groan and buckle of metal alerted us and Caleb was moving before I even had time to think. The north side of the greenhouse was collapsing. We leapt out of the greenhouse doorway right into the Watson's arms basically, and it was too late to do anything about it. Marla had me around the neck with her long-sleeve dress and was giggling in a seriously evil way as she shoved a large glass shard into my back to motivate my cooperation.

Caleb thought about lunging for her or using my ability to throw her, but was afraid I'd be hurt in the process.

"You actually believed all that dribble!" she yelled and laughed more. "Donald was a douche, but he was never running me. He only thought he was."

"I…" I started to argue with her, but I remembered that the vision I'd had of Donald's past would be his perception of events, not facts.

Caleb and Rodney were circling her with palms raised. Walker and another Watson started to inch toward them and I flicked my fingers at them to stop them. Caleb turned in time to see another one coming, so he borrowed the man's fire and set a line of fire between them and Rodney out of the greenhouse debris. They seethed on the other side and I tried to figure out a plan as Marla dragged me. I could feel the glass scraping my back and knew a little blood was running down the back of my dress.

"Let's go for a ride," she said and I realized where we were. The lift. She reached for the rope and opened the gate, all while securely holding me.

"Come on, Marla, stop," Caleb tried to reason. "What are you doing?"

"Going for some girl talk," she said and shoved me onto the lift. It rocked and creaked as she hopped on with me and began to lower it.

"Stop!" Caleb yelled.

"I'm ok, Caleb," I tried to soothe him, but it was no use. I could feel his erratic heartbeats make their way into my chest.

"So," she sang and smiled as she tossed the glass shard over the edge. Her hair was a mess from the wind and her dress was torn in several spots from the shards I'd descended on her. "Just us girls. Thanks for taking out Uncle Ego," she joked.

"Caleb took him out, not me."

"That's right. It was pretty impressive. I could really use that gift." She cocked her head to the side and looked serious. "Now, down to business. My work is not done. I have your blood and I know that there is something in it that will give me some power, it just has to. So, what I want from you, since I can't kill you, is for you to agree to meet me once a month to fork over a supply of your blood." Wow, she was deluded. You couldn't get power from blood. Like she could read my mind, or maybe just my face, she explained. "Uncle Sikes achieved the impossible by never giving up his research and I intend to do the same, getting the results that I want."

"You're delusional," I told her and shook my head at the insane girl staring back at me. "You can't just manipulate everything just so you get everything you want. Don't you understand that your family meddling and being a menace was the reason the imprints were taken away to begin with?"

"Are you talking about the other Visionary? I don't care about that. Of course we've always known what Granddaddy Lionel did. Every Champion in our line has bragged about it for years."

"Bragged?" I said, feeling the warming of my blood.

"Yeah." She held her hand out. Her gloved hand. "Do we have a deal, Visionary?" she mocked.

"Or what?"

"Or I'll send the order to my man who has your precious brother and his star-crossed lover, Jen, locked in your bedroom. For safekeeping," she taunted.

# Twenty Five

I recognized Caleb in my mind and knew he'd heard it all. I gave him the go ahead, but he was caught between saving me and saving his sister. But it turned out it was a moot thought, because I heard Bish's mind as he made his way to us. And boy was he pissed.

Now I was worried because he was coming up behind the Watsons, I saw it in his mind, and he had Jen with him. I begged Caleb to go to him and make sure he was safe. I could handle Marla. He cursed up a storm in his mind, but eventually left with instructions with Rodney not to leave the roof edge.

"So?" Marla was saying. "Deal?"

"No," I answered and gripped the rail of the lift. "No, that doesn't work for me."

I contemplated if I had the guts to kill this girl. It may come to it.

"No," she scoffed. "No?"

"No. I'm not playing into your juvenile plans. Can you even hear yourself? Meet me once a month and give me your blood or I'll hurt your brother?" I taunted. "What was your back-up plan if I didn't go through with it?"

"I already have your blood," she said. "You already can't read any of our thoughts or futures. It'll only get worse for you. And once I figure out the secret that Sikes discovered, I'll finish you."

"Be my guest to try."

She growled a yell for her henchman. When she got no answer, I almost smiled in satisfaction that she had no idea what was going on topside. Then she seemed to catch on. She turned her murderous gaze to mine and sucked in angry breaths through her nose. Then she charged me. The lift rocked as she crossed the few feet between us and tried to ram me against the post on the side. I wanted to fight her off and use my ability, but was afraid she'd fall off the side if I did.

I held her arms back and she tried to strangle me. She was strong for a girl, but I was stronger because I ascended. I pushed her back and she swayed, but caught her balance again swiftly. She charged again.

"What are you solving by this?" I asked as she took a swing for my hair.

"I'm gonna murder you! I'm going to rip your hair out!" she shrieked in a fantastical rage that would have amused me had it not been directed at me. "You're so special and spoiled, aren't you?"

I held her arm above our heads as she went for another swipe at me. She twisted her body, to try to get another hold of me I assumed, but she turned too quickly and her trajectory pushed her right over the edge, breaking the rail on that side of the lift. I gripped the hand I was already holding as she pulled me down to the floor with a jerk as I held on.

"Don't let go!" she screamed. "Don't let go!"

"I'm not!" I yelled back. "Come on, let's pull you up."

"You'll just let me go," she said hysterically.

"Why would I catch you only to let you go?"

"Because you're evil!"

I could have laughed. "Come on and stop being a drama queen."

"No," she said, her voice serious. "No. You'll just let me go."

"I'm helping you, now come on."

I began to pull her arm up, but her glove was slipping. I pulled harder, but it slipped more. She started to freak out and I told her to calm down, but she refused.

"You're doing that on purpose!" she accused.

"Be still and stop thrashing!"

"That's it. If I'm going, you're coming down with me," she promised and threw all of her weight up to reach her other hand for my arm. With all her weight centered and heavy, I felt myself slip an inch from the platform. She was determined, but so was I. Once she started trying to take me down with her, it was game over. I opened my fingers and didn't grip her anymore and she began to slip. Her grip went higher and higher, eventually one of her gloves came off and I felt her offense mark burn into my wrist. She jerked and screamed and fought to hold on, but eventually…

…she fell.

I closed my eyes to the scene of her plunging to the ground below me. I rolled over to my back on the platform and couldn't help it as the tears clouded my vision. I was glad for them. It meant that some part of me was still human and I wasn't the trinket – the lifeless object brought here to bend at their will – that they made me out to be. I could still feel, make my own decisions and accept my own consequences.

I knew Marla would never stop and she'd tried to kill me more than once, but that didn't mean I was happy about seeing her die.

I remembered the battle raging above me. I jerked to stand and pulled at the rope over and over again until I finally reached the top and jumped out of the lift to the grass of the mountain edge.

Half of the greenhouse was a burning heap now. Kyle and Lynne were still tied to the side that was still standing, still unconscious. But I saw everyone left standing off on the other side, so I ran to Caleb's back. He was holding them off by borrowing an ability that shook the ground under their feet. I touched his back and arms to let him know I was there, but he already knew.

*I'm so sorry, baby, but we're in it deep out here.*

*I'm ok,* I told him. *Let's just finish this.*

Jen and Bish were near the wall. Bish was blocking Jen, but not touching her. I thought about what needed to be done. I knew what needed to be done, but didn't know how to go about it.

And they were coming again. The guy who had the fire hands was first. I immediately slammed him with a swoosh of my fingers into the nearest wall. I didn't feel like getting roasted while I was trying to think and I was so over it all.

They started to come at us again and Caleb could no longer hold them all off. One grabbed him around his neck even as he fought and swung to beat them off.

That was when the cavalry arrived. Caleb's beautiful, petite mother jerked the metal railing from the balcony edge and clotheslined the whole lot of them with it. I saw Peter duck and then punch a man's jaw, then he kneed that same man in the stomach. Bish punched a guy, then another guy, then another. Once he punched someone, they were down for the count. Uncle Max was doing something to someone in the corner that I couldn't see and Caleb's other uncle, Ken, who controlled the plants, had a thorny rose bush swallowing a man. Caleb and Marcus went round and round. Caleb punched Marcus' gut, making him retreat backwards.

But it was when Marcus started to charge Caleb again with a broken piece of pipe in his hands that I'd had enough.

That was it. I couldn't take another second of it. My body hummed with untapped energy and I felt it rise to the surface as if I called for it. My arms seemed to rise out in front of me by themselves before seeping to the side. The Watsons all fell back in a wave as if knocked down by some force. The energy ribbons were everywhere, in us and through us and all around us. The energy only seemed to affect the Watsons, and they all rose to their knees in unwilling obedience to it and glowered at me with scared anticipation.

My family looked on as I became what I was destined to be.

"You all have ruined lives. Your family has taken everything you have for granted, and turned our kind into something it was never meant to be. We're different, it doesn't mean that we're better. We're powerful, it doesn't mean that we can hurt the powerless. If anything, we're meant to help the humans and the ones of our kind that are struggling. Your family is the reason that the imprints were taken." They gasped at the implication and called me a liar and worse. I kept going. "And your family is going to be the reason they come back again."

They looked at me, puzzled for a few seconds. I linked my fingers of one hand with Caleb's and begged for him to understand and trust me. He squeezed my fingers in agreement before connecting with me. The energy ribbons filled the air with green light and nowhere was safe from its glow. We began to draw the Watson's power away, their abilities, their very life force, their identity, their place in our kind, their history, and their future. It came away from them in black ribbons of energy that mingled with the green and then dissolved. It hurt to watch the looks on their faces when they felt and realized what was happening, but it was my burden to bear as the Visionary.

They begged and screamed for me to give them another chance and tried to run, but my power refused to let go until it was finished. Marcus was the last to go down and I knew no lessons had been learned for him. His glare was one of revenge, not sorrow. They slumped and fell over in defeat and then it was all over, or at least I thought it was. Rodney came to stand next to me and I laced my arm with his.

"You're something, you know that?" he said in awe. I just smiled. "So when am I going to meet my dream girl? Is there a time frame on that vision of yours?"

I just shook my head at him. "I'm afraid not," I answered, but then I heard a roar behind me.

"No happy endings!"

Just as I turned, Rodney was right in front of me. I was confused as he looked down into my face at first. He wasn't the one who yelled, was he? I heard the footsteps bang against the roof and looked to see Haddock charging us. He grabbed the fire hands guy and tossed him away from Rodney's back. He tripped and fell backward, hitting his head on the cast iron railing.

Rodney tried to smile a little at me, but his thoughts told me of the pain he was in. I grabbed him before he could fall and heard Caleb yell before helping me lower him to the ground.

Before I even really got a grasp on what had happened, a tear slid down my nose and landed on Rodney's neck. "No," I said. "No."

Fire hands had woken up and charged us when our backs were turned. He'd picked up a long glass shard and had stabbed Rodney after hearing him talk about the vision I'd had for him. This wasn't supposed to happen. "But the vision…I had the vision for you to marry your significant. This wasn't supposed to happen."

Haddock bent down and looked at Rodney's eyes by prying them open wide with his fingers. Peter knelt, pushed Haddock's hands away and started his own inspection, but Haddock still spoke to me. "Something changed. Something changed to make the way the vision was supposed to happen be different." He looked at me. "It's not your fault."

Caleb's family looked on Rodney in horror as I turned to Haddock.

"Why are you helping me?" I said, my throat and eyes clogged with tears. It got worse as Caleb grabbed Rodney's hand in a brotherly grasp and they looked at each other.

"I know what it's like to feel like you don't know what's going on around you. You feel so certain about one thing, but everything changes and makes it another." He looked back at Rodney. "I know all about the visions. I know how they work. My family did lots of research on these types of things from the histories." He looked back to me. "I don't know what happened to change it so that your vision didn't come true for Rodney, but that doesn't mean that you can't trust your visions."

I turned away from him, not even understanding why a Watson was helping me. It may not have been the smartest thing to do, turning my back to a Watson, but Caleb needed me. When I turned, it was too late. Rodney was already gone. I pulled Caleb to me and let him squeeze me to him. His skin was almost sizzling with anger and energy, and it seemed to hiss as it met mine and he got a shot of calm.

Kyle's parents had woken him and Lynne. They were all running our way and Kyle's face took on a look that said he understood what had happened. He knelt down with a hard thud to Rodney and ran his hands through his own hair before laying his head down to Rodney's hand. Lynne rubbed Kyle's back. Her cheek was red and there was still blood on her face from where Donald had cut her. I saw in her mind that Kyle had tried to heal her as best as he could, but they saw what was going on with us and ran toward us instead.

Kyle jerked up to pull Lynne to him and buried his face in her hair. I waited, but his touch didn't heal her cheek. He was too upset. I closed my eyes to everything else but Caleb and my own anguish. Rodney had cared for me, saved me, and guarded me. He was family and it hurt so, so bad to know that he was gone so senselessly.

After a while, more people began to come up to the roof. I still hadn't moved and the cries of Rodney's parents were the most wretched thing to hear as we backed up to give them room. Someone put their hand on my back and I turned to see Dad and Bish.

"What happened?" Dad asked and looked around at the destruction. "Did you do all this?"

"Mostly," I admitted through my tears. Then I hugged Dad to me and Bish, too. I squeezed and begged them silently to never leave me. Life was too short for people to be so careless and hateful, and the repercussions of the day pounded down on me. Too much life lost, too much time wasted. Too much hate and bitterness. This all could have been avoided and I vowed never to let things get this bad again.

# Twenty Six

Caleb and I lounged around my now un-charmed bedroom and tried not to think too much. The last two days the palace had been a solemn place. We had a memorial for Rodney, but they were taking his body home to be buried. The Watsons had been removed from the palace. Now human, they were going to have to try to live normal, human lives and be forced to get along just like everybody else in the world. If they found love one day, it would be just that. No imprints, no ascending, no abilities. Justice had finally been served for that family.

And it hadn't been as hard to fight the council and everyone else as I thought it was going to be. We eventually came down from the roof that day, went to the council and explained everything to them. Caleb and I showed the entire people my visions of how and why the problems had come. When the vision of the previous Visionary played out, that was pretty much the kicker. The council apologized for not doing more. Paulo admitted to knowing something was going on with Donald, as did a couple of others, but they didn't want to start digging. I wanted to be angry with them, but the time for anger was over. The time for change and healing was now.

Donald was still a 'statue' of sorts. Caleb borrowed his ability to turn him that way, but couldn't borrow it now to turn him back.

Everybody was surprisingly understanding and even…relieved that the Watsons were no longer one of us. I sat at the council table for the first time and it felt right for the first time, too. The old rules and traditions were being changed on a one-by-one basis. We sat down and stated the obvious ones. Like, it was declared that no council members were to live at the palace anymore. It was too important for them to be with their families and to be here just for the sake of being important and special didn't serve any purpose in my book. I didn't have any complaints about that when I suggested it and I wasn't surprised.

The only problem left to deal with was Haddock. He was the only Watson left and he hadn't been on the roof when a lot of the stuff went down. I later learned that he was the one who let Jen and Bish out of my room. They had planned to use the same gas-like charm that they had tried to use on my father. He saved them. After that, he went to the council and pleaded for forgiveness. He told them everything that the Watsons had done, using my blood, about kidnapping me, about Marla and Donald and their plots and plays to destroy everything and everybody.

Even Marla and Marcus' parents knew what their children were being used for and did nothing to stop it.

So they were good and buttered up when Caleb and I had to state our case and show the Vision. When he'd realized the rest of the family had gone up topside, he ran up to see what was going on and found us over Rodney. I knew that Haddock had no ability because he'd never imprinted. We decided to grant him clemency – gah, I hated that word – since he was so forthcoming and eager to help us, though we still really didn't understand why.

Things were just getting to feel a little normal again. We were going home tomorrow and everything would be sorted out then. Kind of ironically, and sadly, was to find an email on Caleb's phone. Rodney had texted all the Visionary scroll pictures he'd taken that day we were in the library together to Caleb. I had planned to scour and study them. He'd thought ahead, even if he didn't know what he was planning ahead for.

As it was, Dad and Fiona had decided to live at our house, or…his house. That was going to take some getting used to. Caleb was trying to figure out what it meant to be the Champion of our clan. As far as my house, every time I even thought about it, Caleb slammed his mind shut to prevent me from peeking. I assumed he was working on buying our house. He was supposed to have it for me before the wedding.

And I was going to be eighteen in just a couple of days.

There was a knock on our door and Caleb kissed my forehead before getting up from the bed and answering. It was Haddock and my *real* father.

"What?" Caleb barked.

"He has something to say," Haddock explained, "to Maggie."

Caleb looked back at me.

*I'll throw them both out, just say the word.*

I waved him off and came to stand next to him.

"Come inside. I don't want anyone else to overhear." They obeyed and I shut the door. "What?" I asked the man who gave me life and nothing else.

"I'm sorry. I had gambling debts. I was depressed because I didn't have anybody."

I shook my head. "What does that mean?"

"Marla came to me and said she'd give me some money if I'd tell you I was your father," he admitted and looked down at his shoes. Haddock jerked his face up by the man's hair.

"Look at her! She deserves to see your eyes while you tell her how you lied."

I took a deep breath as Caleb and I looked at each other. I glanced back at the man. "So, you're not my father? And you're not a Watson. How can you keep your thoughts from me?"

"Marla gave me something to drink. She said it would make it so that you couldn't read my thoughts and wouldn't see that we were lying."

"And you agreed to this. You agreed to lie to me knowing it was something so hurtful that you were lying about."

He nodded in misery. "I'm sorry. I truly am. I felt like I had no other choice."

I huffed. "What is it with everyone acting like they have no choices? You had a choice! And you chose to hurt me! Get out."

"I am sorry-" he started, but Caleb made a noise that had the man backing away. He left and shut the door behind him.

I hadn't even seen that man since he claimed to be my father and now he comes and says it was all a lie? I squeezed my eyes shut and rubbed them with my fingers. Without opening them, I addressed Haddock.

"How did you know that he wasn't my father?"

He sighed. I opened my eyes and watched him stick his hands into his pockets. He glanced up at me from under his lashes and I had that same strange feeling come over me as before. He was tall, but his brown hair was wavy and thick. His eyes were green and honest. He got a wry, sad look on his face and held his hand out to me. I took his hand hesitantly and let the vision come.

It was him in my house with my mother. He was happy. He was enthralled by her. My mother met him at the flower shop he owned and she made my father out to be a monster. She said he was hateful and hurtful, showing her no attention. That he just wanted a pretty wife to show off to his friends. Haddock dated my mother for almost ten months before she called it off. He had plans to marry her and take her away. He was past imprint age and knew there was no hope that way, but thought he could be happy with my mom.

When she called it off, he was devastated. She gave him no reason except that she wasn't interested in him anymore. He made several attempts to see her afterwards, but she threatened to call the cops. He eventually respected her wishes and left her alone. He had no idea that she had a baby and that it was his. He wanted nothing to do with his family, but he was tied to them by blood. He wasn't in control of the allegiance he owed them if they called for it. He never helped them with their ploys, but would overhear things at the family meetings.

When he heard them say they had the Visionary's blood, that she was a human girl from Tennessee that had imprinted with the Jacobson boy, and they had plans to give them all her blood so they'd be hidden from her ability, he was intrigued. The Visionary! They'd all waited their whole lives for her to return and for his family to so carelessly try to use her was appalling. And more so was when he found out who I was.

Marla was asking them questions at a meeting about the women that they'd been with outside of the clan. No one wanted to speak up, but Marla claimed to need the information. This intrigued Haddock further and he wound up divulging his entire affair with my mother to Marla, but at the end she never told him why she needed it. So he began his own research. When he heard my full name he put all the pieces together.

I was the lost daughter of Sarah Masters, the one love of his life, and he never knew I existed.

So he spent the whole week trying to find a way to help me. He couldn't just leave his family. He wanted to be on the inside, so he could help if I needed him. He could know what they planned, and he knew what they had planned for Bish and Jen in my room and waited until it was clear to save them. Then he went to make it all right with the council.

I opened my eyes to stare at him. He spoke.

"That's how I knew he wasn't your father...because I am."

He looked so ashamed. What was I supposed to say? Come here, Pop, it's all ok? I shook my head. "I'm glad you told me. It was you, wasn't it? The one who's been in my head. Warning me? You were the one who warned me that they were going to hurt my father, weren't you?"

"It was all I could do for you," he said gruffly. "I'd have given anything to know that I had a daughter. I never thought I'd have a family, wife, kids... If I had known…"

"I really appreciate that," I said carefully, "but I had a father. Have a father," I corrected. "I don't want him to find out about this."

"I don't plan to tell him. I won't do anything you don't want me to."

"I just…" I felt Caleb's hand on my back and breathed deep. "I just don't know what to say right now. I'm grateful for what you did, but as far as a relationship…between you and me, I just…don't know."

"It's all right," he said and cleared his throat. "I never expected anything. I did what I did because I felt like I owed it to you."

"But you didn't even know about me? It's not like you just ran off."

"But I still missed *everything* with you. I still was a part of the family that tried to destroy you. I had to play my part in my family. They made me a council member because of the part I played, but I didn't mean any of it. And I was so busy with the council, I didn't know what Marla was planning on the roof, or I swear I would have stopped them. None of what I did was real, except my silent devotion to you." He bowed slightly at the waist. "If nothing else, you are my Visionary, and my only want is to serve and protect you."

I tilted my head in acknowledgment and he stood. The awkward moment grew and I had no other words. I could barely think at the moment. He nodded as if understanding and turned to go. He stopped with his hand on the knob and looked back. "If you ever change your mind, we can come to an arrangement. I don't ever have to tell Jim what I am, but I would love if we could get to know each other."

Then he left without another word.

Caleb wrapped his arms around me, a cocoon of healing and warmth. I had no idea how long I stayed like that, but one thing was sure in my mind. Change was necessary and the truth was always the best option, but that didn't mean that it was going to be a painless journey.

~~~

That night we all got ready for our last dinner together at the reunification. Though it was solemn, it was also a breath of fresh air and relief. Everybody sat with everybody. No council table, nobody serving each other. We all handled our own business and that was what we all needed.

Dad and Fiona were sitting with us, which surprised me. I thought he'd be with Fiona's clan in all things now. Fiona caught me watching them sitting next to each other and smiled.

*Visionary?* she tested.

I nodded, but I mouthed, 'Maggie.'

*Maggie. I just wanted to say that I like what you're doing. I agree with you. Family is the most important thing and I have no intentions of taking your father away. I don't see why we can't be a part of both clans. It makes sense. I've agreed to live with Jim at his house, so we'll be close to you all.*

It was the best thing she could have said to me at that moment. I thought I was losing my dad, only to be thrown a replacement in Haddock. I was grateful to her for embracing our need for change. I got up and walked to her. I pulled her up from the bench and hugged her. It felt awkward, I won't lie.

But she hugged me back hard and Gran, always the inappropriate one, began to spout off.

"It's about time you gave that woman a hug. She's gonna be your step-mom, you know."

Fiona stiffened and leaned back. "Let's just stick with Fiona, if that's ok."
~~~

"Definitely," I answered and smiled, but I got that little buzz of unhappiness again. I looked around the room until I could pinpoint it. There was a girl from another clan sitting near the fire. I went and sat next to her on the hearth and clasped my hands together in my lap.

"Hey."

"Visionary," she said and bowed her head once.

"You seem…upset," I said.

"I don't know what's wrong with me. I just feel this…ache inside me. I mean, I know a lot has happened and everything is different, and with Rodney…I barely knew him, but he was such a sweet guy."

I got it then, and it sucked and it made me angry all over again. This was Rodney's significant; they just hadn't had the time to get together yet. This was the girl I saw in my vision. This was the girl he would have imprinted with, and though she didn't understand it, her imprint was feeling the loss. I rubbed her shoulder and smiled.

There was no way I could explain that to her.

"I know it's a crazy time for everybody," I tried to soothe, "but I have a good feeling about where things are going. Just don't give up, ok?"

She looked up at me for the first time. "You're really nice. The council made out like you were going to be a…" I heard the word in her mind and she bit her lip. "Not nice," she finished.

"It's all right. It was nice to meet you."

"You, too." Then she proceeded quickly as I got up. "Caleb's a nice guy, too. You're really lucky."

"I know," I said and smiled at her as I turned.

After dinner everyone said their goodbyes. We'd be leaving at all different times in the morning. I found Bish in my room when we got back. I hadn't seen him all day and I wondered where he'd been. His mind said he'd been on the roof, thinking.

"Hey," I said as Caleb shut the door behind me.

"Hey." He stood from the bed. "I'm leaving."

"Why? We're all leaving together in the morning."

He raked his hand through his hair, his jaw squared and hard. "I've been thinking and I…think it's best if I don't see Jen anymore."

"Bish…she'll come around, she's just worried," I stalled. "I haven't even gotten to talk to her yet about something that you both need to hear. You'll go mad if you don't-"

"Whatever, I just can't sit here and pretend like I don't want her. I understand if she needs time or whatever, so I'll give her some time and space. I won't be the reason that she's upset. If she wants me to stay away from her, I will."

"Bish-" I began. I was just about to beg him to listen to me when there was a knock on the door and Jen came in without waiting. She hadn't been at dinner either.

"Hey, uh…" she started to ask where Bish was, but stopped after seeing him. She fidgeted with the hem of her sweater that matched her jeans like a gem. "There you are."

"Me?" Bish said and he crossed his arms. "I guess it's good that you're here. I'm, uh…I'm leaving. So you won't have to worry about bumping into me anymore."

She smiled at him. Bish was confused at first, thinking she was pleased with his decision. He reached for the duffel bag that held his clothes and turned to go, but she made her way to him slowly. I heard her thoughts practically screaming across the room and my eyes filled as she spoke.

"After seeing Rodney…it made me think. He never knew who his significant was, and that's a travesty, Bish. He'll never feel the way about someone that I feel about you."

His mouth opened, but he didn't say anything. She continued.

"I never want to take that for granted. And I know now, after seeing it with my own eyes, that Maggie can stop the vision if she says she can." She stopped inches from him and Bish waited eagerly, hoping and praying. She reached up and let her hand hover over the skin of his arm. She looked up at him and he waited. "Do you still want this?" she asked in a whisper.

"More than I want to breathe," he said in a groan.

She smiled, tears filling her eyes as well. She reached up on the tips of her toes, her hands connecting with his meaty upper arms, and she kissed him like there was no one watching, like nothing else in the world mattered.

Their happy visions from the imprint played in front of my eyes as it did theirs and my own significant wrapped me in his arms. It made me smile more that Jen made the decision without me having to tell her about the going mad part. She just decided and it was based on her own heart, nothing else. They were all in and as we watched them imprint, I realized that was best feeling in the world.

To be all in, no regrets, no turning back, no matter the consequences. It felt a lot like freedom.

Caleb tipped my chin up and wiped a tear from under my eye with his thumb. "You're so amazing," he whispered, listening to all my internal rants in my head. "I can't wait for you to be my wife."

"Then let's not wait," I told him and enjoyed the grin that spread across his handsome, rugged face before he took my mouth with his with the promise of much, much more.

Very soon.

# The End For Now

Oh, the thank yous could go on for miles.
Thank you to my God, the readers who have picked up this book and my others as well, you are the reason I do this. It's been SO much fun getting to know all different kinds of people from all over the world who have read something of mine. It's humbling in every sense of the word and I thank you for allowing me to be a little piece of your world. You guys are the best and I love to hear from you! You rock!

Be on the lookout for the fourth and final installment of the Significance series, *Independence*.

**PLEASE FEEL FREE TO CONTACT SHELLY AT THE FOLLOWING AVENUES.**

www.facebook.com/shellycranefanpage

www.twitter.com/authshellycrane

www.shellycrane.blogspot.com

# ~ Playlist ~

1. (Opening Credits) Run For Your Life : The Fray
2. Sail : Awolnation
3. (Meeting Rodney) The Mixed Tape : Jack's Mannequin
4. (Meeting Marcus in hall) Don't Stop : Foster The People
5. Everyone Gets A Star : Albert Hammond Jr.
6. (Caleb & Maggie bedroom) In My Veins : Andrew Belle
7. Not Your Fault : Awolnation
8. Believer : Ben Kweller
9. Sinister Kid : The Black Keyes
10. (Games) Blackout : Breathe Carolina
11. (Ruth) Back Stabbin' Betty : Cage The Elephant
12. Northern Wind : City and Colour
13. (Creeping with Rodney) Too Fake : Hockey
14. (Shower/bathroom scene) Next To Me : Civil Twilight
15. Paradise : Coldplay
16. Give Me Love : Ed Sheeran
17. (Phone call to Jim) As Long As It Takes : Spill Canvas
18. (The dignitary luncheon) We Are Young : Fun
19. Lifening : Snow Patrol
20. Tongue Tied : Grouplove
21. Run : Matt Nathonson
22. (Bish and Jen) Gravity : John Mayer
23. Fader : Temper Trap
24. We're Breaking Up : Against Me
25. Save Yourself : Civil Twilight
26. (Getting ready for the ball) Sweet Disposition : Temper Trap
27. Whirring : The Joy Formidable
28. (Dancing) You And Me : Lifehouse
29. My Body : Young The Giant
30. (Marla and Maggie) I'll Never Let Go : Snow Patrol
31. (Lost Someone) Wish You Were Here : The Sounds
32. (Bish and Jen) Head or Your Heart : Mat Kearney
33. (Theme Song - Maggie and Caleb) Heartbeat : The Fray

Made in the USA
San Bernardino, CA
13 December 2013